OblivioN:

Ad Infinitum Tenebrae

By

Jordan G. Farrell

Oblivion: Ad Infinitum Tenebrae
© 2019 Jordan G. Farrell, First Printing December 2019.
ISBN: 978-0-578-57751-7
Cover Illustration Copyright © 2019 by Jordan G. Farrell
Cover design by Jordan G. Farrell
Book design and production by Jordan G. Farrell

For permission requests, write to the publisher, at "OblivionAuthor1@gmail.com" for consideration.

"Flectere si nequeo superos, Acheronta movebo."

(If I cannot bend the will of Heaven, I shall move Hell.)

-Virgil

Contents

See the way before you...

$$\frac{1}{\infty} = \frac{1}{0}$$

Foreword

uropa exploded in the most violent event to occur in the solar system in three-and-a-half *billion* years. Its tumult was like a bright, second sun suddenly appearing with brilliant, radiant illumination lighting the world. But lasting for only a brief, infinitesimal moment, its illumining went dark in an instant, like an epiphany of genius's clarity being suddenly realized, only to forget, disappearing behind a veil of infinite darkness, forever.

Out of the light, came darkness.

Thousands of vessels in and around the Jovian system charging their capacitors providing their source of motive power were thrown into chaos. The energy released from the Europan explosion set off a chain reaction towards everything connected to the magnetic field lines of Jupiter's magnificent servo. It was so powerful, the resulting power surge overloaded system after system in the physical world, resulting in a cascading explosive detonation chain that rocked all engines attached to it. The grand visible sign of their destruction from afar was a rapid brightening of Jupiter's vast aurora at its poles.

Some ships were part of the chain reaction directly and were destroyed in an instant, while others were damaged so much so they lost the ability to maintain orbit. The unfortunate souls occupying them were left to watch helplessly as they found their oblivion in the rapidly approaching, inexorably looming doom that was to be their grand end burning up within the vast, inescapable Jovian atmosphere. Another group was far enough away so that the resulting shockwave flung them helplessly into unrecoverable orbits, which meant certain slowly freezing suffocation in the inky cold blackness of forever-darkening space.

In the voluminous realm of quantum foam and entangled particles, as the mechanisms allowing mind drives to function, a similar chain reaction of cascading power surges flowed like vectors of overwhelming force through every interdimensional plane interlinked within the System. Every human being and Artificial Intelligence (AI) connected in any way to the mind drive network in the instant of detonation became suddenly aware of everyone else's full experience, as their own, in the deepest most intimate ways possible. All information anywhere from anyone suddenly was given more power to project than the mind drive network was ever designed to manage. This had the effect of providing awareness to all things being done by humanity anywhere, whether they wanted to be kept secret or not, regardless of intention, or choice, or regardless of being right or wrong, and regardless of whom it hurt in the process.

In the instant of cascade failure in both voluminous space, and voluminous time, all became aware in full detail of the events that occurred on Level Zero, Level 3909, Bridgewater Crossing, in the deep ocean, as well as what became of Justin and Jessica— *Forsythe!* —in the days, and moments before. All humanity reveled in Justin and Jessica's *magnifico volumine*, upon their physical deaths. All witnessed their love's grand end as their still-connected metaphysical forms came together as one great being— *soulmates!* — in the hereafter. They witnessed Jessica's non-corporeal form rescue Justin's from being captured and consumed by the Purush, thus wholly giving her to him as a result. Their union was the greatest miracle humanity had seen in nearly five thousand years. God had truly chosen them for some great, and still yet-to-be-revealed, divine purpose.

In the following moment after that great awakening instant, however, every human being and AI connected to the mind drive network was shorted out in an agonizing ripping apart of the interdependency to all others. It was that mind-drive system humanity was wholly dependent upon for survival in the prior millennia following the Purge, and it was all suddenly gone.

But it was an experience that was as close to understanding the divine as humanity would ever reach. And in flying so high, it was indeed a long fall back to the humility of philosophical mud human beings were suddenly thrown back down to. Thus, when the mind drive system ceased to be, all people were quiet and alone once again, and they all wailed.

They called it, *The Ripping*.

Individuals were suddenly torn apart from each other and left alone in the silence of their own thoughts, as pure independent units of humanity, like a falling from grace for having flown to close to the proverbial illumining sun, as Icarus of old. Humanity, in an instant, was thrust into the chaos of *The Infinite Darkness*, as this period came to be known, marked by anarchy, terror and unbridled tumult....

Part 1

Escape

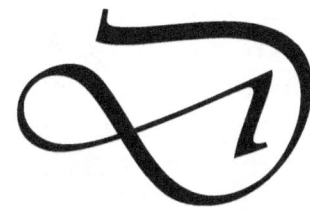aniel and Elizabeth Hawthorne finally were able to get a moment's peace once their adopted children were asleep in their prospective quarters aboard the System Space Vessel, *S.S.V. Deadlight*. He had only returned from Europa station, in geosynchronous orbit around the city of Gabriellium, on Europa, which was humanity's most successful and populous home since the days before the Purge, on the old, good Earth. Elizabeth missed him desperately; his being away for days negotiating the sale of their cargo was very difficult for her to bear apart. They found themselves in their own quarters in the throes of passion as part of their second hour of frustration-relieving love-making, which was sorely needed after months extracting minerals, loading, negotiating with buyers from the Ministry of Resources, and scheduling the load's delivery.

It was the soft, slow passion they enjoyed most. It was the kind of sharing that did not give into the carnal rapid passions of more physical and perhaps violent acts which others may have enjoyed. Instead, it was torturously slow, which built up in the body, like a long tease where increments of arousal were scarcely noticed until the very end, when their minds, bodies, hearts, and souls shared their combined release in a tsunami of force that obliterated their consciousness in a bromide of pheromone-laced dopamine.

Elizabeth was a gentle, sweet creature who enjoyed her husband taking charge and being in control of everything in their lives, from business to the bedroom. He was her safe place, where she could feel free to be totally secure that he would protect her and that nothing ever bad would come to her so long as they were together. She gave herself entirely to him. She devoted herself to raising children, adopting eleven over a fifteen-year period, sacrificing a career in any of the Ministries after transition school to do something real: raising *good* people, and being a part of gathering raw material for human beings all over the solar system they desperately needed to survive. It was her calling. She devoted her life to sacrificing her selfish needs for others', first. It was how her soul thrived in the deepest spiritual way possible for her.

"Oh Dan, Finally!" Elizabeth exclaimed in her mind drive to her husband in a mental conversation between exhausted breaths left over from their last physical achievement. "We've been so busy this month...it's so nice to have some down time. God, I hope we don't have to go back to the Belt that soon. Maybe give us a week or two to enjoy Gabriellium and have some time off. I need some down time." *The Belt* referred to the asteroid belt between the orbits of Mars and Jupiter where the majority of mining activity took place in the System. It was as much a home for the Hawthornes as the S.S.V. Deadlight or Europa ever was, having spent the majority of their adult years hopping from rock to rock, freelancing with various mining companies, guided wherever the market of perfect information guided them.

"Of course, beautiful," Dan replied in agreement, in amorous response to his beloved beside him entangled limb for limb with his. "It will be a nice escape from the routine. We did really well this month and we all deserve some downtime, especially the kids. We can restock our supplies from the arboretum... get some real chicken and coffee... and broccoli. I miss real broccoli... corn and other staples as well."

"You know I can't stand it," Elizabeth remarked playfully, "but... I know you love it so of course. It's expensive, but I'll go without my sweet popcorn if it makes you happy to have your broccoli." It was a conversation they had a hundred times before. But it felt like home having it.

Devotion was Elizabeth's actualizing force.

"You're the best lovey," Dan genuinely offered. "We don't have to blow the whole budget on broccoli you know. We can get both, just less of each. It'd be selfish of me to have you go without. I wouldn't do that to you and the kids."

Compromising was Dan's actualizing force.

"You know I'd give you anything if I had the means. Never doubt that," Dan stated flatly.

"Hon we're fine. I couldn't be more happy. I'm with you and that's all I need. We could live in a hovel, in one of the lower sections, like ten or even three, cleaning floors and I would be just as happy. Never doubt that."

"Ugh. Three? Doing a robot's job?" Dan jabbed. "Not three. Not that. Not for you. And it's way too close to all the noise, and God knows what's on zero. Ten okay, but not three. Don't even think about two or one." They both snickered softly before they kissed one another. A pause. "We'll take tomorrow off and maybe on Thursday take the kids to the city and get to the park. That will be fun for them. I'll get a good room at a hotel near the Spire. It's so nice there."

"Yeah, sounds great," Liz agreed.

Dan Hawthorne was raised in the mining tradition amongst hard spacers who worked for generations in the Mining Consortium. The Consortium was a group of private companies who used their combined collective bargaining power to broker market equilibrium pricing for the raw materials they delivered to the Ministry of Resources on Europa. He was rugged, rough around the edges, and enjoyed his drink probably more so than was considered healthy for a person to consume in a given standard week.

His drink of choice was Scotch whisky, but Kentucky bourbon was a close second. They were algae-based, like all other alcohol was made, but infused with the requisite rye, corn, wheat, barley, *etc.* to give it as authentic a brew as could be made when such plants were grown in small supply in Gabriellium's arboretum. But to Dan, they were as authentic as they could be, having no basis of comparison to tell him otherwise. He only knew that the printed analogs were considered 'the cheap stuff' to most connoisseurs, and he could not bear the thought of chasing back those alternatives with a green, algae-based beer.

Liz loved his carefree attitude and willingness to not adopt accepted social norms as his own. She loved the fact that he thought for himself, made his own decisions, no matter what anyone else tried to make him do or tell him. He was completely self-reliant, and she loved the strength of control the confidence that came with it conveyed. But she also loved the fact that he never swore, as it was a pet peeve of hers since she could remember.

Dan was a miner, a truck-driver and an Eagle Scout all at once, a combination that threw Liz off her feet when they met thirty or more years prior, as teenagers in transition school. They were both each other's first loves, and last. There were never any others and they each had no reason to look elsewhere for something to fill that was missing in their relationship. It was pure devotion, and contentment. Their resulting unconditional love for one another created a warm comforting cocoon of safety that quickly recharged them both.

After hours of slow consummation, it also exhausted them both, like reaching for two tails on opposite ends of the same tiger. Before long, after snuggling quietly, Liz rested her head on his hairy, greying chest listening to his strong heartbeat. His calloused, thick fingers cradled her nude shoulder, and they fell peaceably asleep in each other's arms.

~

The Deadlight was buffeted by a force that launched the Hawthornes from their slumber into the air above their bed only to slam down back into in a chaotic torment that broke their peaceful dreaming in the most unwelcome way possible. Alarms raged across the Deadlight's intercom system in what sounded like two hundred meters of echoing terror as the ship was raked back and forth from an unknown external force. Dan swiftly dove out of bed, hitting the floor as the ship rose and he failed to in time when leaping from the bed. He smacked his chin hard on the metal floor, which stunned him. He groaned.

Liz remained in bed, suddenly terrified. "Dan, are you okay? Find out what's happening! I'll see if the kids are alright."

"Right. On it." He agreed. He rose to his feet unsteadily, stunned, and managed to gain a firm grasp on a vertical handle beside the bedroom door, that was the entrance to their quarters. He staggered with rarely used, atrophied 'sea legs' toward the control center at the front of the ship. Sparks from electrical shorts, and leaking water from plumbing lines exposed as part of the ship's construction for ease of access, were mixing light and water in a chaotic tumult that he could neither dodge, nor avoid. He traipsed through standing water, rising slowly, trying not to think about the risk of electrocution on his way to the bridge. Having reached, and opening the door to the bridge, his view instantly horrified him down to his very soul.

The Ripping occurred.

Dan's view of the Jovian system passed by the view screen in rapid glimpses as the ship was rocked by a force he did not yet understand. Jupiter was retreating helplessly from the ship, and shrunk in rapid succession as the bright, accompanying ongoing flashes of Europa's destruction reached his eyes. The sudden silence of over fifty-million lives shocked and confused him; Gabriellium was gone, as were the outlying colonies, thousands of vessels on Europa station, in close orbit above, all simply disappeared in an instant.

"Attention! Attention! Orbit unrecoverable. Unable to correct! Abandon ship! Abandon ship!" The ship's on-board AI system was calling in repeating cycles to warn its residents of the unavoidable reality that there was no going home ever again, in a soothing, motherly tone designed to relax humans in untenable situations, as had been installed on all ships for nearly a century.

Deadlight's systems were failing all over the ship. Dan was stunned and shocked as his mind began filling with information from Gabriellium, the indigenous Europans, the Purush, Chancellor Manivasagam, Argus, Midge, Tanya, Sherrie Donovan, and most importantly, Justin and Jessica Forsythe. He, as well as Liz, became suddenly aware of their discoveries, the true nature of humanity's progeny, from the printing antediluvian copies of a people who were only supposed to exist in ancient historical tales from before the biblical Great Flood on Earth. The grand malevolence of a divided, hyper-emotive, multi-million-year-old species inexorably trapped within a philosophical conflict appeared before him in his mind. And he saw, as did everyone else, how humanity directly caused their plight, as the experiences of an alien species whose individuals were older than the entire span of humanity's existence as the homo sapient species flooded reality. It was completely overwhelming.

Dan shuddered to the floor as his relatively empty mind filled with more information than any human being was designed to take in at once. The tumult around him retreated in his mind. The thoughts of his wife and children dimmed in the background. His soul heaved. He experienced the union of Jessica and Justin Forsythe, as did all others. His heart exploded emotionally as his awareness of multidimensional time and the experiences in all three dimensions within it burst forth like a Big Bang for his mind.

Dan couldn't move. His body didn't feel like his own, like observing it from afar from a position high above himself.

The Deadlight rocked once again as an explosion kicked the vessel off its yaw even further and his helpless physical form slammed starboard against a bulkhead. Warnings called of depressurization from the ship's AI to abandon ship immediately that was no more urgent than a gentle summer rain on the old, good Earth, in comparison to real experience during the Ripping. Both physical and magnetic-field bulkheads began dropping all over the ship to keep whatever atmosphere there was inside it as a last attempt to preserve the lives of Deadlight's family. For Dan, the tumult continued all around him.

Suddenly, a voice from the ether, from the grand quanta of time's second dimension called out to Dan, specifically, in a loud, but soft whisper, like a child quickly telling a secret, that rocked him to consciousness,

"See the Way before you!"

Dan got to his feet and not yet realizing the Ripping disconnected him from his family, and every other human being anywhere, and focused his attention on the ship's systems. Three of four main engines were gone, completely destroyed. One remained but was barely hanging on to the physical structure of the ship. He glanced at the trajectory and his heart sank.

"Deadlight," he called in desperation, "display current orbital path with given trajectories...," a desperate gasp, "...what happened?" he asked in the only way he knew how to in a moment flooded with adrenalin.

"Europa has experienced a catastrophic explosive event. It appears to have been destroyed. The resulting shockwave has set off a chain reaction of overloading energy vectors that have been transferring to all orbital charging stations and vessels. Capacitance has been compromised, having been overwhelmed by the power surge. There are at least 24,361 vessels that have been destroyed in my field of view, myself being one of them nearly so. We are currently on an unrecoverable orbit that will not return to the Jovian system until 76,292 standard years from now."

"My God!" Dan gasped in a long verbal exhalation that was both a grunt and terror-filled call to no one that could hear.

Deadlight continued, "However, according to the current data I am receiving from remaining ships' internal and external sensors, there is a brief window of twelve minutes, thirty-two seconds where I can reach Titan orbit..."

"Thank God," Dan interrupted.

"...in five-hundred-nine standard years, and forty-seven days."

Dan swallowed.

Deadlight continued, "However, the resulting thrust vector needed from the remaining engine will cause further catastrophic failure and will disconnect it from the remaining intact portions of this vessel. Its failure will cause inescapable exposure to hard vacuum to the majority of the ship, as it is the remaining power source keeping several sections' magnetic seals in place. I may not survive at all as there is a twenty-six-point-nine percent chance of unrecoverable explosive detonation upon my engaging engine four. Physical bulkheads are only functioning in this area."

"What sections are stable enough to survive the thrust vector?" Dan asked hurriedly.

"Section one through nineteen. Beyond that, I will be ripped apart by the torsional stresses."

"So here, the bridge, the mess, the medical section, our quarters, and cryo-station two... God, is that all?"

"Yes sir," Deadlight flatly confirmed.

And then a sudden, cold realization came over him.

"Wait. What about the kids? Where are the children? What about passenger deck three? Oh God!"

"Passenger deck three was destroyed in the initial..."

Dan ran as fast as he could through standing water, sparks and blue lightning back to his wife, where the Ripping was tearing at her soul.

~

Liz was blocked by a bulkhead before she could reach what would have been passenger deck three. Peering through the transparent titanium porthole, she viewed only empty, spinning space that made stars look like streaks across her field of vision. She thought she could make out her children's lifeless bodies as the views swept by, in an auto-punishment event her feelings of motherhood took all responsibility for within her being. She wept uncontrollably.

In Liz's mind and soul, the Ripping was simultaneously filling her with all the experiences that came before. For, every living being connected to the mind drive system, and she, along with all other surviving humans, AIs and indigenous Europans, experienced Justin and Jessica Forsythe's grand union, as well as the Purush's malevolence connected with the family's grand dyadic division at the bottom of the ocean. Voluminous time expanded her conscious awareness to levels beyond her comprehension. Liz gave in to having no choice but to yield to its power over her.

Liz, still in shock at the loss of her adopted children before her very eyes, froze in place in what rapidly degenerated into a profound catatonic state. Assuming the worst, she waited for her oblivion to take her to the next realm in the hereafter. But her husband's rushing form appeared out of the strobe-like flashes of blue-white electrical arcs, sparks, and liquid spray with splashes coming from his footsteps slamming through shallow, standing water. Red flashing warning lights made the scene as eerie and traumatic as any imagined in any event anyone could conjure.

"Liz! Liz!" Dan called. "Liz! Say something!"

His wife just stared out the window where her whole being had been torn from her.

"Liz!" Dan began to cry. "Lovey," Dan softly said as he grabbed her body and held her tight. "God, I know. We need to get to the cryo-chamber. We need to hurry." Dan held her close and she walked hurriedly with him without saying a word but simply wept as her faculties were completely overwhelmed by the rush of too much information and trauma at once. Dan continued to console her. "We can make it. There's a way. Deadlight found a way to get to Titan, but it will take a while. We have to go into cryostasis for a long time, but we can make it."

Liz started to come back around. "What? Cryostasis? What do you mean? It doesn't matter. My babies are gone."

"Lovey, listen," Dan exclaimed over the flashing sparks and sounds of rushing shallow water, "We can survive. We have to. Don't give up. I'll make sure you make it. Please lovey. Stay with me."

"Oh Dan, yes. I love you, *so much!*" Liz softly spoke just loud enough for Dan to hear. She was entering a fugue state and becoming unaware of her surroundings entirely.

"Stay with me lovey! I love you too. We're gunna get through this. Just let me get you to the cryo-chamber."

"Oh... Okay. Whatever you say. You take such good care of me. I don't deserve you...." She trailed off in a muttering mumble that was a series of random protuberances of thoughts and feelings devoted to her husband.

In a couple of minutes Dan and Liz arrived at cryo-station two. In their view a sight that sucked the hope out of them both greeted them in a cold shudder, stopping them dead in their tracks. The room, having been half-destroyed by the forces disabling Deadlight, was crumbling. Three of the four cryo-chambers were hopelessly crushed by falling pieces of debris from all over the room that had flown across the open space, smashing into connecting equipment and systems designed to keep people alive. Only one remained and was intact.

Dan, without a second thought said to Liz, "Okay, we're here. Okay. Let me help you with your clothes." Dan quickly removed his wife's pajamas until she was sans clothing altogether, a requirement for cryo-stasis, and moved her next to the unit.

"Okay lovey. Time to go to sleep. You're going to get to Titan, but it will take a while. Okay? It'll be five hundred years from now. Everything..." an exacerbated pause "...will be different. Okay? It's going to be hard. Okay? But you'll make it. You'll be okay. I promise."
Dan began guiding her to laying inside the cryo-unit as she began understanding the gravity of the situation.

"Five hundred years? What? What are you talking about? What about you? Where are you going to be?"

Dan didn't answer right away.

"Hon? Where are you going to be?!" Liz desperately asked.

"I can't come with you, lovey. I'm sorry. There's only this one bed. We have to..." he buried his dread and sadness, "...say goodbye. I'm not gunna make it."

"No, no, no! You take it. You take it! I'll stay. You go! Please!" Liz tried to escape from the bed.

Dan insisted, "No Liz. No. It's my turn to sacrifice for you this time. You've earned it. And I wouldn't be able to live with myself otherwise."

"I won't either!" Liz became hysterical.
"Yes, you will. I promise. You will make it." Dan changed the subject and called out to Deadlight while Liz grasped at the fabric of his shirt. "How much time in that window, Deadlight?"

"Four minutes, nineteen seconds."

"Okay. And how much reserve power will she have?"

"Assuming this is successful, the plutonium reserve emergency packs can last two thousand years, especially since the life support systems will be off-line. The only power will be to my system on the bridge and to Liz's cryo-pod. Assuming I do not run into any asteroids or obstacles along the way, we will arrive in Titan space in five-hundred and nine years."

"Okay, got it." He turned back to his wife, who was uncontrollably crying. "Lovey, we have to start. You have to lay down."

"I can't, I can't!"

"You have to! We're running out of time!"
Deadlight called remaining time before the launch window closed for it to make the course correction needed to reach Titan orbit. "Window closing in three minutes thirty-seven seconds."

"Okay, okay." Liz relented. "I love you with all that I am my dear, my love. I carry your heart. I carry it inside my heart."

"As I do. As I always will," Dan returned, recalling his wedding vow exchanges with his bride twenty-three years prior. "I love you with all that I am. Know it."

Liz then became quiet and asked blankly, "Why is it so quiet?"

Dan didn't answer and closed the transparent lid, his tears dripping on the surface. Their hands reached for each other's against it as Liz's eyes closed and time suspended for her in the moments with thoughts of devotion for her husband comforting her, in the newfound silence in her mind.

In the infinitesimal moment before the darkness became a blinding white light for Liz Hawthorne, her soul heard the loud whisper of a call from the magnificent volume beyond, "See the Way before you!"

~

Dan took a deep breath, paused, and called to Deadlight in a low, dreadful tone, "Deadlight, begin burn."

"Yes sir," Deadlight replied. "Beginning nine-second burn in four... three... two... one... ignition."

The ship groaned. It rocked as the forces of overwhelming torsional stress pushed the half-destroyed vessel to its breaking point. Deadlight called out, "Burn plus three, plus four, plus five..." until it reached nine, at which point the engine shut down, forever. The ship broke and crumbled into two massive pieces that disconnected all remaining main power to the magnetic fields keeping the air in and the hard vacuum of space out. Dan hung onto a console overlooking his wife who looked at peace in her frozen slumber as all air rushed out of his lungs. His body froze in place, and stars filled his soul that entered the magnificent volume in the infinite oblivion, beyond.

The Titans

Riz Hawthorne slept beneath a blanket of darkness that was both an instant and an eternity for her. In the centuries between the end of everything she knew and her new beginning, history became filled with the stuff of nightmares that was civilization's nearly complete collapse, from *the Ripping*.

Chaos prevailed within the System. With the collapse of the mind drive network, humanity's baser instincts prevailed once more. Those instincts grew from fear and concern into sheer panic, and then into frightful horror that ultimately led to mass-slaughter. Individuals no longer had the knowledge of all human history or each other's insight in an instant to rely on when solving problems, when living their average daily lives, when relating to one another, and most importantly, when simply communicating. They were forced to think for themselves, entirely, for the first time in millennia. Humanity reverted back to a feckless, confused and terrified mob of individuals in the literal sense once more.

People were forced to *talk*—a terrifying prospect in and of itself. Talking was previously looked upon disdainfully as nothing more than a hobby, or a pastime to entertain people in their off-hours, or in their relationships, for whatever purposes they felt whimsy to pursue. After the Ripping, it was all that was left. And verbal communication's failings consisting of misinformation, misinterpretation, misrepresentation, and misguided attempts to glean understanding failed humanity, utterly.

Colonial systems, intended physically to keep life going in some of the most inhospitable environments to human life, were designed to manage thousands of inputs from minds everywhere. Because those systems were so complex, they collapsed quickly and completely, when communication, reason, logic, and finally sanity, did also under objective reality's irresistible force.

Quickly, no one had skills, knowledge or expertise left to run anything. The human race had become so inured to the transformational mind drive technology the species became wholly dependent upon it for survival. That specialization was the root of ultimate failure which resulted in just that: *the failure of human survival*. It's failing was not measured in years or even months, but in mere weeks and even days of chaos and destruction. It was oblivion within an infinite darkness that few managed to survive.

The Luna colonies were the first to fall. Within but three standard days chaos of the tens of thousands of mineral-workers became trapped in varying sections. Water was cut off, air production ceased and the four small cities of less than ten thousand people each, scattered about below the lunar surface died in a horrifying, thirsting suffocation.

Followed quickly, but just as gruesomely, the Neo-Martian cities, re-built near the ruins of the once great ones, like Utopia Prime and Mariner City, managed to keep their systems running longer. However, this effort only provided more time for a panicked populous to begin killing off one another over air, water and scraps of food. Inexorably, over nine weeks, section after section began shutting down, decompressing due to damage caused by riots as well as a complete lack of basic monitoring and maintenance. As the bulkheads between sections intended to keep people alive fell, they trapped small groups, tens or a hundred at a time, leaving them to die in a decompression event that had no comparison in a slow, lingering pain for minutes on end. The temporary survivors were pained to witness the blood-curdling cries and panicked, useless punches by the victims at the bulkhead, as others gazed through the transparent titanium doors, for anyone with eyes to see, waiting for their turn. Ten million Martians were dead in just under nine weeks, a small group at a time.

In the Belt, the Mining Consortium fell apart as basic navigation and cryostasis systems, built and wholly dependent upon the monitoring and maintenance of biological systems via the mind drive aps designed for the purpose, failed. Shockwaves from the destruction of Europa, even a million kilometers towards the sun, still impacted ships' orbits and trajectories to such a degree, those suddenly-ignorant pilots were helpless to correct them as the ships' navigational AIs with versions of dampers also found themselves computationally fried by the Ripping. Only ships without AIs and using antiquated non-sentient computer technology were able to navigate; sorely few of those, perhaps one only, did, however.

Thousands of crews died either by thirst or suffocation in hapless orbits, or worse, badly corrected ones that missed their marks when attempting to navigate to a stable colony elsewhere in the system. Some, navigating back to Luna, like a blind shot at a hopelessly distant target, watched helplessly as their vessels passed the moon of Earth only to see blackened scarred structures, sans lights, and with billowing smoke escaping into the vacuum of space as they raced helplessly to Venus's orbit and the central furnace of the System that was the sun, Sol. Others watched as the sun's glare grew slowly dimmer as air ran out and their trajectories led them to the frozen wastes of Kuiper.

Europa, humanity's heart, with its tens of millions of people (and most anything in its vicinity), was gone in an instant. Except for *The Deadlight* and its lone survivor, Elizabeth Hawthorne, only the Titans remained.

~

The Ripping did not spare the people of Titan as the mob chaos and emotional insanity that marked its passing ensued. While millions did indeed meet their doom, as in the other System's colonies, many of the Titans managed to survive, not because they had some skill others lacked or some inherent mode in their personalities that made them stronger. No. It was, ultimately, for one important reason many survived. It was the one thing all the other colonies lacked, and the one thing that differentiated Titan from all other worlds on which humanity settled: *walkable air*. Titan, with its thick atmosphere of nitrogen and methane at 1.6 bars of pressure at the surface, was significantly thicker than of the old, good Earth, making it possible to walk freely on its surface without a pressure suit. Of course, the frigid temperatures (-180 degrees Celsius, 94 Kelvin) and lack of oxygen presented other, great challenges, of which depressurization, at least, was not one. That was the difference that meant survival for those on Titan versus on other worlds who would have no chance at all.

It was, still, a very slim chance.

Of the twenty-six million Titan citizens inhabiting the pre-biotic world encapsulated within the air-conditioned deep freeze of the outer solar system, it was estimated that less than forty-thousand survived the Ripping. It was an event that likened it to the Purge, where humanity's population was reduced to roughly five thousand individuals, save that it had nothing to do with Earth, but was more about humanity's long history and its first contact with a wholly alien, vastly old, and nearly infinitely intelligent species who saw humans as invaders of their world. In the end, undoubtedly however, the Ripping was another auto-extinction population bottleneck that would be burned forever in all human consciousness, and genome, yet again for millennia.

Titans who managed to escape the cities with breathing augmenters and blankets at least, or hard spacer suits at best, survived for a while, outside the city, on the air they brought with them. Survival instincts kicked in. Scavenging *was* survival. They returned to their ruined homes. The scrapped for whatever functioning technology still worked to make air out of ice, and fuel out of the air, the rivers, the lakes, the seas. They found ways to adapt to the cold through the hurdles of overcoming frostbite, a lack of air and a lack of food. Most perished. Some, however, did not. The few who did survive figured out quickly that everything anyone needed to make heat on Titan was there, right beneath their feet, in the air and lakes. It was just not anything a human being accustomed to those things on any other world would be familiar with. They walked through fuel. They had to dig up the air.

Among the survivors directly after the Ripping, Amadán Dubh managed to find her way back to Mug Ruith, a settlement on the edge of Shangri-La beneath the steppes of Antilia. History recorded her as the first of a line of leaders responsible for the successful re-bourgeoning of Titan civilization by sheer path of happenstance that allowed her to find a working portable reactor, in a maintenance bay that happened to be *mostly* sealed, requiring a few repairs to seal as best she could. It had an airlock, so that she could cut chunks of water ice that she used to make air, heat and potable water with inside where it could stay. Insulation was easier as fabrics from clothing, furniture and even tapestries she collected from the vast ruins were used to place layers of cushioning between walls and the inside air, so that even if it leaked a little, she could still breathe, so long as oxygen levels remained around fifteen to twenty percent, inside.

She used the generator to collect oxygen and hydrogen from the melted ice using electrolysis. The oxygen she mixed with nitrogen to provide her breathing air. She forced herself to adapt to less and less oxygen over months so that she found it tolerable to survive in air that had just eight percent oxygen, however. The extra pressure helped her maintain a livable blood saturation, which settled nicely into a new, survivable equilibrium. The extracted hydrogen she further repurposed as fuel for heat. That heat that rippled the orange haze was like a beacon, a lighthouse in a dark storm for any and all-comers to be guided by toward a safe harbor.

Before long, other survivors found her by the rising heat that made the air ripple obviously as it escaped from the makeshift shelter. In a bit more time, hundreds, then later, thousands of survivors were found, collected, over years, and a new, sustainable colony grew from the ruins of the old. It was a tale of rebirth that was replete in human history, over centuries, over millennia, over nearly thirty thousand years of events that were told and retold to subsequent generations in different forms time and again.

While not wholly inglorious, Amadán Dubh's tale was not one of heroic survival that some who wished to hear about might expect. Instead, her story was of very good luck, persistence, self-reliance, patience and cooperation. But it was mostly *luck*. Luck, luck and more luck, as it appeared obvious to most. Others followed suit out of necessity— *to survive!* — And nothing more.

She prayed, often. She prayed so often, that others who knew her told of how she always seemed to be, "...in a constant state of prayer." As a result, she was considered a quiet, stolid introspective woman, with seemingly the weight of the world on her proverbial shoulders, as if her entire being had humanity's survival in the balance. Some even speculated that she retained all of the information, the flash of collective genius in the Ripping that seemingly all others rapidly forgot in their ultimate mental breakdown. It was said she knew what all knew from the before-time.

More shelters were built around the original out of the scraps of the old, organically, and slowly. Made small, each adding minimal volume, a growth of cubist shelters grew slowly in the frozen orange haze, like crystals precipitating out of a fluid of dissolved solids, invisible to anyone not inexorably connected to it. But its being there, once in existence was seemingly always there, like blocks of brown marble with shiny glints of failing sunlight bouncing off chamfered corners.

Water from the ice that was the "ground," was plentiful. Food was not, however. For many months, food was whatever could be ingested. Animal carcasses were rapidly consumed first. After they ran out, it included the frozen dead millions from the before-time. Before long, however, survivors realized that feeding off of the dead was the surest way to a lingering insane suicide due to the effects of Kuru, a terminal disease caused when consumed prions in human flesh created holes in the brain. But, in the short scope of 'have to,' having frozen meat available for consumption was her, and everyone's best option, even though it was human in origin. And for a long while, the survivors did their best to clear out the long dead and remove them from the settlements, both old and new, and inter them far from their memories.

Amadán Dubh's ultimate tale, however, was remembered not for all that, not for the 'have to' acts or the introspection or for the prayer, or for the fact she was a lucky person in the right place at the right time. She was not even really considered a great leader in history, save for her ability to foresee coming events by some unknown and little-understood sense that no one then or since had an inkling how worked. What she *did* do that changed the world, Titan's world, for its living, breathing survivors, was to figure out how to turn the methane rains into food.

An historical account told of a matter-of-fact conversation between her and her first son, Maltru Riegnis Dubh, where she described how simple it was for her to suddenly become aware that if she went to the ruined arboretum, collected flash-frozen soil and put in it a container with an equal parts liquid methane from a puddle, and water ice, it would react with the bacteria in the soil when she applied heat. Her son spoke about how it would begin a fermentation process that released protein into the water. Once dried, the brown powder was edible. It was then shaped into the *Titan Dubh Grain* that every living human had consumed as its main staple for nearly five hundred standard years since the Ripping.

From that experience, that profound breakthrough of one critical innovation from the creative force of one person, the Divine creative force, Mug Ruith's culture was forever steeped within the source of infinite knowledge that came from the before-time, from the Ripping, and the Divine Spark described in the Way. The Way was wholly reinforced as the only truth in the cosmos to them. Thus, Mug Ruith, to anyone on the outside, would appear like a monastery, or mission, or a vast cathedral complex on a city's scale.

Still, survival relied on reproduction. That mode, millennia-old technology used on Europa and in all the System's settlements, including Titan, genetic printing of human beings was still based on the genomes of 'parents.' Human beings, still sterile, made recovering genetic printing technology the growing colony's only mission for the first generation after the Ripping. Their energies beyond immediate survival, was to locate, repair and recover birthing labs in the old city. Years were spent piecing together the technology and building power systems capable of running it. After a long, slow concerted effort, the survivors were successful in rebuilding a functioning birthing print facility. They perceived that they were successful because of the assumed stored knowledge of the before-time, contained with Mum Dubh to guide them, like a Divine guidance leading them. As the survivors' demagogue, a perception she could not avoid, she naturally insisted, with everyone else, that she be the first to undergo the procedure. In a standard year that followed, she was blessed with her first child, Maltru Riegnis, the first human born after the Ripping, in the new era. He was named for his father, an engineer and the first to find Mum Dubh alone in her makeshift shelter who quickly became inseparable to one another.

Thirteen years after Maltru Riegnis Dubh's birth (the printing process using the slightly altered genetic sequence of his mother and father), he began to show signs that he too was, what came to be known as, "enlightened," as his mother was. Amadán had two other children after Maltru who never manifested the gift, but they still figured prominently in the historical record as well, however.

After Amadán Dubh died years later after a random ground-quake when the ice opened up beneath her feet before she could react on one of her regular walkabouts, Maltru Reignis Dubh was chosen by the few hundred people in the settlement to lead them. He was twenty-seven when she fell. He was her oldest child, and his siblings who never demonstrated the 'enlightenment,' stayed in consul to the new leader of the small surviving settlement, for a time.

Before long, however, the failings of human weakness formed rifts, and divided the fledgling culture, because of Maltru's enlightenment, and the others' lack of it. Maltru's siblings, like in the stories of Cain and Abel, fought with him and each other to such a degree they left, with bands of followers to other regions as a necessary choice to avoid yet another destructive battle for power and control in human history. It was rift that permanently rooted itself in Titanian culture for all time. As a result, deep-seated resentment plagued the factions' dealings with one another since only a few standard years, A.R. (After the Ripping).

The whole series of events leading to the separation was remembered as a unifying moment in Titan history, ironically. For, its division was emblematical of humanity's still strong ability to rise above the tirades of emotionally sourced motives and prevented a final conflict that surely would have left humanity extinct. Thereafter, the family of Maltru Dubh and all his descendants would forever be royalty, both politically and spiritually in Shangri-La. The siblings followed different paths, in their own differing regions and settlements at the time. But for the region of Shangri-La, thus began the metaphysical dynasty that was the family of Dubh, in the city of Mug Ruith, for the People of the Sands, for all time. But all that was ancient history, and few in the modern moment could recall all of the details that came after unless by doing the research themselves and reading about it the Books of Knowledge in the Sanctuary Cloister at the Central Temple of Mug Ruith.

~

In the modern moment, the current leader and beloved Mum to all in Shangri-La, Aibell Amadán Dubh, was named for that pioneering grandmother nearly twenty generations removed. In the anteroom behind the Sanctuary Cloister's main hall, Aibell readied herself for *The Reading:* the annual event when Saturn completed one orbital circuit around the sun (once every twenty-nine standard years). That modern moment, in 509 A.R., or 5301 A.D. to those from the before-time, Saturn's orbital circuit coincided with Titan's own sixteen-day orbit around Saturn (such that a month was measured by two

Titan orbits) and happened to correlate with Saturn's completed one, this time. It was an event that happened perhaps once every thousand standard years.

Thus, its convergence was special to all the peoples of Titan. In preparation of the event, the Reading that regularly occurred every twenty-ninth year was made even grander by making it a celebration of life, of future, and of thriving for all the people, despite all their inherent cultural differences. Delegations from around Titan traveled hundreds of kilometers in a mass migration to Mug Ruith to attend *The Festival*, as it was known, where the leader of Shangri-La performed a ritual that allowed her (or him) to transverse the magnificent volumes of information the Dubh dynasty was blessed (or cursed) with recalling, that would guide the Titans through the next twenty-nine years. It was a reading, a foretelling, a story, and message from the beyond all at once.

The Festival was the time for unity. But the unwritten custom for every inhabitant was for the active refreshing of old wounds, whether the reason to do so was rational or not. Titans thrived on the angst, rifts and drama that poking the proverbial bears' energy produced. It was like a soothsayer's drug: a hopelessly addicting bromide that was both a high and a poison, simultaneously.

Some believed the messages were from the Divine, from God, from Gabriel, or from Jesus, as their way to guide the remnants of human civilization to thriving once more. Those who still believed in the Magnificent Volume after the Ripping were of that camp. Others believed they were from the dead, ghosts, demons, and manifestations from Hell itself. Those rejecting the notion of life's direct connection with higher orders of time but carried the faith of an omnipotent master giving all His subjects a destiny, were of that dark and terror-filled philosophy. Most saw it as bleak and hopeless, as a way to give up on any future whatsoever. And yet, there were a few, perhaps more aware of the voluminous realms than most, who understood how time's multi-dimensional nature allowed for the storage of vast amounts of information in "places" that could be accessed in an instant of relative, local time. That camp became the voice of reason, logic and sanity to the others, a fact that fueled deep resentment of a cold perception of how life progressed.

But those people, the people of reason, had not yet arrived inside the walls of Mug Ruith for the Festival. It would be a long while before that delegation, known as the People of the Seas, from the city of Ergon, *Vinculum Mare* (the Connecting Sea), and their leader, Manannán mac Lir, would walk through the gates of Mug Ruith and explain it once again.

In the meantime, Cassius Boll and his delegation from the people of the hills, from the triple cities of Áed Rúad, Díthorba, and Cimbáeth, would stride into Mug Ruith seated high on the mechanical walkers they used to navigate the crags of ice along the equator, beyond Xanadu to the east. They would be a never-ending source of energy, haughty boisterousness and partying fervor that all of Mug Ruith looked forward to in order to break themselves out of their stolid introspective, and mostly silent lives, with shouts of, *"Carpe diem, et cras enim moriemur* (Seize the day, and tomorrow we shall die)!"

When the delegations arrived in such a manner, it was anticipated as a glorious unifying time for all Titan, a celebration of all time, at least on its surface in a moment in celebration of that specificity: the *moment*. The past and future were turned utterly away, and in living today did all celebrate that unique infinitesimal point in their lives.

Despite the fact the three great regions (Shangri-La, Kraken Mare and Xanadu) were separate and distinct cultures in every way, from politics to economics, from faith to feelings, this grand event, this guiding force was common to all. It was the grand unifier, from three into one people, *de tribus unum*, for its presence in their lives. And as a result, *"de tribus unum"* was plastered on every surface, sign and pamphlet a person could see inside the walls of Mug Ruith during the Festival. It was the only thing in the cosmos they all, every printed man, woman and child on Titan, relied upon that was bigger than themselves, bigger than all of them combined, that gave them a common, shared purpose beyond the rudiments of survival. It was in that phrase that rooted their hopes and dreams for the future.

Beneath the surface, however, old cultural rifts, like infected boils, festered and leaked all over the hearts and minds of three peoples that would be hopelessly opposed for the foreseeable future.

~

"I probably think that's quite enough," Aibell Amadán Dubh stated frustratingly. "How much do you think I can carry on my head alone, anyway?"

"Yes Mum," came the respectful reply from Grace Blieh, a high priestess and current dressing assistant who was helping Aibell robe for the Reading, which would be the climactic launch of the Festival. "I have to say though Mum, you look stunning. The costumers have outdone themselves this time."

"It's all very nice," Aibell forced. She abhorred the ostentation, much rather preferring a simple priestly vestment, minimalistic, in order to elevate the Reading, and not herself, to the high awe that it deserved.

On her head were sculpted images of the embodiment of man and woman in a circle, alternating twice, crouched and bowed in reverence, like a crown in silver, bent forward as if protecting what rose from the center like a radiant fountain of stars that glistened and twinkled in the sparse twilight of oxygen torches lighting the room without a flicker. It was dreadfully heavy and kinked Aibell's neck intolerably.

On her body were layers of heavy robes, woven with metallic threads, fine, made of platinum, gold, and copper, in layers of fine, soft "cloth" that were embroidered with cabochons of colored glass of reds, blues and yellows. Her breather was gilded, and gracefully covered her nose and mouth, exhaling white "steam" from two ports at a thirty-degree angle from both nostrils that pointed up and away from her eyes, towards the top of her ears. The angle of incidence was custom-measured for her precise ear length so that the point of her nose was connected to the streaming white gas as lines pointing precisely to the tops of what was left of human ears in all Titans. The shape completed a widening V-shape from the ear-tips when intersected by her chin's point at the base of her jaw that was both aggressive and powerful, a symbol of strength of the ages, a vision of power all could understand.

"But it's all very Gaudi. Ugh!" Aibell stated to herself in a way that sounded nothing more than a muttered thought to Grace standing next to her in a full-length mirror imperfectly made of polished aluminum.

Grace caught the utterance, however and asked, "What's 'Gaudi,' Mum?"

"What? Oh, never mind about it. I was just mumbling to myself," Aibell deflected.

Aibell's stature was tall, for a Titan. Being one-and-one-half meters tall, she 'towered' over her one-meter subjects who looked up on her in awe in large black eyes behind the palest grey-white faces any human being could possess. Humanity had adapted (both by evolution and engineering) since the Ripping, in order to maximize efficiencies around consumption: shorter, less massive beings, required less air, food and water to survive. Large black pupils allowed far more light sensitivity in a place where Sol shone like Luna's full moon disk as seen from the iridescent seas on Earth.

Skin pigment paled naturally in the absence of Earth-equivalent ultra-violet exposure that could not be matched anywhere on Titan, and no spare energy to afford such a luxury. Skin also calloused vigorously, creating a shield of dead, frostbite-resistant material that gave individuals protection from one-hundred-degree Kelvin breezes that peeled it in sheets naturally over weeks and months as a sort of molting process that became as normal as any other bodily function one experienced. One prepared, however for public events by vigorously shaving down the callous so that the 'skin' appeared as smooth and blemish-free as could be attained, a process that became an art form that turned into a whole industry blessed with great demand, and wealth.

To an outsider, Mug Ruith appeared to be populated by nearly earless, pale dwarves with large blackened eyes to those from the before-time, before the Ripping and before the Purge. Despite their relatively small stature, Titans were actually also somewhat gaunt, with limited calories to build anything in the way of strong muscles, while musculature itself adapted to smaller frames allowing muscular bulging in the legs to become most prominent, and highly desirable. However, having little in the way of food, save Dubh's Titan Grain, which over centuries was contracted to, "dubgrin," and a few, luxuriant examples of printed proteins of 'chicken', which became, "shkin," or 'rat,' which became, "shrot" in the modern dialect, nutrients were scarce to build more strength than was minimally needed in order to survive.

Nature found ways to adapt, as well as how technology did. And its relative high gravity, perhaps three times that of long-gone Europa, which became "Yurpa," Titans had relatively large, bulbous heads that were supported by short, more muscular legs beneath long, thin torsos, attached to short arms, with thickened calloused hands and fingers. Fingers totaled four, counted three plus a thumb, as what used to be called a 'pinky' was genetically removed as useless, or even a detriment, it being historically the usual first appendage to succumb to frostbite. Another was the large external ears that succumbed even faster in Titan's frigid air in the early days after the ripping, or A.R., as did large, pointed noses.

Smaller humans meant less to cover, to insulate, which meant lower consumption in nearly every area required for survival. Oxygen consumption was reduced by two thirds, calorie consumption by half, habitat volume by half also, which meant less energy to heat, less air to fill. Water needs were reduced by a third. It was systemic adaptation by necessity, a 'have to,' in order to begin again on a whole other world that has as much in common with humanity's source planet as fire had with ice. Thus, as a result of the adaptations, nearly three times as many people thrived at one meter tall (or roughly three feet in the ancient system) than three-meter (nine-foot) tall

Europans could persist otherwise. Creation was always creating while nature was always finding a way.

"Well I think we are just in time, Mum," Grace stated forgetting the awkward reference. "The clamor outside must mean the Ergon delegation has arrived." Grace looked out the window on behalf of the now seated, statuesque Aibell. "Yes, there's Manannán mac Lir now. Crowds have formed near the gate. The parade is becoming a real one now. Ah! And there's Cassius Boll! They have at least twenty walkers, with *him* in lead. I wish I could learn to ride one!"

Aibell laughed, "Surely you can't be serious! I would not have you associating with such barbarism. Perish the thought," she ended flatly with a dismissive waving gesture.

"Yes." A pause and then a small sigh came from Grace. "Perish the thought Mum," she agreed, peevishly. She sighed, introspectively deflated as she sat in a relatively grand hall that was marked only by several pillars positioned at regular intervals in a circumference around a furniture of polymer, recycled from the ruins of the old build, in a dull gray color, where all ornamentation was considered an over-luxuriant pursuit that had no place in Titan's value system—at least within Shangri-La's austere norms. All walls were like deep crimson tufted pillows in regular points that intersected in a cushioned grid around the room that was the insulation keeping the air above water's freezing point inside. A dull orange sunlight and Saturn's grand beauty cradled the sky as her glistening diamond necklace jewelry of vast rings around her glowing yellow-belted face graced the view through an orange haze of frigid tholins, methane, and nitrogen. Rays of dim sunlight formed brightened spots of the floor of Mum's chamber as its perceived radiance passed through several transparent titanium windows, installed in regular intervals between the pillars, embedded in the walls all around them. Browns and oranges and pinks prevailed. Blues and greens were wholly absent from the world, lending an ever-present foreboding under the Titan sky despite Saturn's protective gaze.

"I suppose we should make our appearance. Greet our guests. Light the torches..." Aibell trailed off. "...I need to open..." another exhaled pause "...but I think that will be coming quickly and not take much effort." There was a sense of repose and perhaps confusion in her tone, or perhaps is was that of awe, or overwhelming revelation.

"Yes Mum," Grace replied as she walked towards her beautifully dressed sovereign. "Take my hand and I'll lead you, as always, Mother." Grace said the words, the script as it were, as was required by the ritual of the Reading that marked the beginning of the Festival as a long course of interwoven ritual tapestry among the revelry of overt boisterous celebration, and the quiet whispers of corruption in dark alleyways. Aibell had no care for either, especially in that moment.

"We will meet the other two after, as is the custom, although my stomach can't seem to keep down the idea of being in the same room with them," Aibell revealed.

"Yes, Mum," Grace agreed, minimally.

"What would you have me do Grace?"

"Yes, Mum? Do, Mum?" Grace, forever obedient, forever about optics, and minimal volunteerism when it came to her sharing an opinion in response to a barely endured question, cautiously asked.

"Yes, Grace. What would you have me do if you were in my place? I permit free discussion. So please, offer your perceptions."

"Yes, Mum. As you say, Mum." Grace paused and thought for a moment and offered, "I would deny an audience and shut off the flow of dubgrin for them. They will not relent to provide those needed minerals, and with only four ships coming from mining missions per year, we must be resolute to extort what we all need from those Hill People. We can and should be doing it ourselves and not relying on outsiders for our needed materials. And if I may, Mum, they *disgust* me, and their arrogance and insolence are enough to make me vomit. They advantaged upon us wrongly. They are like animals with big ships and big mouths, the latter being more loathsome than the former. I loathe them. I loathe them all! They are nothing but animals acting as animals! Ugh!" Grace let loose and gave Aibell the validation she was looking for that echoed the sentiments within her own heart.

"So, you believe they are hopelessly steeped within the selfish wail, then?"

"Yes, Mum. Woefully so, Mum."

"And therefore, you believe they are beyond guidance—beyond hearing? Have they no ears to hear?"

Grace bowed her head in an almost embarrassing, guilty pose and answered, "Yes, Mum. I do, Mum. They have none, Mum."

"I see, Grace. And do you see them with the Spark?"

"No mum. They steal what they need from the People of the Seas, they blast their way through the hills mining for scraps of minerals they sell to both our peoples, and they can't even produce their own dubgrin! We trade so much of our stores for the scraps they provide us, and for what? Just so we can keep the peace a bit longer? We are better than that, Mum."

"Thank you, Grace, for being honest with me. 'Thou shall not deceive,' eh Grace?"

Grace forced a smile. "Yes, Mum," through a slight, and obviously forced snicker.

"I see. I see. I see what you see, Grace." A pause and a stare. Then a breath. Then a thought. Another pause, and then, "Resume normal speaking permissions now. Lead me."

"Yes, Mum," Grace reverted back into her subservient and stoic mode, took Aibell's delicate pale white, four-fingered hand, and made their way out the exit door toward the antechamber where Aibell Amadán Dubh would meditate and open, before performing the Reading high above the Central Square.

~

At the end of a long, darkened hall, sans windows of any kind, Grace led her sovereign to the resonance antechamber: a nearly fully blackened room, without windows and only a small methane torch to cast any light at all on a small polymer table. There were piles of cushions of all kinds, styles, fabrics and shapes where Aibell Amadán Dubh would sit in Om in a near corner for minutes, hours, or even days, depending on the need for the message, before she executed the Reading. Grace was left by the odd and opposite corner of wherever Aibell chose to take her place within the small dark cubist volume, with only a small seat protruding from the metal wall where she would rest patiently before attending to her Mum's every need as it arose.

Several hours passed while the Festival raged on outside the walls, to the complete obliviousness of the two within the resonance antechamber. Haughty drunken laughter and a general ruckus became the din of white noise to the citizens of Mug Ruith as they awaited the Reading. All of Titan looked up as its tidally-locked orbit around Saturn saw Sol hide behind her limb and their world darkened for twelve hours. The Festival became lit only by the few dim methane torch-lamps constructed and placed around the streets and in the windows of residences and business alike.

It began to rain.

Aibell Amadán Dubh sighed, took a deep breath and reached for Grace's guidance with a shaking, quaking hand. It was a sight Grace had not seen before in her Mum since being entrusted with her care nearly seven standard years before. In the methane light, Grace noticed blood running from her nose and what was left of ears from under the silver sculpture upon her head. Grace let out a wholly uncontrollable gasp of inhalation.

"Lead me, child, as is your duty. I permit no other action."

"What is wrong, Mum?"

"Never you mind, child. It is your time now. Remember what happens here."

"Yes, Mum," Grace begrudgingly agreed, horrified by the view of her sovereign within her gaze. Grace took her hand and Aibell rose painfully to her feet. In another nine paces, Grace and Aibell Amadán Dubh were outside in the dark and in the rain, under a tapestry of cloth that echoed the snaps of methane droplets colliding with its surface. The Reading commenced.

Aibell Amadán Dubh, Mum to all of Shangri-La and religious center of the Three Regions, and symbol of hope and unity for all peoples forever more began amidst gasps of shock, awe and horror at the bloodied, beautifully dressed towering woman high above the crowds:

"The future and the past will collide! There is a voice from the past, the future, from the moment, from the ether, from the volume that blasts its way through the cosmos for all to hear! 'See the way before you,' are the words! There will be one from two, who come, from the beyond, from the past, that will be the future for all peoples everywhere..." She trailed off as she lost her balance on the high patio above the Festival of terror-filled attendees. Grace took immediate action to hold Aibell up by her right arm that instinctively reached for her as a leaning post. The crowds gasped in fear at her unsteadiness.

The sovereign continued through her clear pain, "Giants will walk among us! The one! Elizabeth! The two! Justin! Jessica! Remember the Ripping! Remember what has been forgotten! Remember the Way! Giants of two shall stride from one, will fall from the sky upon us and bring quiet to the world. And then, you shall all have the peace you so deserve! You!"

Aibell pointed to the entire crowd in an arching, achingly slow gesture, "You all have turned your backs on the Way before you and you will suffer the wrath of your choices steeped within the selfish wail!"

Aibell staggered once again, blood pouring from her nose ears and eyes at the climactic point to all who quickly reflected her anger. She continued, "Death comes for you all! The sins of the past will be paid in the future! The way is dark and giants will stride among us! The one from two will deliver the rapture on the great blue world to all!" The 'a' part of 'all' was screamed in an extended cry reverberating over loudspeakers that was only matched by the dead silence of the crowd, the shock of the thousands of faces in a stone-faced glare, and the methane drop-snaps of collisions with all things solid in Mug Ruith.

A shot rang out.

Aibell Amadán Dubh's head exploded in a ball of ice and fire from within her now tilted headdress, her brain matter splattering over Grace Blieh's body as she stood helpless in emotional turmoil, shock and tears. The crowd gasped. Rage erupted. The world was dark. The imminent end was all the future anyone could see.

The Rage of Grace

eath rained down from the orange haze above as a pack of black autonomous drones fired magnetic railgun shots indiscriminately at the helpless crowd with repetitive (and distinctive) 'whooshes,' and inexorable 'pops,' that were explosions of methane air, superheated oxygen pellets, and pink-sprayed, sublimated flesh. Guards fired back at nimble and seemingly intelligent drones that dodged oncoming fire easily and effortlessly. The hordes scrambled and broke apart into their triadic groups attempting to find safety under metal roofs while the rain of lethality claimed life after innocent life. Grace Blieh was immediately shuffled back inside by four Ruithian guards who covered her body with their own, protecting her with their lives. Screams of terror flooded the air.

Manannán mac Lir ran with his people from Ergon who made their way to one of the market areas where shelter in the form of raised security doors doubling as roofs in their open position shielded them. As he settled in a relatively safe place with dozens of his people, he peered across the square to observe Cassius Boll, seated high on his walker, in the open, his people behind him to the eastern wall of Mug Ruith. He grinned ominously.

Within another seemingly endless moment, the shots from above ceased and the lowering pitch of the automatous drones, and bringers of terror, fled away out of sight, to the east. Cassius Boll and his entourage fled just as quickly through the main gate and headed in the same direction crying, *"Carpe diem, et cras enim moriemur!"*

In the dead silence that came at Boll's departure, cries rang out of the wounded and helpless grieving as Manannán mac Lir observed the bloodied square. It reminded him of numerous records of other massacres from history the People of the Seas recovered over the centuries after the Ripping. He shuddered. Beside him were his most trusted advisors, Dreil Brughin and Carmella Heed. He rose. His advisors rose. His people rose behind him.

Dreil, with alarm stated, "We must leave, excellency! It's clear that Boll has thrown the gauntlet down upon Shangri-La. We must return to Ergon as quickly as we can to avoid getting brought into their conflict, clearly. There is already an eighty-four-point-seven-two-percent chance we will already inexorably be dragged into it, which rises the longer we remain."

"I am quite aware, Dreil, quite aware. I see the figures too. Still, I see a larger pattern. This conflict has been simmering for over four hundred years between the two regions. Why now does Boll choose *now* to escalate? It is not logical, nor reasonable to provoke Mug Ruith into war. They will lose their supply of dubgrin, a famine will likely result for Xanadu and the triple cities..." he trailed off and sighed, paused and continued, "No. There's something more here. Something that doesn't fit the pattern of rationality that appears too obvious to me."

"*Too* obvious, Excellency?" asked Carmella. "This surety carries high statistical validity. I strongly caution against any choices based on an emotional reaction... sir," she quickly added 'sir' as a reinforcement of her respect for her leader.

"I know, I know, Carmella. I assure you I am not," mac Lir confirmed. "This doesn't make sense to me. I therefore must investigate it more deeply. Moreover, I believe it's our duty to support the leadership of Shangri-La in the immediate days following this assassination."

"Concur," came the unified agreement of mac Lir's advisors that was genuine based on the reasoning of their leader's position.

"Let us enter the Cloister then," mac Lir motivated.

"They won't allow it," Carmella stated flatly.

"They will," Manannán replied as if it had already happened in his mind. He turned to the crowd of huddled, but slowly strengthening resolute of his people behind him and called, "Tend to the wounded. Work with the Ruithian guards and have them moved to the hospital. We have only twenty healing pills, use them wisely," he ordered as he gestured to Dreil, who immediately reached into a pouch on his left forearm made of metallic fabric that glistened slightly in the dim torchlight. Dreil began distributing sealed healing pills recovered over the centuries after the Ripping and gave them piecemeal to sectional leaders of groups of nine that was the cellular structure of Ergon society.

Ten people led by one, of which made a Section. Ten Sections made a Centum and were led by one from within the Centum. Ten Centa formed a Millum,

Bimillum, Trimillum, and so-on, until finally the leader of the People of the Seas was automatically placed as a function of pure mathematics as the leader of the Transmillum. In the modern moment, the Transmillum consisted of just over two million lives, all living in the vicinity of Ergon, Vinculum Mare, in the region of Kraken Mare, in Titan's far northern polar areas. But in the far gone history of Ergon, the Transmillum was the *first* Centum.

Carmella, Dreil and Manannán mac Lir turned and walked slowly to the Cloister temple where they were instantly met with Ruithian guards who firmly pressed their rail-rifles at their chests.

"You shall not go further, Ergonite!" The guard warned, pressing the barrel of his weapon deeper into mac Lir's sternum.

"Such rage, I understand. However, you must permit me as well as my advisors to enter, for we wish to offer support to the Lady, Grace Blieh Dubh, whom I presume will be known as *Amadán* Dubh, from this point."

"You presume much, Ergonite! Our Mum still lies dead up there, and you *presume* to enter the temple?!" The guard's tone escalated but died quietly through the rain. The crowds silenced.

"I warn you, friend, without my help in this very moment, the probability of Shangri-La's long-term future survival grows short!" Manannán mac Lir screamed as loud as he could, over-emphasizing his willingness to out-perform the guard.

The argument caught the attention of the emotionally shattered Grace Blieh—now Amadán, Dubh. She raced outside, still bloodied from Aibell's demise, crying, and interrupted the verbal exchange, "You! Guard!

Allow them to pass immediately, at once, you! These are our friends! I permit it and that's all you need to know."

"Yes Mum," came the guard's peevish but submissive reply. With that, the arguing was over. Manannán mac Lir and his colleagues were guided inside a place they had never been allowed to set foot in before.

Manannán and the others were led to the central room where Aibell had dressed, her wracks of vestments, albeit plain, were plentiful as they hung on multiple metallic frameworks designed for their display in the open, each being like a rite of passage as she elevated herself to Amadán status. *Grace* Amadán now inherited it all as the same rite suddenly, and violently, passed to her, whether she earned it or not; whether she was prepared for it, or not, as a burgeoning woman of just eighteen standard years.

Grace Amadán paced in her bloodied vestments rapidly, taxing the standard white titanium-polymer breather all Titans wore so that it rhythmically groaned loudly trying to keep up with her heightened metabolism. She ripped it off her faced after it dawned on her she was safely inside an oxygenated room. She was incensed. Grace's rage was not hidden, was not filtered. Her huge black eyes widened enough to scare anyone from the before-time into a horror-filled terror for their lives in an instant with her raw anger to fuel it. She stopped and glared in mid-pace at the three Ergonites with her blood-sprayed pale tortured face that was wrangled with angst.

"What do you know of this, Manannán?! Carmella? What about you, Dreil?! Surely you must know *something*! You have all the technology around you to monitor everything. So, what do you know?!" Grace lunged forward to the Ergonite trio in an aggressive gesture that anyone could read, let alone someone skilled in reading the art of kinesics in others.

Manannán held his ground and allowed her to approach closely, which was an act as severe as one of actual physical contact in Ergonite culture, which valued a one-meter zone of personal space as an extension of their physical form. To cross it was the same for them as physical assault committed by punching someone in the jaw. Manannán allowed the moment to pass, while Dreil and Carmella gasped in disgust.

"Grace," Manannán asserted, "you must calm yourself or you will be unable to make rational decisions in this critical moment. I recommend you sit." Manannán gestured to several of the other priests in the room with them to get other garments for Grace to change into with a swirling motion of his hand toward one of the racks of vestments. "Fetch water and a cloth for our Mum to clean herself with. Dress her according to her wishes. Fetch a biscuit," which was dubgrin-based, of course, "and prepare some cooked, hot shkin; some tea. Yes, bring the tea first, once she is clothed and cleansed properly, as the Mum of Shangri-La ought to be."

Manannán turned back to Grace as he crouched before her. He took her hand and requested, "Please, Mum, sit with me here. Let us calm ourselves."

Grace nodded in agreement, as the adrenalin began retreating from her physiology. She undressed hurriedly, without care or shame. Before she could sit, the priests came with cloths, warm water, and vestments. The priests prepared to wash Grace, dry and re-robed her once again, all before Manannán and his advisors. He turned away out of the engrained sense of personal space, respect and privacy that was instinctual and automatic.

"What's the matter Manannán? We're not as uptight as you Ergonites. It's just a body. Relax!" Grace chided. Grace was cleaned and ritualistically clothed after several minutes in a silence that became deafening before long. Then she sat slowly in the sea of cushions, fabrics and pillows that was the floor.

Grace, from a bowed head position, raised her face to meet Manannán's eyes directly and said, "There will be war."

Manannán looked square back into her eyes and stated flatly, "I know. I see it too."

"The bodies. The burning. It's everywhere. Right in front of me."

"Yes, Grace," Manannán agreed. A pause, and then, "Mum, but consider the logistics. The triple cities will not fall by might alone. They cannot simply by the numbers. Mug Ruith is only one-and-half-million, Ergon, two. The triple cities are over eight! We will fight with you, Mum, but we have to seek another way. They will cut down your armies with all those ballistics they have."

"Yes, insidious those things are; spherules of carbon filled with superheated oxygen that explodes on impact igniting the damn air all around us! Who needs rocks, when you can just use the air to disembowel your enemy?! Those animals! They can't manage to make a single dubgrin, the easiest process in the world to replicate, but they spend their energies to make *those* things! They're repugnant. They must be wiped off the face of the world!" Grace re-agitated herself quickly and rose to her feet once more.

Manannán grabbed Grace's hands above her and gently guided her down, looking into her eyes the whole time, never losing the gaze-lock he put on her. She calmed and re-seated herself before him.

"What am I to do Manannán? I can pray all I want. I can refer to Gabriel all I want, for hours, days, weeks even! And all I'll find is, 'Their sole purpose is to deceive and create strife, error, confusion, anger, and resentment, further amplifying the noise of the wail. They are the noise that creates nothing but noise!'"

"Yes, and of course the obviousness of, 'If there is a person who cares only for what his neighbor has or does and does not give thanks for the blessings he himself has received instead, he is of the selfish wail,'" agreed Manannán, "...page forty-seven if I am not mistaken."

"You know your *scripture*. Good! You have earned some more of my respect Manannán. But I see not the Way before me. The Way is dark."

"I suggest you meditate, grieve. Take some food," Manannán gestured as the shkin and biscuits were served before them both. Carmella and Dreil also received their portions and partook as they listened intently to the conversation before them. "I will begin the interment process for Mum Aibell, sad as that will be for me. May I work with your people?"

"I would consider it an honor, Manannán," Grace assured. A new calmness came of over Grace like a warm wave of surety that was quietly growing in her heart and mind. She looked at Manannán who continued his deadlocked gaze upon her.

"The world knows you are young, and untested," Manannán offered. "Perhaps this is Boll's motivation. I have confusing thoughts on that however, Mum."

"As do I," Grace agreed, trailing off in a moment of introspection. Then she blurted, "Sometimes you have to be a little selfish to rise above the status quo, you know."

Manannán, startled, opened his gaze further, and asked after a momentary pause, "Those are wise words, Mum. But they are not yours."

"No, of course not. They are Jessica Forsythe's." Shock entered the chamber among all within eyeshot of Mum Grace Blieh Amadán Dubh. Stunned silence gripped the room. Even Manannán stepped back one small pace in response.

"We shouldn't mention... *her*. It's bad Karma," Manannán deflected and quickly changed the subject.

"True, regardless," Grace flatly stated, like putting up a wall that was like an immovable object to anyone trying to penetrate it.

"So, what of the words?" Manannán deflected once more. "Mum Aibell's Reading... So confusing. I am struggling to recall the precise phrasing, but she referred to the Jessica, speaking of which, and the Justin if I recall... Giants..." he trailed off in the thought, "...the ones responsible for Yurpa's destruction. Why would they be anywhere near Mum Aibell's thoughts? Their evils and steeping in the selfish wail nearly destroyed us all... trying to touch God. Disgusting... I can almost feel a shudder and a sick feeling in my stomach when I think of them."

"As do I, my friend," Grace affirmed, "but I sense a deeper meaning. Somehow there may be a false premise to be cautious of. I'm not quite sure. The Way is dark."

Carmella then approached and interjected, "I have the transcript at the ready, Mum, my Lord. Allow me to recount it."

"Of course, go," Grace stated flatly as mac Lir nodded in agreement.

Carmella recited and said, "The Reading was as follows:

The future and the past will collide. There is a voice from the past, the future, from the moment, from the ether, from the volume that blasts its way through the cosmos for all to hear. 'See the way before you,' are the words. There will be one from two, who come, from the beyond, from the past, that will be the future for all peoples everywhere. Giants will walk among us. The one. Elizabeth. The two. Justin. Jessica. Remember the Ripping. Remember what has been forgotten. Remember the Way. Giants of two shall stride from one, will fall from the sky upon us and bring quiet to the world. And then, you shall all have the peace you so deserve. You. You all have turned your backs on the Way before you and you will suffer the wrath of your choices steeped within the selfish wail. Death comes for you all. The sins of the past will be paid in the future. The way is dark and giants will stride among us. The one from two will deliver the rapture on the great blue world to all.

"Quite ominous," Carmella added. "Clearly she was more emotive in her delivery. A failing, certainly. On face, I would conclude easily that the end of Titan was coming. Perhaps she knew of her impending demise. Perhaps she knew something about the assassination plot by Boll already."

"Perhaps she let it happen! Perhaps she *knew* it would," Grace exclaimed, "somehow!"

"Maybe," Manannán added. "I am not so sure of anything. As you said, Mum, the Way is dark."

"But who is this *Elizabeth*?" Dreil asked. "I have nothing of a significant historical contribution by anyone of that name in Yurpan history. Accessing archives now, Lord." A few-second pause and then, "Complete. While several thousand individuals of given names, 'Elizabeth' or with common derivations do appear, no one stands out in the historical record that would link Aibell's Reading to them. I'm at a loss, Lord. Mum."

"Then, 'one from two,' 'giants,' *etcetera*, 'future for all peoples everywhere,' sounds like a prophecy or something," Grace analyzed. "Or a couple of them."

"Indeed," Manannán thoughtfully agreed. "But any prophecy normally brings the promise of everlasting life, or something, not the end of everything. Not the rapture. The quiet of the world may mean the destruction of all human life on Titan for all we know."

"That would surely make it quiet!" Grace exclaimed.

Dreil added, "No. That's too simple. Too obvious. We're missing key variables. The razor cuts both ways."

"Occam's Razor, Dreil?" Manannán replied.

"Indeed, Lord," Dreil agreed. "Disproven centuries ago as the root of false premise in all human history."

"Really?" Grace chided peevishly. "Disproven by whom?

"Bad Karma be damned, but Justin Forsythe in his uncovering of the AI subculture on Yurpa before the Ripping. No one expected centuries of culture thriving beneath an underworld in a main one that held full disclosure as its ideal. His words were, 'truth is always stranger than fiction.' It was proven time in memorial throughout the broken record of pre-Yurpan history, and in the Yurpan history we have managed to cobble together. The Yurpans themselves, the voluminous nature of the cosmos, the Divine realms, all described and known by the indigenous Yurpans as a function of their natural existence... The mind-drives, and their ultimate destruction of civilization because of the foundation on which they were built, the list goes on. Both he and Jessica did contribute that. However, as we all know, they destroyed Yurpa. They destroyed us. Thus, giving us their ignoble status in our culture today."

"Ugh!" Grace cried. "They make me sick! And Aibell said they're coming here? *Here?!* We must prevent that at all costs."

"We are straying from the proper course of logic and reason in favor of irrational emotions," Manannán stated flatly. "It is irrational to conclude that two humans from Yurpa who died a half-a-millennium ago will be raised from the dead to bring us extinction, in some kind of rapturous event. They are not coming here. They cannot, because they are dead. It is reason, logic, pure and simple. But I still do not believe this Reading to be a religious event, but a scientific one."

Grace asked, "Yeah? Why's that?"

"Because of something Aibell said. She mentions, 'the beyond, from the past, that will be the future.' That sounds like the voluminous time realms to me."

"Yes, we all know that some Ergonites still have some sort of access... *somehow.* You did manage to steal the one working printer on the whole planet from the Progenitor, Amadán Dubh all those centuries ago, too!" Grace poked at the rift between Mug Ruith and Ergon that was its own centuries-old scar. Maybe you made mind drives using that and now you already know everything that will ever happen."

"That is... that is impossible. The one working printer we have cannot print barely a shkin let alone a quantum engine. I assure you, that technology is long-dead and well-beyond anyone's capability. Be comforted, Lady," Manannán soothed. "I am not trying to provoke you, assuredly."

"Yet, you have..." She let out an exhale of aggression that was as volatile as ethane and flame as she leaned in purposely close to his face well beyond the one-meter imagined line of personal Ergonite space around him. Another punch in the jaw.

Manannán continued with acknowledging her emotional acceleration, "The fact remains we do have access to a great deal of information from the before-time and information that was stored in the voluminous time dimensions using a working quantum computer. Your people have a perception of it also, hence the Readings. But yours is in a different way, it being hereditary running in lines of daughters for generations. You sense it. You perceive it, without a device of any kind. Your innate abilities, honestly, can be traced back to centuries even before the Purge! It runs in families, and in yours, clearly."

"Flawlessly correct as always, Manannán," Grace released in both tone and gesture, like releasing a choke hold around a prey animal.

"We mustn't quarrel, Mum. It is not productive," Manannán pleaded.

"Yet, we quarrel!" Grace refused to relent as her eyes narrowed.

Manannán did, however. "I will not."

"Very good, Manannán. Very good. You see who your Mum is now, yes?"

"Indeed, Mum," Manannán submitted. "That was never in question, I assure you."

"Very good." The pissing contest was over for the moment. Grace continued, "Whatever form these two coming abominations take in our world, I will control it. I will do whatever is in my power to prevent this rapture, extinction, destruction from ever happening. Is that clear, Manannán? When whatever it is that is coming Aibell saw comes, I will be the one to catch it, and kill it, before it starts."

"Yes, Mum," Manannán replied flatly. He became introspective and calmness overtook his demeanor, as if a glistening of insight lit a way before him, and him alone.

Then Grace, also thinking she found new levels of calm in the moment absent from her recent memory stated ominously, "I see it. I see the Way before me."

"What way?" Manannán asked seriously.

Glancing out of the sides of her eyes, after a brief silence, Grace matter-of-factly replied, "For the Reading, I have given you my position. For Boll," she laughed haughtily, "For that *thing*, it's simple, really. We shall give Boll what he desires most." Grace laughed haughtily that resonated in the chamber.

Manannán looked down and his kinesics connoted trepidation. "Relax, Ergonite, *de tribus unum* is now *ex multis duo.*"

Manannán sat down, and a broad smile came across his face, as if knowing precisely what she had in mind before her revealing it. He sighed. I see it too. I see the Way before us both. Indeed! Let us give Boll what he desires most!" And they heartily finished their meals and began preparations to exercise the funeral rites of Aibell Amadán Dubh, Mum to all Titan and the Three Regions. Then he muttered under his breath, "the Way lies."

A barely-noticed Sol then spread its dim light on the world once again.

The Grace of Rage

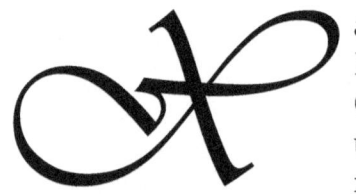anadu, the Triple Cities of the Hills, Áed Rúad, Díthorba, and Cimbáeth, regaled in the triumphant return of an eight-million person strong populations' godhead, that was Cassius Boll and his legion of twenty-five glistening walkers. In the Main Square, the common space centrally located between the outskirts of the Triple Cities and kilometers wide, millions flocked to the theatre districts and rallied to the media centers where they watched in amazement their great leader demonstrating once again how his power and glory were paramount in their lives. Layered in fabrics, heavy boots, facial breathers and eyewear of all kinds made the crowds appear to be an army of scrapping, rugged pioneers eking out a living from rocks and bones. It was not far from the truth in the cold. But they were far from starving, helpless or powerless. All loved Cassius. Cassius loved all his people. He was their savior, their godhead, their caregiver...

...their *everything*.

Cries from the din unified under an everlasting, slow chant, "Boll! Boll! Boll!" slow and low, so that it was a powerful hum of perfectly unified anger and joy in the moment of one thought, expressed by the exhalation of one great breath, by the largest group of people on Titan, in unison. For them, it was the personification of sweet revenge over a long-dead divine power that no one in the Triple Cities believed in any more.

"Boll! Boll! Boll!" echoed against the cubist buildings in the three directions anyone could see in the Main Square. Tall and metallic, and coated by brown tholin dust, the edges peaked through the orange haze of Titan's dim atmosphere such that one may have felt like they were swaying in the breezes, or floating on a writhing sea.

Having seen the events—the *assassination!*—of Mug Ruith's holy leader, televised either in their homes, or preferably in a voluminous mob within the theatre districts in the Main Square (a party no one could conceive of missing unless taken deathly ill), the people of the Triple Cities finally came to understand their power on their world. Power was the bromide of choice for them, and one they drank wholeheartedly. Power was as much their god as Cassius Boll ever was.

The Regents of Áed Rúad, Díthorba, and Cimbáeth prepared to meet their leader in the Main Square, coordinated the return with the populace and ensured that the warmest of welcomes would meet Boll and the legion. For Áed Rúad, there was the broad and stout Conrad Holmes. For Díthorba, there was the relatively tall and graceful Reyna Mead. Finally, for Cimbáeth there was the rising star of Xanadu and likely next in line to The Chair, Xavier Rademacher.

Xavier Rademacher was a rising star in every way that mattered. He won nearly every physical contest since he was printed, among those his own age, women and men included. He had a singular, infectious wit that everyone gravitated towards as being the proverbial, "life of the party." As far as popularity contests were concerned, one would be hard-pressed to find anyone who was not nearly as enamored with Xavier, as they were with Cassius, especially with the throwback blonde locks and dazzling, massive steel eyes that contrasted wholly with Boll's much darker, throwback skin tone and large brown eyes.

Even for a time, a whirlwind rumor spread around the Triple Cities that he and the very discriminating, Reyna Meade, were the hottest item on Titan. Though never confirmed, it was never denied either. If Conrad Holmes was the man's man on Titan, it most certainly was Xavier Rademacher that was the ladies' version.

Barring Xanadu's social elites' populist drama among the Regents, however, nothing compared to the stature of Cassius Boll in both areas of relating to his people, men and women alike. For the male population, Boll was the teacher-father that taught them how best to be a man, be self-reliant, be strong and most of all, be stolid in every aspect of their lives, especially in celebrating life. For the female population, he was the father figure, the caregiver, the provider, the strong shoulder that any person would be a fool not feeling safe leaning on, or crying on. Weakness in either was wholly denounced, and all movement away emotional forces that drove them forward, energizing the self to overcome or to celebrate was replete in the culture.

Men and women were entirely equal. None were perceived as weaker, or lesser, or *anything*-er, relative to one another. Whoever was strongest, fastest, smartest, more creative or productive were simply *better* than those who were not, based on performance in the moment, and were rewarded accordingly. Failure was not an option, and the word, 'can't' did not exist in their lexicon. Excuses were punished severely. Taking ownership for failings was rewarded.

The people of Xanadu and the Triple Cities were the most resolute culture to have arisen since the Ripping, as was demonstrated by their unqualified success at recovering the human population relative to those of the other two Regions and their host cities. As a result, the People of the Hills, both women and men were respected, and sometimes feared, outside Xanadu equally as well, as fierce and unpredictable. They were most likely similar to the stature of ancient Norwegian tribes, commonly called, 'Vikings,' in personality, save for the bloodthirstiness. Still, no one dared provoke them needlessly.

Cassius Boll rode triumphantly to the center of the Main Square and disembarked, his feet falling the two meters from the top of the titanium 'animal' that functioned directly into his brain via liquid-metallic protuberances that integrated with him through his hands. It was itself, semi-intelligent, almost AI in nature, and given a name when 'born.' Boll named his walker, "Urso," having read stories as a child about bears that roamed the old cultures of Earth before the Purge. Cassius took a liking to their ferocity, strength, and unceasing persistence, to the point of being obstinate. It spoke to him like an image of himself as he looked within a mirror.

Boll climbed the stairs to the central square, elevated nine meters above the ice-ground, and the millions of loving, loyal subjects, that were, for him, his extended family in his charge. He spoke in a deep, plain tone that echoed through the thick orange haze as it was amplified hundreds of times through the Main Square via a microphone awaiting him and speakers placed throughout the theatre districts. He waited for the chant of, "Boll! Boll! Boll!" to slowly diminish which seemed like minutes of him staring resolute at the fabric-layered masses of encrusted pale-skinned faces adapted to the chill.

Boll said, "My family! What has needed to happen *has* happened! The witch of Mug Ruith is dead!" A deafening roar overcame all electronic voice amplification and Boll was forced to exhibit his stolid, resolute patience with all those he loved.

A few seconds passed, and Boll continued, "The centuries have been brutal. For over five-hundred standard years we have endured here since the Ripping, without anyone's help, foretelling, assistance, or fated guidance! We, the people of Xanadu have thrived despite the lies of false gods the People of the Sands have forced upon us! The so-called annual messages from the so-called 'Mums of the Sands' have misguided all people on Titan and everywhere! Those pacifist priests have been controlling us everywhere in the System for *millennia!* Now, finally! It all comes to an end. Now!"

Another long roar from the crowd interrupted Boll, to his great pleasure.

He continued, "Today, I have taken the first step toward the future of humanity that places *us* in its center! Tomorrow, we will wipe the face of Titan of all those who oppose us! War has come. *Our* war! And it will lead to our salvation! Not by some made-up divine god, not by some false premonition! No! By *my* choice! By *my* hand! By *my* will and *my* heart! I will wipe away the stench of superstition and mysticism put in our culture by long-dead, misguided humans from a world that no longer exists! A storm is coming! *My* storm! By my power do I blaze a new world before us that is the might of Xanadu for all time to come! *Carpe diem, et cras enim moriemur! Carpe diem, et cras enim moriemur!*"

The crowd erupted with a clamor never before seen on Titan or anywhere in human history since the Purge.

~

The following day, a mass of metal that were ten thousand walkers began the long march out into the western desert, towards Xanadu's salvation from the tyranny of religious dogma and fated existence. Pale faces riding meters high with huge, darkened eyes loyally and steadfastly formed columns behind the will of their god-like leader as they marched. The walkers' spiked bipedal legs made a thunderous cracking sound as the penetrated deeply into the rock hard ice-ground, ensuring a slip never would occur, like a billion silver spiders headed together to claim a prize that only one would attain.

~

"And so it begins," came a barely vocal whisper, rasped and deep from the dark from behind Boll's seat in the Main Residence. "Once this is done, you will be *god* to them. You will be their... *emperor*. You *get* me?"

Boll snickered and turned, looking skyward toward the ceiling, toward the source of the question. He said, "Of course I do. When this works, and I know it will because of those trilobites out there still living in the past of false premises, I will rule this world. My rage will ensure it. And everything will be finally right after all these millennia... after all the lingering failures. Finally! It will be right again. So, yes. I get you!"

Out of the darkness and into the artificial methane flame light strode a three-meter-tall white giant, with platinum blonde hair and pale blue eyes toward Boll's relatively child sized throne. The giant placed his gigantic right hand on Boll's left shoulder and said, "Yes, my friend, my *emperor*. We will get what is ours, has been ours for forty millennia and we can finally rescue my people from the ring."

Boll sighed. A thoughtful pause came and he stated, "We'll need power to run it. To run one that big..." he trailed in thought and finished, "...to get it working. We need lots of power... capacitors. That's the one thing we cannot make here. Not yet."

"We will," the tallness flatly affirmed. "We will have exactly what we need. You get me? We need patience in the moment, however. You will have it with discipline and patience. Everything starts with the first one. You get me, Cassius?"

Another long drawn breath drew in Cassius Boll's lungs, like the gathering of fuel for his soul. He exhaled slowly in the dim light, taking a sip of dubgrin rye. He looked down, slowly, paused and said, "I see the truth of it, Argus. I see... *everything*.

~

The march of a what appeared to be a billion silver spiders stopped before the great city. Its blazing white polymer-titanium blend towers was dirtied only by the brown and orange hazes that the Titan air soiled its bubble with, like fine dust from a great cinnamon desert. Lights were replete on every surface, powered by electricity and the lot of ivory spires domed in a bubble of perfectly breathable air where a million people lived out their lives in relative peace so far from the forces of chaos at the equator. Those lights' reflections drew delicate, graceful lines in the reflection against the slowly crashing ethane waves of Vinculum Mare's shoreline.

The city of Ergon, its unsuspecting inhabitants, and loquacious and wholly distracted military swam in their blanket of conceited, comforted assumed safety as the thousands of two-legged metal spiders came over the eastern hill. Above them, hundreds of vast, winged machines, like those on the ground, but with two massive slowly flapping Kevlar wings, instead of legs, cast long shadows against the frozen ground and began bombing runs around the perimeter of the dome. Superheated oxygen instantaneously ignited the ethane and methane vapors in the air, creating massive blue-white explosions that shook the ice beneath them all. Bombs, like the bullets that killed the Ruithans, were twenty times larger, and created a force that was to the twentieth power more destructive.

The dome fell quickly.

The spiders rushed in.

Ergon, Vinculum Mare fell.

Thousands of Boll's troops rushed in and captured key centers of power, communications, recycling, and resources. People, who normally refrained from emotional outcries, did so in a wail so loud that Boll's soldiers joked about being able to be heard all the way to Earth. Any who resisted, died instantaneously at the hands of walkers, its Xanadu riders, and their magnetic rail guns, or titanium blades. Resistance, if any, died quickly. Those who surrendered were herded like tied cattle to hastily-dug pits meters deep and wide where hundreds of thousands were pushed into.

But for most Ergonians, it was *genocide.*

Before the standard day was done, most of the population of Ergon was dead, dying, or captured. Most were not the latter. Some of the captured elite were rounded up and placed in a make-shift detention camp in a guarded public square in the center of Ergon, across from the Capitol Building, on display for all Titan to see. Over one-hundred thousand Ergonites in the camp, and many others more in the chilling prison pits from every walk of life were all that remained to witness the fall of reason and logic. Those in the pits died in hours. With it any hope died for finding a path toward civilization once more after the Ripping.

The people's weeping would not relent.

Then finally, it came.

"Excellency! We have it. We have it!" Xavier Rademacher exclaimed over the radio, speaking directly to Cassius Boll in The Chair, Argus dutifully by his side.

Boll and Argus glanced at each other and smiled. Boll replied, "Good. Secure it. There will be a visitor shortly. It will be gone before you know it. Keep that area secure. Continue the interrogations."

"Yes excellency," Xavier obeyed.

Argus left the room.

Ergon burned. In the city center, Xavier Rademacher coordinated the migration of Ergon's remaining population to Xanadu where their fates were as yet unclear.

Materiel transports followed the silver spider walkers in the supply line that ran south to the Sands, where Mug Ruith stood, wholly unaware of Ergon's sacking.

Anyone in Mug Ruith, who was worried about war, was worried about it coming from Xanadu against *them*. No one was even looking toward Ergon, not Grace Blieh

Amadán Dubh, and not certainly Manannán mac Lir. The only thing that told them both something was wrong were a few spotty radio transmissions railed in chaos, explosions, screams and frantic calls for backup and assistance, which lasted only minutes.

Before long there was the gloating announcement and parade of elite Ergonites in the pen, then the cry, "*Carpe diem, et cras enim moriemur!*"

After, there was only static from the Ergonite channels.

The transports traveled longline to the center of a burning former beauty of human creativity. One at a time, each was filled with the last remaining survivors of a genocide that would burn in Ergon's cultural psyche for millennia in the future, and none who were once from Ergon would ever be the same again. The chaos of the mob had once again triumphed over reason, logic, sanity and civilization as it had so many other times in human history since the Purge, and certainly, before it, like the burning of the Library of Alexandria so many millennia before.

~

"What are they looking for Manannán?!" Grace screamed at the broken man before her, limp and morally destroyed. "What do you have?! What is it!? Tell me! Tell me now! Is it a printer? *The* printer? The one you people stole from the Progenitor all those years ago?" Grace kicked his body as hard as she could in asking while Carmella and Dreil were physically held at bay by Ruithian guards protecting their Mum.

Through Manannán's tears and spit, from the floor, he cried, "No! That *puny* thing? That was non-functional centuries ago. How do you think we were able to build

Ergon to the beauty that's there today?" He caught himself. "That *was* there?" He paused and took a tortured breath. "That will never be again!" He sobbed. "Two million lives! Gone! ...by savages with pitchforks and torches screaming at the sky!" He wailed, uncontrollably.

Grace stopped him and asked sharply, "What do you know Manannán?!"

Through Manannán mac Lir's dire, desperate cries, he called out as loud as he could muster, "We... have..." He gasped and gulped for air. We have... a printer. A gigantic, beautiful printer. We *had....*" He trailed off in his grief. *"That's* what Boll wants. That's what he's after.

"You... What?!" Grace was incensed. "You have a full printer, from before the Ripping. Running. Intact?! With not the power it needs to run it?" Then came a pause and a breath.

"Liar!" she screamed.

"It's true. But not what you think. It was here! It was already here! By the sea! By Kraken Mare! Right on the coast, waiting for us! It was there, just... just sitting there, when my people arrived. I'm telling you!"

"...and you withheld this information from me. From *us*. From *everyone* on Titan... for five-*hundred years!*" She let out a scream no Ruithian ever heard a mum let out in their collective memory. Guards' stiffened and took a step back, slightly.

"We did not set out to deceive you, assuredly," Manannán pleaded.

Then there was along, calming pause before Grace responded.

"Yet... ...you have... deceived, omitted and lied!" Her eyes shut and let her mind take her on a steeping journey that to anyone outside was personified by another exhale of calm aggression. It was a stunted growling grunt which was as volatile as ethane and flame as she leaned in purposely close to his face well beyond the one-meter imagined line of personal Ergonite space around him. She motioned to her guards. There would be no further punches delivered to his proverbial jaw. Not this time. The line drawn in the orange air was deeper and fixed than it ever had been. Instead, she motioned swiftly in her mind to her loyal guards. And in the next moment, the Ergonite delegation was silenced before her, permanently. Then Grace Blieh Amadán Dubh warmly welcomed the furious rage steeping within her mind and very soul.

She then opened her eyes and gazed upon her last allies on all of Titan, objectively alive but emotionally gutted, who pleaded for *her* help. Their imagined demise, dwindled in her mind and she again saw the man she held in such high regard return to her. And then she remembered why she was so enamored by him.

"Save me from *me*, Manannán. I beg you."

Then Boll's forces were at her walls.

Fight and Flight

xplosions rattled the oldest city on Titan as the cries of death and pain filled the air. Grace, Manannán, Carmella, and Dreil ran to the Reading platform and saw the thousands of shiny walkers hundreds deep as far as their eyes could see in both directions of their field of view, to the east. Mug Ruith's security and modest military, on high alert after the assassination bravely confronted the invaders at ingress after ingress, only to be smashed by oxygen bombs and pellets in blue fire and pink snow.

Boll's forces poured in like a flood of water after the breaking of a dam, relentlessly laying waste to anything, or anyone, in their way.

Grace stared inevitability squarely in the eye.

Manannán saw it in hers.

"We need to run, Mum. We need to run, now!" Manannán pleaded.

"Run?! I don't run! I cannot. I *will* not," Grace entrenched.

"We *must*. We must run, or we are all dead. Right here. Right now," Manannán parried. "We will run or everything that Mug Ruith is and ever was will be gone forever. You may not care about your own life, in some sort of warped sense of martyrdom, but I for one, cannot, *will* not, have your blood on my hands, and that of our entire culture for that matter."

"It's not *our* culture anymore! Is it!?" Grace screamed.

"In the moment, no," Manannán agreed. "But do you want that to be forever?"

"No. Of course not," Grace relented.

"Then we need to go. Now!" Manannán ordered. "Let's head to the southern gate."

"Yes, it's rarely used. I doubt Boll's walkers will focus much on it. We may be able to slip out," Grace offered. She motioned for her twenty-three dedicated guards to follow the foursome, knowing full-well they would lay down their lives to protect hers, and theirs.

They went back into the cloister, quickly fitted rebreathers and insulation garments on. Dreil instantly began running down a list of survival gear needed for a long journey:

"Oxygen generator. Local printer. Water purifier. Dubgrin still. Extra clothes. Goggles. Boots. The Way."

"We don't have all that in here!" Grace yelled. "Oxygen, yeah. Water-purifier, ok. Clothes, boots, the Way. Fine. Forget the printer. Grab some sacks of dubgrin from the gray cabinet by the bed. Get the guns! Ammo! We can't carry any more! We need to go!"

Explosions rocked the cloister and debris from above began to fall to the fabric and cushion floor.

"Hurry!" Carmella yelled.

Dreil grabbed seven sacks of raw dubgrin as instructed and placed it inside his pack, which weighed him down more than twice his accustomed carrying weight. He grunted his adaptation to its force on his back. "Got it!" he cried.

"Run!" Manannán called.

Stairs to the ground seemed endlessly long and monumentally challenging to navigate as panicked adrenalin flooded the four's bloodstreams. All around their ears were the sounds of explosions and dying cries.

Reaching the bottom, the main door greeted them to the outside where Grace stood between it and the others. "No. Not here. They'll be watching this for my escape. There has to be another way out."

"Okay. Where?" Manannán asked.

"I don't know. I never used any entrance but this one. We don't have time to be hunting around for secret exits!" Grace trembled.

"We need to make a break for it," Manannán offered. "We all go at once through this door, make our way to the southern gate. Pray some of us make it."

"We cannot just—!" Grace stopped in mid-sentence, seeing the futility of protesting any further. She sighed. "It's the only way." Grace looked at the people she'd come to know and love for most of her formative life as protectors of Amadán Mums over the years. She gathered her strength and ordered, "All of you will rush through the doors and keep us in the center. Hold them off as long as you can so we can get away south. I know you didn't ask for this. But it's the only way the Way is showing us. The Way is dark, except for this. Your sacrifice will be rewarded in the Magnificent Volumes. I'll pray for you, always."

Her guards all snapped to attention in response, verbally accepting their orders with bravery and honor. There was no need for Grace to explain further. They knew their duty, and they knew they would offer their lives up for a far greater purpose.

Grace called, "Go!" and the doors swung open to the conflagration that raged outside. The group of twenty-seven made their way out as a unit and was immediately noticed. Blue fire rained at them from afar. Merely fifty meters separated them from Boll's main army battling the remaining Ruithian military resistance.

They moved. Fast.

As the pursuing army closed in rapidly due to the walkers' larger strides and power, Grace's last gasp for escape in the form of the people and allies sworn to protect her she emerged with fired back relentlessly. As they did so, they moved around the cloister building, the only cylindrical structure in Mug Ruith, and took shelter by remaining in the blind behind the circular wall as they moved.

Boll's forces closed in. Fast.

The protection from guns and the shapes of walls began to fail them. Guards on the outer perimeter of their cell protecting the jewel within it began falling as the angle of view that blinded the walkers grew narrower and narrower.

But Grace's cell finally reached the southern wall.

Amongst closing gunfire and falling comrades Grace called out, "There! Eight meters! Go!"

Carmella and Dreil looked at each other ominously. Carmella cried, "We won't make it! There's not enough time!"

"It will have to be!" Grace cried back.

Five meters.

"There's no time! You can't make it!" Dreil exclaimed.

"There is no 'can't!'" Grace yelled. "We make our stand here then!"

"Shoot for the legs!" Carmella cried out. The guards obeyed and walkers began falling. Fast.

Grace took Dreil by the head, looked him dead in the eyes and said, "Buy us time. I just need time. Please." Carmella was next to both and knew what her Mum was asking. She looked at Dreil and with a glance they both knew what needed to be done.

Three meters.

Dreil came out from the center of the group, Carmella closely following.

One meter.

Eyes from the guards glanced at them quickly and knew full-well what was required of them. Then Dreil yelled, "For our Mum! Attaaaack!"

With that battle cry did he, Carmella and the remaining guards rush toward their attackers as Grace and Manannán rushed through smallest of openings in the barely noticed southern gate.

They ran. Fast.

Dreil, Carmella and the guards, aiming their pistols at the walkers' legs proved an effective strategy, albeit obvious one. It gave the smallest number of people with the greatest military training in two devastated regions, to hold the line for their mission of a lifetime: *buy us time*. With it, the team bought not just seconds, but whole minutes, as Boll's walkers advanced no further against the fiery tumult unleashed by Mug Ruith's last stand, at least for a little while.

The brief pause in forward progress only emboldened Boll's forces, however, who regrouped slightly and backed away from the piles of fallen walkers piling up in front of them. Then, using the pile as a hill, the next onslaught came over it, and from the higher position, took aim at the remaining guards, where they quickly and finally were put to rest. Carmella and Dreil's lifeless bodies fell so that each other's large black eyes were each other's final solace as their end met their new beginning in voluminous time.

One meter. Five minutes. That was time enough, but as expensive as the rarest of jewels, paid for by twenty-five lives at a price of five lives per minute, or a scant twelve seconds per life.

Grace and Manannán ran as fast as their short legs and weighed-down statures could, carrying what was left of their supplies. Beyond the walls of Mug Ruith was a vast open cinnamon desert of frozen ices, and blowing grains of black hydrocarbon sand against an orange translucent sky. The battle raged behind them: a known threat and blisteringly loud. The way before them was its opposite: unknown and silent. Yet they still ran.

Grace looked up at the haze and saw something new in the sky that was nowhere near Saturn and her other moons. I white point of light, bright like a sun appeared where no sun should have been. She said as they ran, "What *is* that? Do you see it Manannán?"

"I do, Mum. Not certain what it is."

"It's not a comet or a meteor is it?"

"No. Definitely not a comet. Not out here. We wouldn't see it, not like on Yurpa when they could. Not a meteor either. It's in orbit. It's not falling."

"What is it then, a ship?"

"That'd be a big ship if we can see its reflection all the way down here. Nothing we have is larger than a two-person vessel, even back home." Manannán paused and suddenly reaffirmed that his home was utterly gone in his mind. "No. ...nothing like that anywhere in orbit around Titan, that's from Titan."

"Well it seems to be pointing the way south, just being over the horizon there. We're going where it is, I guess. It leads us."

"It would seem so," Manannán agreed.

Titan's merciful breezes covered their tracks rapidly in the black sands while the craggy terrain made by water ice "rocks" formed spikes and other jagged features that made excellent hiding places from the pursuing army. Islands of crag replete with cave-like openings between the sands left Boll's forces to search them all in pursuit, slowing them down to a crawl.

And they ran.

Grace tired first. Inside the hundred-and-third craggy spire of ice and sand (or other random number that could have been assigned to it at the time) she and Manannán came across they entered a darkened void that led deep beneath the surface. Not too steep but sufficiently below ground to keep their heat signatures out of sight of hunting drones, the two decided to risk a rest and to take stock of their situation. White breath torched the empty air around them both.

"I'm thirsty," Grace flatly stated. "Do we still have the water purifier?

"Yes, Mum," Manannán replied just as flatly, as he began to stop ignoring his own exhaustion. He pulled it out of his pack and could be barely seen in the nearly absolute black of the void the two found themselves. Grace began picking up ice chunks off the "ground" and handing them to Manannán who placed them inside the cylindrically-shaped water purifier.

"Here," she said, referring to another chunk of frozen water as she handed it to Manannán. I have the dubgrin so if you're hungry..." she trailed off, still breathing heavily.

"Yeah," Manannán said, "we should eat. Might be the last chance we get for a while. I'll even have some salt after the purification cycle is done with the water."

The cave was silent for a while as the pair were stunned and defeated in ways that ran as deep as any childhood trauma could have. As adults, the survivors of Boll's aggressions, the presumed last of their prospective regions, were stunned into agonizing silence as the blue flame and pink snow was all they saw in their minds for a long while.

"Today's my birthday. Did you know that Manannán?" Grace blurted.

"Happy *print* day then, Mum," Manannán emphasized. "So, all of nineteen standard years now? Huh. Trying being thirty. You're still a child in many ways, Mum."

"It's not that young. Stop it. I got us out of *that* mess didn't I?"

"Yes..." Manannán reflected a moment. "You did, at that. That was quick thinking I admit. But the cost..."

"Damn the cost! We are still here to fight another day, right? If we were dead, it wouldn't matter. But it does, so here we sit! Do not presume to lecture me Manannán mac Lir! You'd be dead and frozen solid if it weren't for me..."

Manannán stopped her in mid-rant by saying, "...if it weren't for those twenty-five people who died, you mean. Right? Carmella and Dreil? You mean *those* people. Right, Grace? And what about all the others who died? Your whole city is probably dead! Just. Like. Mine. So save your self-indulgent glorification if you don't mind."

"Fine," Grace relented, as her anger and sorrow mixed in froth like oil and vinegar dressing being poured onto a bitter salad.

More silence.

"Manannán," Grace asked, "where should we go?" We just can live out here in the wastes. We'll die for sure once the dubgrin runs out. I cannot make more. Not without a fermenter." The water purifier hummed softly and emitted a low, yellow light that was the heat source doing its job. The light went out indicating its task was complete. Manannán poured hot water into two cups he had in his pack, its steam blanketed the air around them. He pulled out the collection tray that revealed white crystalline salts that he sprinkled on her white, molting hand. She smiled at him.

Manannán sipped with her. He answered, "I know of a story told to me as a child about a place far to the south that has seas and is full of life. It's a child's story. A fairy-tale, as they used to call them. It's called Wonderland."

"Wonderland? What does that mean? It's a land of wonder? Or will I wonder about it when I search for it for weeks presumably and not find it?" Grace asked sardonically.

Manannán answered, "It's a children's story. You know, for ones who were just printed. They don't know anything and they barely know how to speak. But basically it tells of a lonely peaceful giant who knows everything you do who lives by the southern lakes, in Romo. The story says if you're good then the giant will reward you by giving you wondrous gifts, hence the name. But if you're bad he will punish you by taking away something you hold dear. 'Good' is being logical, reasonable and calm. 'Bad' is being emotional, hyperactive and irrational. So, it's what my guardians used to instill the merits of my peoples' rejection of as much emotive expression as is possible in favor rational, calming thought. It's a child's take on the fundamentals of the Way before the Way is introduced."

Grace blurted, "Ha! That *is* a good tool for that. Wish I thought of it." She grunted and growled then said, "I wish someone would have told it to Boll when he was just printed... or their whole damn region for that matter!"

"I couldn't know if he did or didn't."

"Obviously," Grace charged. "What's this giant's name anyway? Does he have one?"

"He's called, 'The Midge.'"

"'The Midge?' That's an odd name," Grace commented taking another warming sip of hot water. Then, in the distant air they heard a low humming getting slowly louder. Unbeknownst to them both, the steam from their freshly purified water was rising like a white plume into the orange haze of Titan's atmosphere, that was like sending up a flare for a rescue neither of them wanted. Manannán and Grace figured it out and rapidly dumped their water onto the ground and snuffed it with their boots, covering it in frozen ices until all heat was dispelled.

Manannán then said as they hunkered down in a corner of the cave, "Seeker drones. They must have seen the steam coming up through the opening. If they're far off they may not know exactly where it was coming from, or can figure out if it was artificial or just some natural cryo-volcanism. We must remain still. Don't make a sound."

The sound of drones, however, got louder as they approached. The pair covered themselves completely in all of their garments and layers keeping in the little warmth they needed to stay alive in the frigid environment. They looked helplessly on each other's exhalation vapor that was like beacons of white steam that rapidly evaporated before them. At the peak of the drones' volume they heard them stop and hover above their transitory shelter, inspecting every thermal eddy in the air for any signs of human life. The two held their breaths for what seemed to be an eternity before the drones became satisfied the vapor, they saw from a kilometer away, was a natural phenomenon that had simply ceased.

They sat motionless, nonetheless, for several more minutes, far beyond the point after the seeker drones' waning hum could no longer be heard by either of them. As they sat, they each relented to steeping fully into what would be a permanent state of fear.

Without warning, in the absolute black and deafening silence of the space around them a pattern of white particles of light zig-zagging appeared before them. Their ears rang. The aberration's winking and particle's vectors were so random that no eye could follow or predict. As a whole, its dim light formed a strobe-like randomly rapid blinking form so that the afterimage of a curvilinear voluminous shape appeared in the dark and in their eyes, like the morphing shadow of a dream.

Its light came with profound warmth that steamed the ice walls and floor of their crevasse in a loud hiss that stunned them further.

The pair gazed at it in silence, holding their breaths and catatonically freezing their blinks in shock of the adrenalin and electricity they both felt overwhelming their skin. Suddenly the white lighted form stopped all motion and a single bright flash over lit the entire cavern they occupied that momentarily blinded them both.

And in the next moment they both heard in their minds, like a young child's whisper telling them a quick secret, say, "See the way before you!"

And in the next, they found themselves floating above Titan's vast atmosphere, in orbit with Saturn's looming bulk dazzling their senses in abject awe. Before them, they witnessed a silver liquid metallic saucer approach what was left of the *S.S.V. Deadlight*, extract what appeared to be an ancient cryo-pod through the gaping wreckage of its massive bow. The equally gargantuan wreckage of the stern was none-too-far distant, spinning slowly but wholly and completely separate from its other half. The silver disk, like mercury's quicksilver namesake the size of a building, returned to the cinnamon sphere, descending faster than anything they'd seen before, to the southern polar region in what appeared to be barely longer than an instant of linear time.

And in the last moment, back within the glacial crevasse, the bright blinding white light disappeared as quickly as it began, and all was silent, dark and frigid once again.

The Rabbit Hole

Slumber was disrupted rudely by the grand mountain, Selk's awakening nearly a kilometer north which shook the ground in violent lurches that broke Grace and Manannán's dreamscape into fragmented shards. One of the largest and most ancient cryo-volcanos on Titan, its eruption was not only feared by the inhabitants of Mug Ruith, but practically worshiped as a profoundly beautiful, yet haunting event to behold. This was because what erupted from its peak was not lava, but steam and liquid water from the belly of the cinnamon beast that was their home world that bathed the world in blue and white for moments when water-snow fell among the ethane rains.

Residents of Mug Ruith would look beyond the crumbling ruins of the old city, and the blocks of buildings of the new, to gaze upon a white froth that added superheated oxygen to the ethane and methane-saturated atmosphere which expressed its discontent by spontaneously igniting in a brilliant blue-white explosion that rocked the sky in a thunderous hydro-technical fireworks display. Its shockwave was a welcome warm breeze that no other individual had any hope of experiencing in their lifetimes, most anywhere else on Titan who did not live in Mug Ruith. Thus, when the quakes came, the entire city prepared to feast on the experience, as if filling a hole they forgot needed filling.

This time, however, Grace and Manannán had no forewarning of small Titan-quakes, which were so very common on the moon. Hiding from the drones in the crevasse they found themselves and then deciding to rest for a longer duration to be sure the drones passed them over gave them the advantage they needed to move forward later, when Boll's walkers were far away once again. Neither of them knew the fate of the citizens of Mug Ruith or what would come of them under Boll's thumb.

Grace sank.

Literally.

"Manannán!" she cried, "Oh god! Help me!" Shaken by the ground's rumbling himself, he was jostled to the same state of alarm he found Grace in. He acted quickly to pull her from a rapidly expanding crack in the ice floor where she lay. The wall shook and began to fragment and crumble. Panic set in quickly.

Manannán yelled, "We need to get out of here now!" as he pulled Grace by her arms to a flat section of the floor still relatively intact that was rare real estate in a crevasse so small. "Go!"

Grace obeyed and ran up the gradual incline toward the orange sky a few meters away. Before she could reach it, another quake rocked the hole as Manannán was reaching for the supplies in his pack when the crack that nearly swallowed Grace, swallowed it instead. Ceiling chunks of ice were breaking free and landing on Manannán's body, forcing him to retreat, leaving their means for survival behind, utterly.

Manannán scrambled up the shattering ramp where Grace's hands were outstretched waiting for him to appear.

"Here!" she cried to him. "Take my hands!"

The sound was thunderous and the vocalizations from each of them were barely audible to both. Grace gasped as she pulled with all her strength to help her only remaining living friend on an entire world escape from the collapsing respite that was their home, if only for a brief time.

Snow fell in a stark white flurry that was like fallout from a nuclear winter, replete with old-city ruins in the distance as they both gazed in mesmerized agape slack jawed at the wondrous beauty of Selk's magnificence. Blue bomb after blue bomb rocked the cinnamon sky as shockwaves could be seen rippling through the dense haze above them. The snow's intensity increased and began accumulating at their feet.

"Beautiful!" Manannán muttered to Grace as he broke his gaze from Selk and placed it squarely upon her. Blue reflections of Selk's expulsions made Grace's eyes look like sapphires, the brightest he could have imagined against the resolute orange of everything else around her above her waist. And below it, stark contrasting bright white snow added twice as much light to everything that was there before. She glowed in his view.

Grace's eyes remained locked on Selk, unaware of Manannán's change of focus. The snow piled higher and the moment was broken by Manannán offering, "We need to find another shelter. Quickly, Mum."

"Oh. What?" Grace's mesmerized catatonia took longer to return from as a child would to break its attention from a new and challenging puzzle to solve. She continued, "Oh right. Yes, of course. Let us press on south and follow the guiding star there." She pointed at the second sun, still bright enough to pierce the snow, which appeared the hours before their brief slumber. Then memory fragments of their experience in orbit began flashing before them.

"What was... we were above the sky," Grace remarked. "There was a massive ship, or two of them, or maybe it was one broken in pieces."

Manannán added, "Yes and the saucer. Then the pod I saw just floating towards it. Then it disappeared faster than anything I've ever seen, into the haze. I think what it took was a cryo pod."

"A what?" Graced asked genuinely as she began walking through the snow looking for another craggy ice formation that perhaps housed another opening for them to gain shelter.

"A cryo pod, Mum. It's ancient technology from before the Ripping. People used them to curtail the time lost visiting Mars, Earth and Luna from Yurpa. Here too. That was over five hundred years ago though. No one's been doing that since then. No one goes back to those old worlds any more. So, no need for cryo pods to keep people from aging years alone in space, driving them mad."

"I see," Grace said confusingly, having no concept of the distances between planets or the time it took anything would take to get there. "You seem sad about it."

"I am. It's been a dark time to live. I've seen so much from the old records... we're so... *small*."

"Small? Yeah, I guess compared to all those old worlds working together with millions, maybe even billions of people, it must seem magical to you, like you were born in the wrong place and time." There was silence for a moment in somber reflection of their reminiscing over memories of worlds they never saw or experienced directly. Then Grace added, "So, I assume though, retrieving a cryo pod would mean there is someone in it to retrieve, right?"

"Yes. Yeah I agree with that. Presumably so, Mum," Manannán affirmed, trudging through the snow beside her as they crunched between distant rumbles. "It's all academic you know."

"Academic? Why?" Grace asked.

The somber moment was reinforced with, "We have no food, water, or anything to make air out of. We will be dead in a few days. We might get fifty or sixty kilometers south but that's so far away from Romo and Ontario Lake over nine-hundred from here."

"So what," Grace agitated, "we just die then? Without a fight? Right here?! That won't happen. Not as long as I'm still breathing. We will find a way, Manannán. Trust me."

"Find a way or *make* one, maybe?" Manannán offered sardonically. "Not likely."

"Obviously," Grace affirmed. "It worked for Justin Forsythe, and Hannibal for that matter, and it will work for me—for *us*. It must."

"Out here, in the middle of this... all this... nothing?! It's snow. It's orange. It's brown. There's nothing here to make water from the ice, or air from the water we don't have," Manannán relented to his objective view of the situation with contempt. His kinesics revealed his relenting helplessness.

"Huh! You're supposed to be the logical, rational and scientific ones around here my friend," Grace poked, "you Ergonites, yet here you sit with nothing creative to add, nothing to offer, no innovation to reveal, feeling sorry for yourself! You might know power and circuits, but real innovation is the creative force! Build something new? Not you. Not you Ergonites. Build what's been tested and proven. That's your philosophy. And you wonder why your people have drifted from the Way almost as badly as Boll and his have."

"I'm only being realistic, Mum," Manannán replied humbly, defeated.

"And so, what about it? That vision or whatever we had. How do you explain that? How did we end up in vacuum... in orbit... in a moment of time? Then only to be returned back here in another and then to be so exhausted we slept for nearly fourteen standard hours with barely a recollection? Was it as dream? Together, both of us at the same time? No. Why can't we remember everything about it, every detail? I just see an image barely moving, and then another with saucer bursting into the atmosphere faster than I could imagine. Was it real? Were we even really there? What say you?!"

Manannán relented to the obviousness of the flurry that could not be answered by stating simply, "We can't know. But I bet that star up there is the ship's reflection."

"Huh. Yes I probably think you're right about that. But we can't know what happened? Why the hell not?!" Grace's rage was creeping back into her personality that was so forceful tens of hours before back in Mug Ruith. "You're supposed to have access to as much of the old records of our history as there are to be gotten, and yet you sit here, dumbfounded, just like me! You are no different. You are no better than us Ergonite." Grace rushed away in the deep snow toward the southern star and nothing but orange and white thickened atmosphere before her.

"Mum!" Manannán called, "Please wait! Mum! Mum," getting no response. Then he yelled as loud as he could, "Grace Blieh Amadán Dubh!"

She stopped dead in her tracks. Turning around slowly she marched back to him and looked him dead in the eye, and ordered, "Do *not* presume to address me by my full name... *Manannán!* You have not earned that right! Any past familiarity is gone now after all... *this!* Know. Your. Place."

Manannán exploded. "It doesn't matter Grace! Everything's gone! Everything that was great about us is gone! We don't matter anymore! Can't you see that?! I don't care about your title and I sure as hell don't care about your tirade! Our ways are done! Can't you see that at all? It's all been for nothing! The Way has led us to a dead end. Your Way had led us to nowhere. The Way is not only dark, it's *dead*. The Way is dead!"

Grace ran as fast as she could back towards him and slammed into his body, tackling him in the snow. He defended himself, rolling her over as she flailed in a desperate attempt to punch him with all the fury she had in her mostly frozen frame. Manannán rose above her, breathing heavily, as she, and offered his hand to pick her up.

"To hell with you, Ergonite!" Grace raged.

"Yeah, well to hell with you too, Ruithian. But we need each other to survive out here. So you're stuck with me. So get over your little tantrum and move on already."

She spat an empty, dry breath at him that vanished in a puff of white steam and falling powder from her rebreather, to her exacerbation. "You feel sorry for yourself, which is worse than being angry," Grace pointedly charged as she peevishly grasped his hand.

"I don't know." Manannán grunted as he lifted most of her weight out of the snow. "Getting angry over something you have no control over is more of a waste of energy than accepting your fate in melancholy foam."

"It's giving up!"

"No it's not. It's accepting the facts."

"No it's not."

"Yes. Yes it is," Manannán stated flatly.

"No... It's not!"

"Yes it is," Manannán said more flatly as the sparring continued, emoting precisely the opposite of what Grace was attempting to escalate.

"No! It's not!" Grace was at her wit's end with the childlike banter. "Aaaarg!" she cried and stomped off ahead of Manannán back toward the second sun in the sky.

"Would you like a healing pill, Grace? I think you might be succumbing to..."

He was cut off by, "Go! To! Hell!" that came in the loudest, most blood-curdling scream Grace could muster. Its sound died instantly in the falling snow and dense air, five meters away from her intended target.

Then, Grace sank, again.

Literally.

Manannán watched her form disappear downward before his very eyes at which point the point of the argument was lost upon him as his adrenalin rushed forward pushing him to where she fell. Then Manannán fell with her.

With snow all around them both, they clamored out of their respective piles and rose to their feet. Looking they could see Titan's dim cinnamon sky far above and impossible to return to. Manannán pulled a small flashlight from his belt, one of the few things saved from the crevasse that was still useful, and shone the light forward.

"At least we have some light," Grace muttered. "Not much else, but we have that."

"Are you okay, Mum?" Manannán asked hesitantly.

"Yes. Fine, thank you."

"Okay then."

"Where are we?" Grace asked as she gazed down a massive, cavernous tunnel, meters tall and wide that spread before them like a tube of infinite darkness that had no exit.

"Some kind of lava tube, they used to call them. It's not made by real lava, obviously, but hot liquid water instead of molten rock," Manannán explained. "And we have no choice but to follow it and look for a way out."

"Obviously," Grace charged.

Manannán rolled his eyes behind her as she stormed off ahead of him, retrieving her own flashlight from a pocket in one of her multi-layered garments. He followed, nonetheless, despite her impossible obstinacy.

The pair was like matter and antimatter, which walked together into the vast unknown before them, but resisted getting too close for fear of mutual annihilation. Minutes, seemed to drag on for what was like years as monotonous wall after monotonous wall passed them by at a slower and slower pace as their energy-reserves waned.

"How long we been walking?" Grace asked in a most languishing way.

"I estimate four hours, thirty-three minutes, give or take the duration for me to state it."

Grace gurgled in disgust and rolled her eyes as she said, "Fine. Close enough already. This better not be a dead end or we're done for."

"Forever the optimist."

"Go to hell," came the sharpened spear of resentment from Grace.

"You can do better than that," Manannán retorted.

"I can. But I won't. You see? I'm better than you. So I won't grovel like an animal on the ground."

"Yet here we are, both, *under* the ground, eh?" Manannán smiled to himself, which was not lost on Grace.

"Go to hell. Again! Just shut up already." Grace marched off faster and ahead of Manannán once again as the spark beginning to ignite the gasoline between them was striking.

"As you wish, Mum."

"That's right. *Mum.* Better."

Manannán smiled once more, in abject defiance, a gesture of which Grace saw this time. Grace sighed and stark silence followed them once again.

"I said titles don't matter before," Manannán broke in after several minutes, poking the bear. "It's just you and me now, as equals. How's that making you feel, hmm?"

"Shut the hell up!" Grace blasted back.

"Aaaah! I see you are handling the change in stride. So mature! So in control! So resolute! You're an object to behold!" Manannán was pushing for the shear fun of it. "What a great leader you *would* have been!" He laughed overtly.

Grace rushed him. This time, he knew what was coming and he absorbed all of her momentum without moving an iota. She flailed again on every part of his body, nary feeling a blow and picked her up so that she hung before him a few centimeters off the ground from her armpits. Her anger and rage replete in her contorted facial expressions, wrangling eye movements and shaking body was enough to break her down completely before long and she relented at long last to a deep and uncontrollable crying, desperate sob.

"What are we going to do!? We're going to die. We're all going to die! We only have thirty hours of air left! There's no way out of this, *thing*! My home is gone!" Grace was sobbing uncontrollably through rapidly freezing snot and tears that built up on her already peeling face. She gave up, finally, completely and hugged the only person who cared enough to get through to her where it really mattered shattering her ever-fragmenting defensive walls, and cried into Manannán's fabric layers.

He hugged her back.

She calmed after a few minutes and stood before him, holding him warmly.

Manannán said, "We are going to find our way out of this mess. There has to be another way out of here. These things are like tunnels with fingers that go in all directions. There's vent holes. We see steam coming from them all over Titan. This is no different. We just need to keep going, make good choices, and get a bit lucky."

"Ha!" Grace half-laughed through her tears. "You people don't believe in luck."

"You're right, not generally. But in this case, I need to make an exception."

"Faith? Is that faith I hear creeping into your cold soul, Manannán?"

"Well, perhaps. I know how it works. But I, *maybe*, after that, well, whatever that was that happened before, am rethinking my premises."

Grace stood back and looked at him in a way that was like looking at something old, that had suddenly become new again and said, "Maybe there is hope for you. For us both maybe. Hmm?"

"*May* be," Manannán agreed.

The silence returned. Before long they stopped in their tracks.

Grace asked, "Is the tunnel curving? There! You see that? There's a light...barely there. You see it?"

"I do!" Manannán replied with fervor. "It's so bright it's reflecting off the walls ahead of us. They look blue!" With those words they were certain it was not a hallucination and they instantly and ran towards it.

As the running pair came around the arching tunnel the slowly brightened. After a few seconds of breathless running, they came upon something they never expected to see.

"What the...," Grace blurted.

"That looks like a fermenter, in operation," Manannán observed.

"Are you sure?" Grace asked. "It's enormous!" The source of the blue-white light was a box-shaped machine over two meters tall and wide that glowed in sections that were stages of cycling atmosphere and water. In front of it was a pile of dubgrin that spread as far as the eye could see down the rest of the darkened tunnel that was up to their knees as they waded through it. Grace's walk was stopped by something deep under the piles of grain.

She looked down and said, "What's this?" She reached down and felt around through the dubgrin. Finding something long and hard to grab, she pulled it out and screamed.

"Oh my god! Oh my god! It's a bone!" Grace yelled.

Startled and visibly nervous, Manannán replied, "Yes, a femur. Big one too."

"Oh wow. Who's is it you think?"

"I haven't the foggiest. Let's start digging."

"Digging? I'm starving!" Grace cried as she dove into the piles of dubgrin with her hands and ate it by the handfuls, only to launch a grimace on her face that illustrated her profound disgust.

Grace spat it out and said, "Ugh! It's stale, or spoiled or something. It doesn't taste right."

"Maybe it's old. Here. Try some from the hopper directly," Manannán offered.

Grace took and reluctantly tried a few grains. The same look of discontent came over her facial features. "Ick! That... that's not food."

Manannán took some for himself and chewed vigorously, not permitting him the wincing indulgence of discontent Grace displayed. "It's got way too much alcohol. It's over-fermented. That's why it tastes this way. We might get a good buzz from it though."

"A good buzz? Seriously? We need food! Not shots!" Grace was becoming exacerbated again. "Help me find something more."

"You know, by the looks of this fermenter, if that's what it is, it's so large, and looks as though it'd been cobbled together with other parts that don't belong together. See? There. Behind the radiant coil. There's the power supply. That looks to me like an old portable fusion generator. Wow. The decay rate of the..." Manannán trailed off and paused. Then he said, "I concur. Let's dig around and see what's here. Somebody was here, at some point, a long time ago."

The pair felt around the piles of fermented grain where the femur was pulled and before long a pelvis, ribs, and finally a skull were extracted, all cleaned and polished like they never carried flesh.

Expanding their search they crept further away from the radiant light of the dubgrin fermenter into the darkened continuation of the tunnel. A part of the wall that formed a shelf rose from the Dubgrin, and as Grace walked ahead of Manannán, she gazed upon piles of clothing, cloth, tapestry, boxes of parts, gadgets, tools, and fasteners of all shapes and sizes. The shelf expanded deeper into the tunnel wall, which strangely appeared unnatural to Grace and she asked, "Do you think this was carved out of here?"

Manannán shown his flashlight on the corners and faces of the walls above the shelf which clearly made visible cut and chisel marks in the raw ice wall that formed a tall hollow over two meters in height, twice as tall as either of them could reach. Beside all the containers of scrap, tools, and parts was another shelf, about a meter high with parts and other tools on it. Grace shined the light on the wall above it and jumped back as she was surprised to see writing which read:

"Property of Amadán Dubh – Keep your paws off if you value your life."

Grace looked at the writing confusingly and asked, "What's that say? I can't really read it very well. The letters are so misshapen; it's barely words to me."

"Well now," Manannán blurted with a sense of intrigue he'd not felt since before the war, "that is very interesting. Those characters are from a period in our history that came before the Ripping, Mum. You see how the 'A' has a line through it in 'Amadán?'"

"Wait! That word is 'Amadán?'"

"It is, Mum."

"How can that be? It looks like 'Uruduz' to me."

"Ha!" Manannán let out an exhalation of laughter for a moment, a rare event lately and replied, "Right, the 'A' written looks like our 'U' as an upside down triangle, the 'm' an 'r' and so on. I see why it's confusing. But here's what it says, in a language that's over five hundred years old: 'Property of Amadán Dubh – Keep your paws off if you value your life.'"

"What's a '*paws*?'" Grace asked genuinely.

Manannán laughed again and explained, "'Paws' plural of a 'paw,' are the feet of a for-legged mammal that used to be with human-kind on the Earth millennia ago. I've heard stories that some of them made it to Yurpa with the first colonists, but the records are sketchy and validity is questionable. They kept them as pets."

"A what? Pet? What's that?"

"An animal people used to keep as companions for emotional support. They were called 'pets' because you'd pet them, like this." Manannán started stoking Grace's face in a slow way awkwardly that made her grimace before him.

"Ugh! Why would anyone want to do that? That's just weird."

"Yes, a bit, I guess. But I think this means 'hands' in a way that belittles would-be thieves into thinking twice about stealing from her."

"It can't be Amadán's. It just can't! The Progenitor, herself? No way!" Grace was becoming flustered at the realization.

"I think so, Mum. She was the one who started scavenging and looking for ways to survive out here. The stories are spotty, and I'm sure a bit exaggerated, but look. Here. At all this! This is Aibell. It has to be."

Then Grace noticed something tucked away in the back of the shelf-like table carved from the ice. She reached out, moved some gears that were covering it and picked it up. It was made of two plates of aluminum metal, of which Grace could not identify, that were joined together in the center by two brass metal hinges, like a

book. On the front Amadán's name was written, or
scratched into the metal, and beneath her name were the
words, 'Book of Records.' She opened it to find no pages
inside, but just the backs of the two metal plates. On the
reverse side of the book's cover was finely engraved letters
she could not read and grunted her discontent as a result
as she handed it to Manannán.

He took and opened it, his face lighting up when
seeing the fine letters. He said to her, "Oh my god! Do
you know what this is?"

"No. What?"

"I think this is a record, a journal maybe, of
everything Amadán Dubh did out here. What she went
through, how she went through it! This is amazing... and
unexpected. Want to know what the words say?"

"Absolutely!" Grace exclaimed.

"Okay," Manannán agreed. "Ready? It reads:

*'If you idiot beasts can read this then maybe
you've come a longer way out of the darkness
than I've given you credit for. I've been
surviving out here God knows how long, a
couple of standard decades perhaps, and all
I've known is pain. This bloody cold is worse
than death. So if you've made it this far out
then I commend you because not many could.
I don't care anymore though. I don't care
about you or providence or destiny or any of
that garbage. I just wanted to survive. And I
care about me. I did this. I made this
possible—prevented our extinction by
adapting faster and better than anybody else.
Not bad for a Resources accountant. And I
got lucky. I believe in luck more than the*

Way or in the volumes or any of it. Luck is what got me here, and a little common sense. Since the collapse of the mind drive network hasn't affected me, I still access knowledge from somewhere, or some-when. I hate it. It's too much. But I figure if anything I've done in my life means anything, there should be a record of it. And if you ugly beasts of rank bacteria are still alive to get here, you must be smart and tough enough to figure out how to access the data in this book. The data is stored in dimension two. The black rock on page 2 is of the printer so deal with that. If you know what that means then you'll be able to piece together the hows and what-fors on your own. If you don't, then it doesn't matter. You're just animals then and it won't mean anything to you anyway. I'm so sick of being cold. So I'm going to get even more stinking drunk than I already am and end it in a hot blue blaze now. I'm done. Later.'

The two of them sat motionless in shock and amazement after reading the entire message together. Grace just stared at what was to her the meaningless etched scribble in the metal, dumfounded and uttered, "That was, *interesting.*"

"Understatement I would say, hmm?" Manannán added. "History says Amadán died on one of her walkabouts in the desert when a quake collapsed the ice beneath her feet. She was presumed killed by it. Her body wasn't found. Looks like we found it. Well this place is certainly no accident. She came here all the time! The last time then she doused herself in alcohol and pure oxygen and then made a spark I guess."

"Clearly," Grace agreed. "Plenty of it all right here coming from that monstrosity." She pointed to the fermenter. "She was the Progenitor. She kept the Way alive for us. But in the end she hated everything about it. She thought it was all a bunch a crap. And she left us to carry on *with* the Way and *without* her. I have so many questions and issues with this that I can't begin to get my head around it all."

"There's so many questions I have too, Mum," Manannán added. "But in the end, the most important thing about what she said was that her mind drive was still working. That's incredible to me. How could that be?"

Grace grunted her ignorance.

Manannán deflected after a pause, "Well, at least we know how she got drunk. She messed with the mix ratios on the dubgrin fermenter. That means I can adjust them back to normal and we can eat and drink... water. But a stiff drink sounds good right about now."

Grace looked up genuinely and said back to him, "At last we finally agree on something. Don't mess with the fermenter. I'll get used to the taste. So will you." Before long, their exhaustion and imbibed spirits took over their conversations.

~

Grace, fully imbibed blurted loudly, "So let me get this straight, Amadán was an 'accountant?' What the *hell* is an 'accountant?!'"

"It's a person who counts. A lot!" They both let out a hearty laugh filled with stupor and gusto in a haze of alcoholic oblivion.

"Well that sounds exciting. What did they count?"

"Numbers." Another burst of laughter. "Lots of numbers."

"Why the hell would anybody want to do that?"

"So they can balance."

"Balance? Balance to what?"

"To itself."

"Whuuuh?" Grace was rocking helplessly as she laughed to herself.

"Yes the whole point was to balance so that there was no remaining amount. It was called a 'reconciliation.'"

"Balance to zero?! That's beyond insane! It means they are going through a whole litany of gyrations to get to nothing! Literally!" Grace yelled.

Manannán laughed with her, "Indeed! I mean it's like they spent their whole professional life literally making nothing, zero! A literal zero sum game! Ha-ha!"

"A what?!" Grace was lost again but laughed anyway.

"A game that gains or loses nothing. So it doesn't matter. It's pointless!"

"Aaaah!" Grace was in stitches. "Pointless! Their lives were pointless! Oh my god that's horrifying. No wonder Amadán hated her life! Ha-ha!"

"Yeah well maybe she felt free of it for a minute, but then the cold and surviving stuff kind of took away the rush!" Manannán was laughing at Grace's uncontrolled laughter, as much as the conversation.

"Wooo!" Grace fell over onto her back on the pile of dubgrin they were sitting on. "Accountant! That should be a verb! Ha-ha!" Through the ongoing laughter and deep inhalations, she continued mockingly, "Hi. My name is Grace Blieh and my life is so pathetic I'm accountant-ing and that's it. I accountant! I accountant so good I'm always a zero! Ha-ha! I'm invisible because I accountant!

So you can't see me! Ha! Ha!" Laughter echoed through the tunnels and drifted into silence once more.

"Grace," Manannán said, "I think you should have some water now. You're way gone." He snickered.

"Whuuuh?! Me? Not more than you Ergonite!"

"I'm thinking so Grace."

"Ugh! I told you not to c-*call me thaaaat!*" She belched the words and fell over entirely down the back of one dubgrin hill and between the next.

"I rest my case."

"Okay, Manannán. You're kind of right. *This* time. Don't let it go to your head though."

"I wouldn't hear of it." Manannán picked Grace up by her hand as she willingly took his for the needed assistance trying to walk in meter-thick dubgrin dunes. "I'm getting tired. I'm thirsty."

Grace's energy, so boisterous just moments before deflated rapidly and she began to yawn. "Me too. I can just sleep right on the dubgrin if I had to. Might be comfortable."

"Better than the ice floor and shelf I'd bet. Warmer too. I might just do that actually."

"I hate you," Grace whispered in his ear leaning on him to prevent falling again.

Manannán knew she was playing and played along. "Yeah, yeah. I'm irresistible. I hate you too Grace."

"Sleep with me," Grace muttered.

"Um, Mum...Ah, Grace, that's probably not a good idea," came the stunned response.

"Do it. You know you want to. I don't mind. Not like there's anyone else around better."

"High praise, Grace. Now I'm definitely a 'no,'" Manannán stated posthumously. "Besides, you'll just hate me more after you sober up. And I don't want anything like that. Fun or not it would be for me. I want you to want me when you respect me enough to without being delirious."

"Whuuuh?!" Grace rolled her head on her shoulders.

"Just lay down here. I'll lie down next to you and we can keep each other a bit warmer, but that's all. Layers stay on. And it's way too cold in here anyway."

"Oh. Okay." Grace faded slowly.

The pair lay down between two dubgrin hills and allowed their exhausted souls to finally rest. Just before Grace faded completely, she whispered to Manannán, "Thank God for you. You saved me. I love you for it. Don't forget it. I'm scared. Just hold me."

Manannán didn't reply as she fell fast asleep before his own weary eyes. He drew her close and placed his arm around her body and fabrics and fell asleep facing her finally peaceful eyes.

The Case for Slavery

assius Boll had a problem: he had conquered the whole world! Now that he had it, however, he didn't know exactly what to do with it once gaining it so... *easily*. While his plan to divert all eyes from Ergon to Mug Ruith with assignation of Aibell was genius on his part, as he would tell everyone around him on any occasion he could, he honestly did not expect it to fall in days, let alone hours. The Ergonites barely put up a fight. The oxygen bombardment leveled Ergon's protective dome in a matter of minutes, and Ergon froze in fear, and its own analysis paralysis.

While killing most of the population injected Boll with a rush the likes of which he had never experienced, there was still a weak sense of guilt that plagued him; like somehow survival and conquest for the betterment of his nation's own peoples' future was not justification enough to remove from Titan all evils from the old world, from before the Ripping. He surmised that if the future would belong to the Triple Cities and Xanadu it was a simple matter of removing the competition. The best way to do that, he concluded, was to erase it, because if one needs to forget the past and allow the future to flow unfettered, one needs to destroy it, utterly.

Still, many Ergonites survived and now Xanadu was stuck feeding an unproductive population. He could simply let them starve or freeze, or any other passive method of eradication that didn't waste now depleted and expensive resources. But a lingering thought kept appearing is his mind to make use of them, somehow.

Mug Ruith was another matter entirely. As keepers of the Way and the lies that embodied the very reciprocal of all that he believed in, Boll kept as many of them alive as was possible. Boll wanted to defeat them, in every way a person could be defeated: physically, mentally, emotionally, *and* spiritually. He wanted to ensure the world knew the rightness of his leadership and for all time have that rightness on display for the world to see as meandering herds of useless humanity demonstrating where taking the wrong path leads, as animate reminders and trophies.

Argus approached from his anteroom beside the main hall of Boll's High Chair, his nine-foot tall towering form leaning constantly to avoid knocking his head on the trusses supporting the ceiling and various lit methane torches dimly illuminating the grand hall. The dim light cast even longer shadows of his form in multiple directions and contrasts that depended upon the proximity to the lights and their distances from him.

Approaching Cassius Boll Argus said, "You cannot just drop over a million useless parasites in the middle of nation and expect it to survive, Boll! That's more than ten percent of your population. Who's paying for all them to eat? Where will you put them? You'll start a revolt if you're not careful. You get me?"

"It's a problem. You got that right, Argus. But I want them here. I want everyone to see them every day of every year until they're all dead. They will serve as a reminder of my absolute power and righteousness over them. My people will *love* me for it. Rebel? Bah! Never! They will parade me down the streets of the Main Square for a year! You overthink it Argus. This is about glory! Not economy."

"You listen, Boll, and listen close. I have been doing this sort of thing for longer than you and your pathetic puny mind will ever be able to comprehend. I build nations, *great* nations."

"They all failed if I remember your history, Argus."

"Ha! A fair point. But it was... necessary to *let* them fail. The weakness of your race never fails to... astound me. But perhaps it was my failing to have chosen ones with such high hopes only to watch them crumble to vices, hubris... and ego. Don't fall into that same trap Cassius. You get me?"

"What by depriving me of my final triumph? I will ensure that my legacy, *Xanadu's* legacy, drives humanity forward for all time and not those troglodytes. We have taken the first and largest steps toward that goal. *War works*! We win! And to the winners go the spoils! *Carpe diem, et cras enim moriemur!*"

Argus let out a laugh of resolute joy in sharing of what was the obviousness of Boll's argument. Having yielded nothing, however Argus pressed, "Yes we all will die Cassius, eventually, even the Ruithians."

"Well they don't seem to think so. They believe in the afterlife, like some changing of direction in 'voluminous time,' they call it. I think it's all nonsense."

"Ha! My dear friend... the cosmos is far larger than, and I mean this with utmost respect of course, your fragile little mind can possibly conceive of! Energy never gets destroyed, only diverted."

"Or absorbed," Boll stated flatly.

"Ah! So it does. Well done." Argus snickered to himself.

"Death is the only real thing, Argus. Everything else is just... well it means nothing because it's so small relative to everything, every-when else. Life is fleeting! Death is eternal."

"I'd forgotten...." Argus rolled his left temple with his fingertips.

"You have. How many iterations are you on now? Nearly two-hundred-and-sixty?"

"Two-hundred-and-fifty-three."

"Fine. A lot. But why? Because you fear it. You fear death. Death is the absolute. Life is the blip. The exception. The dumb luck of an animal suddenly becoming aware that it *is*."

Argus's demeanor retreated. Then he added, "...and in a cosmos of infinite volume, time volume, our blip that is our lives is nary but zero by comparison. One in infinity is the same as one in nothing."

"Exactly! That's the spirit!" Boll rolled in his dominance over Argus on this point, and he enjoyed playing it whenever he could with him, at least until he reached the line and attempted to cross it.

"Careful Cassius. Know your place. Remember where you were before I showed up here on this orange iceberg. You were Aibell's little dog. That wasn't so long ago... you get me?"

Cassius retreated peevishly and let out a, "harrumph" that was mostly a stunted grunt of white frozen steam jetting from his face. He coughed to cover up his insecurity and diverted back to the problem by remarking, "We can put them to work. They have to eat. We have to eat. We need more buildings. We need more scavenging. We will use them. As they used us, but this time it will be for something tangible. There will be something to show for it. And... they will suffer, which pleases me to no end."

Argus smiled broadly. "So you'll employ them? *That* could get costly."

"Yes, but at least we would get some value from their worthless lives. Better than what we've gotten to this point. They think they've contributed by supplying dubgrin to Ergon and to us, and we let them just so we can get something out of them besides a bunch of guilt and superstitious nonsense. We never needed their dubgrin. You know that. But you're the one who said to keep letting them think they were the only ones who could produce it. Ridiculous! A child in formative school anywhere in Xanadu could replicate it in their bathroom."

Argus agreed but kept leading, "Think about this though Boll: over the millennia, human civilization has been destroyed time and time again. I know *you* don't want to remember it, or recall it, or even think about it, but hear me out."

"I'll allow it," Boll reluctantly agreed with a vast exhale from deep within his gut.

"Thank you," Argus replied so that the 'yoo' sound at the end of the phrase went far longer than was necessary. But in his mind, it was most warranted. Keeping Cassius in line was for Argus like keeping a rabid tiger from jumping out if its cage with cage door wide open and fresh meat in his own hand. His method was simple but effective: stick and carrot. But mostly, more stick worked best. Except this time. This time, the carrot would win the day.

Argus continued, "As I was saying, civilization has risen and fallen countless times in our history... countless; and most of the time it wasn't as a result of a natural disaster or an extinction event like those that destroyed the dinosaurs or trilobites..."

"The what? Di No Soarz? What are those?" Cassius asked lumbering over the pronunciation.

"Never mind," Argus sighed. "The point is this, Boll: civilization rises when populations come together and work to a common purpose: to survive! To be safe, to live for the future and *not* for the moment. The moment is for the animal, by default, because it cannot afford to think about anything else. Why? Because it could get eaten or killed by a bigger animal at any waking moment of its life. You get me?"

Boll nodded.

Argus went on: "When people work together for a common purpose they thrive! There develops a division of labor that permits excess free time that allows for growth, ingenuity and technological advancement that builds wealth! That's what builds nations. That is the mechanism that builds and maintains civilizations. When they don't, it collapses... *utterly*."

Cassius interrupted and asked, "So what does this have to do with the Ruithians? They're the opposite of coming together for a common purpose. Wouldn't you say?"

"I would. I would indeed. Arrogant sniveling little brats, all of them." Argus took a breath and continued with increasing fervor in his voice, "Now take for example what happened right before the Purge. Human civilization thrived and advanced technology to heights it had rarely seen in all history, approaching even the glory of my Gibborian empire. But in the end it collapsed... *utterly*. Why? Because fewer and fewer people contributed to the civilization that supported them. They turned on it, claiming it owed them their existence as a right. As a *right*! Can you believe it?

"A greater percentage of populace not only didn't contribute value, they taxed its value into economic oblivion because of that twisted premise: 'I exist. Therefore, I'm entitled to everything everyone else produces, as a right.' Obviously, a 'right' means that it applies to everyone. So what happens? No one produces anything because they have a right to persist without contributing one calorie of labor. It's the very essence of a parasite living off of its host. The host dies because the parasite overwhelms it and kills it... *utterly*. You get me, Cassius? Those Ruithians are the very parasites sucking the life out of everything your people want for the future. Can you get your head around that?"

"Yes, I can," Boll agreed heartily. "People are lazy! They'll do nothing so long as they get food and pleasure in the instant they want it from somebody else!" Boll laughed. "Of course, I am guilty of such indulgences myself on occasion!" He laughed again.

Argus, laughing and smiling agreeingly with him went on:

"Brief luxuries not withstanding given by those willing to voluntarily in exchange for some value, but you got it Boll! Ha-ha! Exactly! They'll let their own bodies rot around them if someone enables them to do it. It's the very posterchild of the fallacy philosophies of the Old World before the Purge even! There's nothing especially sparking, divine or otherwise, inside their rotting flesh as they consume in a day more food than can feed a legion for a week! Spark, bah! If you do not work them, if you do not give them a task, a chore, a reason for getting what they want, they will let themselves consume themselves right into oblivion, if enabled!"

Boll chuckled in agreement and reached for a dubgrin pipe. He gestured to offer one to Argus, who nodded in acceptance. Boll packed the bowls with the blend of dubgrin and chemicals which were designed to slow the mind, and deprive oxygen to the brain resulting in a slight euphoric effect. They shared an ethane lighter and puffed in the dim air within the great hall of the High Chair of Xanadu and flooded its space with thick grey smoke that rose quickly to the ceiling. Argus's pipe appeared four sizes too small for his hand, but he managed aptly. Boll closed his eyes, and allowed the euphoria to wash over him. He paused, sighed and said, "My people are not like that. Not one bit! My people are strong! And they will stay that way. I will make sure of it."

"Yes Cassius. They are indeed strong. We must keep them that way. Together. Look at you sitting on your laurels already when there's work to do. Complacency is already creeping into your culture. We must do everything to prevent that or that parasite will feast on you."

"How?"

"By putting these aimless trophies to work. They should work not for themselves, not even for you, but for their very *survival*. You say they're animals? Treat them as such, *as* animals, living in the moment because their next could be their last if they don't produce for food, water, air and shelter. Keep them so worked they've not the time or the energy to even *think* of anything else! And get everything you need, production goals, quotas, expansion plans faster and cheaper than you thought possible. And then let everyone else... *watch*. You get me? How's that for a trophy? And make everyone accountable for keeping them in line. That's how we get the masses engaged and keep them strong."

"Oh Argus! I love it! I love it! But let me ask this: faster, better *and* cheaper? But how? I still need to feed the wretches. I need to produce air and water for them to consume.

"They will produce it. None of your citizens will be required to produce one milliliter of oxygen more than what they produce today. The only thing they will need to do is to supervise. With weapons and other... *methods*... that will motivate them that I will teach you. They will *have* to. You *get* me? We are going to build a whole new economy over a whole new sub-class."

Then it hit Boll like a gut-punch. "Slaves! Make them slaves! Ooh! Wonderful! Argus you are a man of many, many talents! But this is your best lesson by far!"

"All great civilizations began in slavery. Not as slaves, obviously of course, but by enslaving the weaker. As soon as it stops doing it, the economy collapses within a couple a centuries. Sumer, Mesopotamia, Assyria, Babylon, Egypt, Rome, Britain, America... and they cannot complain because their own teachings condone slavery! Not the Way precisely, but certainly their ancient text called, 'Bible.'" Argus stopped himself and said, "I know you have no idea what I'm talking about but you get my meaning, yes?"

"I do, Argus. I do. But we have the Ergonites' printer. We can manage to make almost anything! What do we need slaves to scavenge for if we have that?"

"Cassius, you are a dear a trusted friend, and with the utmost respect I assure you that you are sometimes a complete idiot."

"Watch your tone, giant!"

"Let me explain. The printers only work when there is raw material in the form of basic elements available to use to print whatever it is you need. Those elements are quite rare out here, by Saturn. You will need your slaves to find them in the ruins, refine them, and store them so that printer can be of some use. Think of how many walkers you can have with that massive printer at your disposal! But you can't print them without titanium, magnesium, germanium, gold, platinum, or power them without uranium, neptunium, or plutonium. Where do you think you'll find those last ones, out in the desert? No, there's tons of them in the ruins accumulated over centuries from the Belt, just waiting to be exploited."

"Okay, okay Argus. I get your meaning. We need to grab all we can. The more hands we have, the more we can grab in short order. I get you."

"Good," Argus concluded. "There is another matter we must mitigate."

"And what's that?" Boll was becoming weary as his mind was reaching its low absorption limit of new information he marked with a frustrated exhalation.

"The risk of subculture infiltration. We don't want these new slaves of yours developing some kind of underground society like what happened on Yurpa that might surprise you a century or a millennium from now and take over what you're building here."

"Yes. I see the truth of that, Argus."

"Right. So what you need to do is to figure out a way that these Ergonites and Ruithians can be identified by anyone at any time, that's permanent."

"Permanent? How do propose I do that? Cut off an arm? That kind of defeats the purpose of having extra hands to fetch materials, wouldn't you say?"

Argus chuckled. "No. Nothing so... grandiose. A simple brand should suffice."

"A brand?!" Cassius was taken aback by the suggestion. "Branding, even for me seems a bit... barbaric."

"Oh come off it Boll. You just slaughtered two-million people this week. Nothing is too barbaric for you now!" Argus angered. "Put it on their faces. Right above their eyes. It's never covered up and it will always show. The molt is very thin in that space. 'E' for Ergonite, 'W' for followers of the Way... *Wayfarers* you might say. The brands will be black against the pale molt, and will never molt away, if done correctly."

Boll exhaled a long-drawn smoke from his pipe and exclaimed, "Ooh! Argus! I get you my friend! I sooooo get you! It's brilliant! Marvelous! My trophies will be easy to spot, even from far away. I can even pass an edict down that says no one is permitted to cover their foreheads for this exact reason." Boll reflected for a moment and added, "So this subculture problem you mention comes with another issue I think. They'll want to print children. What about the children?"

"Children? Ah, yes. Very good, Boll! I'll make an emperor out of you yet. "If you permit it you run the risk of this subculture worming its way into every dark crevasse in Xanadu. You must not let that happen. So the solution is simple: do not permit it."

"Simple?! It's *genius!*" With that, Cassius Boll's laughter echoed and resonated through every hall and chamber within an earshot that flooded the atmosphere with his delight. "So will I own them all? Obviously a new market for slaves will be created. My people will want one or some of their own."

"No! That's the trap, Boll! If you permit individual ownership of slaves to do the things your strong people now do on their own, they will become the very parasites you seek to destroy. No. If there is to be private ownership, then it must be in association with mining, scavenging or something else that produces a value to everyone. No slaves scraping your molt for free. That's the trap. It's a business! Not a spa!"

"I seeeeeee!" Bolls 'E' drew out like a blade in the dim. We start private companies to divvy up the slaves. Set a franchise price, perhaps. All comers. First in, first out, gets first choice. We can do a lottery to determine who gets their order in line. The entrance fee is the franchise fee. The lottery will be the talk of Xanadu in the Great Square for weeks! Months even! I can draw it out...make their anticipation build up until no one will think of little else! Yes!" Boll's mania peaked and he took a drink and smoke in one motion, rose and hugged Argus around his waist, the highest point on Argus's body Cassius could reach. "I thank the cosmos every day for having you by my side! You have given me so much! I can never repay you."

Argus grinned and replied, "Rest assured, Cassius. You will find a time when you can, and you will. But for now, today, you needn't worry about it. I'm here to... *serve*."

Out of the Fog

anannán woke first to a twitching, dreaming Grace, seemingly running in place from some unknown demon through the fog of a weary and sleep-dulled mind. His head cried out in pain from the aftereffects of the alcohol-saturated binge-eating contest the two shared after being pursued by Boll's forces for seemingly endless hours, which became seemingly endless days. The sound of the fermenter working overtime, by hundreds of years, with its clicks and whines kept him company along with his lonely, hot breath that dissipated as fast as he could generate it within the super-cooled, tholin-saturated nitrogen atmosphere. He decided to take the moment of solitude to heart and permitted Grace to sleep to her heart's content while he collected his thoughts and resources.

The first matter he attended to was air. His reserves were nearly ninety-percent depleted, leaving less than fifteen hours to live on. As he approached the fermenter, he quickly assimilated its control mechanisms, found the oxygen outflow valve, detached the ambient atmospheric carburation unit from both that and the water evaporation condenser and injection manifold, then attached his own air supply assembly injection line to the fitting. To his relief (and surprise) the two fittings, one made just months before and the other, a half-a-millennium prior, fit perfectly, as if engineered by the same person, on the same day, and built in the same hour. To himself, he quickly came to realize the profound importance the Progenitor was. She designed and built the equipment all Titan used in Manannán's time as *"standard equipment – never to be changed,"* as was taught in formation school to every newly-printed person as the proverbial, *"Lesson Number One."*

Standardization and uniformity in hardware designs were an engineered benefit, in that for everyone on Titan, spare parts would be not only plentiful, but everything possible would be interchangeable. Manufacturing them would be both indispensable and inexpensive, due to the economies of scale that the mass production of such things across the world provided. Obtaining them would be easy, since they would also be cheap to obtain. Even five hundred years later, that formula was still working perfectly. In the moment Manannán mac Lir tapped his oxygen coupler to that of the original, presumably prototypical version of a fermenter, it stood before him like a monument to a once great being.

He sighed as another wave of headachy beating flowed across his skull. It would take about twenty minutes to recharge his oxygen supply. He thought when Grace awoke, she would do the same. Still, with a hangover so bad that he was enduring, hers likely would be far worse, and fresh water might be the first on her list of priorities to consume; that, and maybe a whole *handful* of healing pills, to say the least.

Grace squirmed and moaned slightly in her slumber. Manannán's gaze was diverted as well momentarily but returned quickly to the fermenter's overwhelmingly mechanical works, where gears, pumps and hydraulic arms swung, pushed, spun and rolled in a beautiful dance of mechanics and chemistry. It was wholly mesmerizing to observe. He followed the mechanical path to its logical conclusion, mapping and burning it all into his memory, in every detail, so that it would be retained for all time within his consciousness.

He waited in silence until the recharging cycle was complete, demarked with a green light and a chime. Still, Grace barely stirred at the objective interruption to her dreamscape. Looking around the cavern he felt the urge to explore more deeply into the water-lava tube on his own. He quickly changed the fermenter's configuration to begin producing purified warm water and left it in rotation with a large insulated container of which was one of several strewn about the Progenitor's workstation. He looked at the darkness to his right and began slowly walking down its inky throat.

Manannán began carefully shining his light on the walls, floor and ceiling, searching for anything else Aibell Amadán Dubh left behind so many centuries before. Prior to making nine paces, he noticed a carving in the ice-wall of a circle, bisected by an arrow that pointed to his intended direction. At the end of the carved arrow was a spiral, also deeply carved into the rock-hard ice. He sighed in a startle that rattled his mind momentarily.

"Well, I certainly didn't expect this. What are you telling me Amadán?" he asked aloud to himself.

He shown his light farther down the shaft in search of any landmark that the symbolism may have referred to in his view. Not finding any, he continued walking methodically, recording every image, every view he observed in his mind.

Manannán enjoyed the sudden opportunity of silence and solitude—alone with his own thoughts for a change after everything he—*they* just went through that dismembered their lives entirely. After a few hundred paces around to the left slightly on a curve and following the left wall, not able to see the right one, he felt the ground give way down a slope. Still looking, he finally found the dubgrin dunes shrinking so that the grains crunched under his feet against the ice-anvil that was the ground. He drove on, and down as the ground led him.

He passed several openings in the wall, all earmarked with deeply carved exes denoting the obviousness and futility of exploring them on his own since the Progenitor had done so already and found they were dead ends of some form or other. But, white steam escaped into the immediate air around his face as his labor intensified and his excitement level rose when he saw an abrupt right turn at an ice wall blocking his forward path.

At its end, before him he saw another carving in his light. It was that of a circle with a vertical line from its ninety-degree tangent and a perpendicular arrow to that with heads on both ends, one left and one right. He looked right and saw the declination sharply increased in the ice floor down to a much deeper destination. Correspondingly, the symbol carved at the right of the right-hand arrow had another curious spiral at its end.

"Decisions, decisions," Manannán blurted into the dim. The left-hand arrow had a new symbol at its end. This one was a circle with a ring around it. "So that's

Saturn..." he faded in his utterance, thinking aloud, "...and that's in the sky at the surface on a clearer day...so that must mean it's the way outside. Simple." He felt a keen sense of satisfaction with that basic analysis knowing that there was indeed a way out of the tunnel system and it was already mapped. He felt a sense of calm overtake his previously adrenalin-filled physiology. "So much less work to do now. We can feel pretty safe here for the moment. Maybe exile won't be so bad. This is a welcome reprieve to say the least..." He trailed off in a muttering collection of soft noises.

He decided on right, toward the spiral.

Manannán took a breath and started down the steepening decline toward whatever the spiral pattern in Amadán's symbols meant. Before long the ground began leveling off without much drama and a steady but consistent declination downward greeted him with an ambient glow far ahead in the distance. Alarmed, he hurried his paces and began slipping some on the ice floor. Correcting his footsteps for the new conditions, he adapted his gate so that he prevented his boots from leaving the surface as well as resting his left hand on the ice wall he followed.

The sliding made Manannán's foot-slide noisy and it echoed through the halls, rapidly revealing the complexity of channels and other tubes spreading their way through Titan's ice crust like strokes of lightning through a meandering fog of ignorance. The glow brightened.

Manannán squinted painfully to make out what seemed to be so far in the distance generating the light. But all he could make out was the brightening cool glow as his welcome destination, hurrying along as fast as he could without falling and sliding utterly to the end.

It didn't work.

The grip of the ground gave way and sliding was the inevitable consequence of his hurried impatience. With nothing to hold onto but his flashlight, the wall began speeding by faster and faster with each failed attempt to use it as a brake with his cold fingers. He tried jamming his flashlight into the ground, the wall, anything he could at speed to slow his slide which only served to cause him to spin and lose orientation rapidly and completely. He relented as the far-off glow grew rapidly in his spinning views to let go to see what destiny awaited him at the end of the line.

Manannán stopped with a thud, his acceleration was stopped rudely by a flat embankment that stunned him, causing him to exhale a painful, "Ugh!"

Performing a self-diagnostic on his body, he decided that despite the fact that he right ankle was unnaturally behind his right ear, the twisted knee that gave way to allow such a position, while excruciating, was not dislocated. He took a moment to recover his posture, retrieved his foot and placed it against that which stopped his fall.

He muttered aloud, "This looks like it was *made*." Standing, Manannán rose up with a painful grunt to be greeted by a wall for which he stood below the embankment by only a few centimeters. It was made of metal, braced behind with welded components, springs and legs. Its face was layered with fabrics and tapestries woven in centuries past that was over a meter in thickness. "Ha! Cushion! I thank you!" Manannán spoke to the invisible sky above him to Amadán.

He tested his right leg under full-weight and proceeded to inspect the barrier which went around to his right as far as his eyes could see in the now nearly full brightness of the glow behind it. Stiffly, he passed his left hand on its uppermost part and used it as a railing to prevent any further mishaps. To his left the light glow warmed and he observed a fogging of the air above it, which had a rising motion that evaporated quickly in the frigid air around him. It slowly swirled like the view of a storm, mirroring itself from all angles he viewed.

Walking in amazement at the light's brightness, Manannán's eyes struggled to adjust to the intensity. He squinted perhaps for the first time in his life with a bit of pain to remember it by. It was gold light, but not purely, but more like the net effect of several colors combining into one; deep blues, reds, oranges, yellows, and blue-white emissions reached his mind and scrambled his perception of it.

"What in God's name?"

He followed the railing he was using further and finally reaching the end of the line, he faced the right hand wall of the tube, where he was surprised to see carved steps, a woven-aluminum guide rope leading back up the shaft to his right. To his left was what appeared to be a gate.

Startled at the irony of the staircase he said loudly to himself and Amadán, "What? You couldn't carve stairs on *both* sides? Would've saved me a mess of hurt! Just saying, Amadán!"

Hearing nothing except the breeze he chuckled to himself and faced the gate, released the centuries-old hasp and walked through.

Before and beneath him was a winding staircase that followed the outside walls of a massive spiral formation in the ice, around a central shaft, that reminded him of the insides of a seashell he remembered seeing in the archival records in Ergon. It appeared bottomless.

But towards that unreachable bottom, the light showed bright. He followed the carved stairs, slowly winding their way downward, until reaching a large platform of both partly carved ice and metallic engineered structure.

He stood in awe of the view.

The ice walls all around Manannán were aglow with pale colorations that blended into an overarching cornucopia of golden light. Above, below, in front, and behind did radiance come. He squinted more tightly so that his massive black eyes were mere slits across his face.

"Amazing!" he cried in bated breath that barely shown a diffuse opacity coming from his lips due to the discovered warmth of the spiral. The echo of his call resonated like an amplified sound system in the spirally-shaped resonance chamber that was this spiral seashell he found himself. Manannán took a breath and just stared for a few moments, soaking in the relative warmth of the moist air around him. The ice-walls glowed and glistened in the same heat he involuntarily was basking in.

Then he turned toward what was behind him, and approached the glowing, glistening wall. Getting closer, almost so that his face touched the ice, the glare on his hyper-sensitive eyes being nearly too much to bear, his eyes zoomed in on the area before him, magnifying it tenfold, and to Manannán's amazement, witnessed the least-expected eventuality he could have imagined.

Before his eyes, were radial glowing animals, slowly moving across the surface of the ice, which left a trail, like a long divot behind them.

Manannán gasped and said to himself, "They're eating it. They're eating the ice!" The creatures were globular in form, which surrounded a central nexus with radial thick spokes of matter that glowed different colors as they moved. Zooming in closer with his augmented eyes, he could see calcium "teeth" breaking off chunks of the frozen water, which was its food. Zooming in further, to ten-thousand times magnification, he could see molecular chains and chemical reactions happening in real time.

"I wish someone were here to share this with. This is incredible!" he spoke aloud to the light. He asked to what he saw on the wall, "What are you, creatures?"

He paused in amazement and then began analyzing out loud just for the sheer joy of it.

"They are consuming the hydrogen in the water, electrically separating it from the oxygen using some kind of natural electrolysis and metabolizing it with all the volatiles in the atmosphere! But it looks like they like the acetylene flavors best. They breathe their food and eat their air. Astounding! Oh wow! Look! They're exhaling methane... more methane than what's already here! In the ices there's dissolved solids: carbon, calcium, silicates, copper, iron, magnesium. Huh! Water-ice as food, ethane, butane, acetylene as air... electrolysis burning them, causing the colored light show and heat! Lots of heat! Incredible!"

Manannán touched the wall with his fingers, and chemical glow smeared across the ice face. His finger glowed yellow, blue and red with the residual bromide of radiant life he took for the shear wanting to know what it felt like, tactilely. He tapped his left temple and began to rub it gently for a purpose only he knew for and the glow transferred to that spot on his molting white head as a badge of honor.

Then it dawned on him. The shape of the ever deepening spiral wasn't natural geology. It was *dug*. The microscopic radiant creatures ate their way into the natural pattern, like that of a nautilus from the old, good

Earth. The Golden Mean everywhere around him in plain sight to behold: the hallmark of life everywhere. Manannán zoomed his gaze back out to normal perception with a whizzing noise and took in the full beauty once more, sighed and made his way back up the carved steps to the gate a changed person.

~

As he approached the dubgrin dunes of Aibell's base camp, he saw Grace sitting, hunched over and sobbing as she buried her face in a cup of steaming hot water.

"Grace?" Manannán asked. "Are you alright?"

"Manannán!" she cried. "Where the hell have you been? I thought you left me here; abandoned me to rot in this dubgrin oasis to die a lonely and quiet death!"

"Don't you think you're being a little dramatic?" Manannán retorted. "I went for a walk while you were asleep. I recharged my air assembly, and made water for you to drink—I figured you'd need it more than the air at first given your... performance."

"You're a real prick, you know that?"

"Enough. You were way beyond yesterday and I thought of your needs first. So don't start lecturing me like a brat. I'm done with all that."

"Oh! Are you?! Well excuse me for reacting to waking up utterly alone! It was terrifying for me!"

"You're never alone Grace. I'll see to it. Now that's enough of the emotional tirade. Let's settle down. I have something I need to tell you."

Grace sat back down peevishly after rising to scold her benefactor with a thump and a sigh as her aching head reminded her of her body's dehydration. Reluctantly she replied, "Oh really? What's that then?"

I know why Amadán built this place, and kept coming back. It's amazing! It's alive and amazing!"

"Amazing? Alive? What's so amazing?" Grace asked sardonically.

"I'm calling it, 'The Nautilus.' It's a vast spiral of heat and light, and *life*! It's more beautiful than anything I have ever seen in all my years!"

"Nautilus? What the hell's a nautilus?" Grace asked impatiently.

Manannán laughed at the ignorant question and calmly showed her the way before her.

Down and Out

he exiled pair made their way down the right wall of the shaft, where carved steps and a braided aluminum rope were mercifully constructed centuries before to prevent the slip-filled paces of Manannán's first fall. Grace lagged behind complaining of her still slipping footsteps she could not avoid due to her fresh hangover symptoms that had just begun to present themselves in earnest through her exertion. Manannán wearied of her lack of mettle.

"Grace," Manannán called out from several paces ahead, "you need to pick up the pace. There's no reason for you to be so clumsy. Just walk normally. You'll be fine."

"Easy for you to say," Grace pointedly retorted. "My room is still spinning over here, and it's not like you gave me a healing pill or anything. You don't care about how I feel or what I'm going through. All you care is about yourself. So shut it!"

Manannán sighed. "I know you don't mean all that so I'll just ignore it. Ridiculous baby, you are. You know that?"

"Shut up."

"Yeah. No. I don't think so. Not after last night. I know your heart. You're scared. I get it. You lash out because you're afraid. You allow your emotions eradicate your reasonable judgment and bite the hand that feeds you."

"No I don't."

"Yes, you do."

"No. I don't."

"You do. And you know it."

"Shut up."

"Nope."

Grace relented and sighed in an overmuch, overloud protest against the objective truth that he was right. Then she blurted, "I still hate you."

Without missing a beat, Manannán retorted, "Good. I hate you too."

"Great. Now that we have re-established that, I can die alone, cold and afraid, and faithless in every way. I hate you, so I have no faith in you. I have nothing to go home to because I have no faith in anyone else anymore. And the Way is dead! So I haven't even God to show me the way back to my faith!" Her emotional outburst grew louder and more desperate with each statement.

She continued, "I have nothing! Everything that I am supposed to be is dead! I should just be dead! Why did I even bother to run! I should have let Boll's walkers blow my head off like everyone else!"

Grace fell to her knees, screamed in terror through tears of agony, desperation and loneliness she had never experienced before, and relented to the deepest terrors in her heart that broke through the pain of the blasting hangover-induced headache and dehydration. Her heart darkened to a cold, black cinder before Manannán's eyes.

Manannán stopped, turned and made his way back to her, grabbed her whole, wrenched rocking body and held her as tight as he could as she collapsed in his arms on the ice staircase.

"I just want to die." Grace stated flatly. Then she rapidly muttered through sniffles, tears and terror in a clear psychotic break, "Please just let me die. What's the point? Even if we get out, where are we going? South? To some Wonderland from an old story? That's all crap you made up for my benefit, I'm sure. We are going nowhere. We are just going to die out here, alone, cold, frozen and afraid. Even if we can get out, Boll's walkers are everywhere. We might just walk right into their grasp anyway. Nothing matters. We don't matter. I certainly don't! I can scream with all the force in my being and it will be like everything I am evaporating into a sucking hole of nothing. It doesn't matter anymore. All that I am, the infinite power of spirit is nothing when it's sucked into an infinite vacuum of black and cold."

Manannán held her tighter as she rocked and he with her. He said softly, "You matter to *me*, Grace. And that's enough to be greater than the black hole of nothing you see."

"Shut up," she instinctively snapped back.

"I care about you. I won't let anything happen to you Grace, while I'm still alive. You're all I have in the whole world."

"But I hate you."

"No you don't."

Grace buried her face into his cloth layers and sobbed. Through the tears she relented and said, "I've had a crush on you since I was fourteen. You're amazing. I've loved you for years. There. I said it. You happy now?"

Manannán held her tight, her glistening, tear-filled eyes longingly gazing into his. He took a deep breath and removed his rebreather. She saw this and did the same, and they kissed one another softly but deeply, like famished souls finally gaining nourishment. He felt her body relax as her final barriers and defenses collapsed in his arms, for once and all time.

Grace said softly as they broke the kiss, "I love you so much. Don't ever leave. I beg you. I can't live without you."

Manannán calmed and savored the moment. In another moment he said, "I have come to love you, to protect you. You are all I need. You are, to me, the very thing that completes me and makes me whole."

"Oh Manannán! I'm sorry. I'm sorry for being such a..."

"A bit..."

Grace cut him off immediately, slapped him on his shoulder and said, "No. 'Pain,' I was going to say. But whatever. Yes that works too."

They smiled.

Manannán reassured by adding, "We're in this together, and together we'll get out. I promise. There's always a way."

"You're my way, Man," Grace said softly.

"And you're mine, and will always be," Manannán replied.

In the cold and in the dark, the pair found a spark of hope within themselves, and permitted their hearts and bodies to show the love they made for one another in all the physical ways two people could.

~

A few hours later, the two dressed and glowed in the calming peace their love-making provided, like a long-needed safe escape for both their tormented souls. They continued their walk, close together, Grace clinging to the guide-rope and to Manannán's draped cloths equally for support, in silence. Manannán pointed out Aibell's signage carved in the ice as he described his journey there not long before. They continued.

Grace then caught the glow.

"What is that?!" she asked excitedly.

Manannán replied joyously, "That's the Nautilus."

"Let's hurry. Show me!"

"We're going, we're going. Be careful," Manannán called as she began briskly walking carelessly down the carved steps, rushing to see the wonders she could only imagine were causing the light ahead of her. Manannán followed.

Grace arrived at the gate Manannán found before, opened the hasp and made her way down to the cordoned off platform, aglow in colored light and warmth.

Studying the phenomenon similarly to how Manannán did only hours before, she excited and blurted, "They're eating the ice! It's life! They're alive! All of them...millions of them! Everywhere here! All the way down there!" Grace pointed down the spiral, leaning precariously over the metal fence preventing her fall.

"It's spectacular, isn't it?" Manannán asked.

"Spectacular? It's *miraculous!*" Grace offered gleefully. "I want to go down! I want to see the bottom. I have to know where it all starts, or ends or wherever it does whatever it needs to do."

"I don't think that's a good idea. We'll never make it back up. We have nothing to climb up with. It's horribly steep and you can't even manage a few icy stairs."

"Watch it, Man. I'll start hating you again," Grace quipped.

"Bring it," Manannán retorted and smiled back.

"Okay," Grace continued, "If we can't go down, can we go up a little? The center shaft is right here, and I see a flat top only what, ten meters up there?" Something flashed in the light from where she was looking at the top of the central shaft.

"Did you see that?" Grace asked.

"See what? No. I didn't see anything," Manannán replied.

"Watch," Grace ordered. "Wait for it."

The flash returned.

"There!" Grace exclaimed.

"Yes!" Manannán agreed. "What is that up there? It looks metallic."

They both zoomed in with their augmented eyes to see what they couldn't at a normal zoom, barley making out an object just out of sight, in the dark shadows above their heads.

"I can't make it out," Manannán stated.

"Yeah, me neither," Grace agreed. "Can we get up there?"

"Same problem. Nothing to climb with."

"I know," Grace relented.

Manannán studied the ice structure of the central shaft and began working out footholds and handholds, mapping them in his burned memory, searching for a way at least he or one of them could climb to the top. After a few moments he said to her, "I can get up there. But there's only room for one. You'll have to stay here.

"Bullocks. Fine," Grace blurted peevishly. "But how are you going to get over there? Jump across?"

"Precisely. I've mapped out the stability points and footholds in my mind, and have calibrated my body for the jump."

"You what?!"

"Never mind. Just watch." With that, Manannán climbed on the metal fencing, stood, and jumped in one swift motion, sticking a perfect landing on four grab points invisible to Grace until the very moment of his clinging to them. Then he turned back toward her and said, "See? Easy!"

"I guess for you! Okay. I'm impressed now."

"Oh, so *now* you're impressed. I see how you are."

"Shut up!"

"Yes Mum."

Grace watched her beacon of light climb what seemed to her precariously to the top of the life-filled, color-glowed ice-shaft. After several minutes, Manannán reached the top and was stunned.

He called from above, "My God!"

"What! What is it?"

"I don't even know if you'll know what I mean when I tell you."

"What are you talking about, Man? What the hell is up there?"

"It's a spaceship."

"A what?!"

"Well a probe, of sorts, I guess."

"A probe?! From what? Where? What are you talking about?"

"Well it says 'ESA' on the side. I know what this is, from the history record fragments."

"What?! What is it already?!"   Grace was in suspense.

"It's the Huygens lander."

"The what?!"

"It's called Huygens. It was the first man-made object to ever land here from Earth, over five thousand years ago."

"It's what?!" Grace was even more befuddled after the explanation. "Five thousand years? What the hell are you talking about?!"

"Quiet, Grace. I'm studying this."

"Excuse me! Don't start talking to me like..."

She was cut off with, "Shut it already!   I'm thinking!"

A relented sigh came from the air down beneath him. "Well... hurry up then... I guess."

"Grace. Enough. Just wait a few minutes."

"Fine."

In the forced silence Grace contemplated the wall, and the creatures busy at work making their lives. In a moment she did not contemplate, she heard a call like a child's voice telling a hurried secret, "See the way before you!"

Grace, startled asked aloud, "Did you hear that?" When no answer came, she dismissed it and continued staring at the glowing colorful organisms in silence. Not even five minutes passed when Manannán jumped back onto the railing and onto the platform where Grace watched his acrobatics in amazement and welcomed him with a hug.

"I missed you," she said in his ear."

"I know."

"What'd you find?"

"It's amazing. It's nearly perfectly intact after all this time. Its shiny aluminum surface is like it's the day it was built! And I know where the creatures came from."

"You do?"

"I do, indeed! They're from Earth! They're microbes that travelled all the way here from earth that were stuck to the hull of the lander. Maybe only a few survived the journey. But the ones that did managed to adapt rapidly and are now thriving right before our very eyes! It's truly miraculous!"

Yet again dumbfounded, Grace's mouth dropped agape, speechless in the moment. Then she said after a moment, "How can you know that?" A pause. "Never mind. Nature is always creating. This is the creative force in action, Man. God *is* here, right before us both!"

"Well I tend to think that the microbes adapted to the climate conditions rapidly, certainly, and after that..."

"Rapidly?!" Grace blasted, cutting him off. "How long do you think it took them to eat their way into the cavern like this?"

"I see. Yes, maybe three thousand years!"

"And leaving what, two thousand to radically remap their genome or something to become these things?"

"Something like that..."

"And does evolution work that quickly?"

"Not usually..."

"So what other explanation can you give for such a dramatic and radical change to a harmless bacteria into an active feeding colony of multi-species water-eating, butane breathing microscopic grazers?"

"I have none. At least not right now."

"That's right. You don't because you know full well that *this* is the Way before us! See? There *is* a light in this time of seemingly never-ending darkness."

"Yes Grace. So now you have me and God lighting your way. The day grows brighter by the moment!"

"It does, Man, it does. And I am happy suddenly!"

"How quickly things change!" Manannán yelled out to the cavernous void.

Without missing a beat, Grace exclaimed in return, "My faith renews!"

Manannán genuinely smiled with her and remarked, "You need air. We've been out longer than I planned."

Grace checked her air supply seeing red on the indicator dial telling her she was down to her last hour. Her eyes widened as panic set in. Manannán, always prepared, took a deep breath and detached his own breather to her supply pack and transferred some of his own air to hers. Before a minute was up, her gauge was back in the yellow, giving her three additional hours, and he quickly reconnected his own and took a needed, deep breath.

Manannán stated flatly, "We need to go back and charge us up fully once more."

"Yes, you're right. Let's go," Grace agreed.

Within an hour they were back to the dubgrin piles and fermenter. Manannán connected Grace's air supply to the massive machine and within minutes her air supply was fully charged. He topped off his own in a few more minutes and converted the fermenter to water.

"We've got a long way to go. Best we stock up."

"So we're leaving?" Grace asked.

"Well, yes. Yes we are ...going to find Wonderland and the Midge. Right?"

"I guess. Why don't we just stay here? We have everything we need. No one will ever find us," Grace offered.

"We found us. I mean, we found this place by accident. So did Amadán, presumably. It can't be that difficult to find," Manannán replied.

"Yes but it's better than being out in the open dunes, on foot, with our body heat pouring out as a beacon of wavy air for the world to see," Grace reasonably asserted. "What if Boll's walkers are wandering everywhere when we get out? What then?"

"All reasonable questions."

"You bet they are. I say we stay."

"We can't. They'll find us."

"They'll find us anyway. At least we can form a defense here."

"Futile. I do not concur."

"Then what is it then? Why must we leave?" Grace became more desperate.

"They'll find us... probably no matter what choice we make. But what they cannot find is the Nautilus. That cannot happen. Boll we surely destroy it."

"What? Why?" Grace panicked.

"Because it supplants Boll's supreme authority. It illustrates for all to see that there is a power on Titan greater than his, and he won't stand for it. Trust me. He will blow this place to hell and us along with it before anything else to make sure there would be no memory of it."

Grace thought about the words and said, "*He* would remember."

"Be that as it may, we must leave, before he finds this and us in it. If we travel carefully outside, around cover, we'll make it."

"We have about five days of air, and we can ration our water and food I guess. We can make it the whole way to Ontario Lacus, if that's where we're going."

"It is," Manannán confirmed.

"No one's been there before who's come back to tell us about it. Not to my knowledge anyway. There's no reason to go. Why would anyone go down there? It's not like Kraken, Man."

"No you're right. It's superfluous. We have everything we need, or needed in Ergon, Mug Ruith and the Triple Cities. No need to expand. Yet the story..."

"Your story, Man. Your story your guardians told you as a new one. How do you know it's true?"

"I don't. It's a hunch."

"A hunch?" Grace fumed. "We're traveling five-hundred kilometers to the south pole on a hunch?! Are you mad? And what about when we start running out of air again? What if there's nothing there to recharge with. We're dead. Stone. Cold. Dead."

"Possibly I *am* mad. But it just feels right."

"Bullocks on that. We should stay here. Damn the microbes."

"That would not be the Way, Grace."

"I know. I just don't like it, 'tis all."

"That I know clearly well."

Grace sighed. "I know you're right. And you'll protect me. I know you will. I believe in you. But I reserve the right to complain when we can't find decent shelter for sleeping."

"It may be rough out there. There may be nothing but pasty ethane mud, tholin dust and ice rocks to rest your head on."

"Ugh. Yes I was afraid of that. I'll just sleep on you, if that's alright. I mean, where else would you have me sleep, hmm?" She sprung her sleep trap.

"Aha! I see now. Yes Grace. You can rest your head on me. Of course, my dear."

"Good. About time you started seeing things my way."

"As it is you say, Grace." Manannán smiled at her and rubbed her forehead with his, kissing being inconvenient with covered mouths most of the time. "Shall we get going then?"

"Yes, I command it. We are leaving." Grace raised her voice in an auspiciously commanding tone, as if it was her idea all along.

~

Grace and Manannán walked for several hours, following Aibell's long-aged carved ring-world signs along dark corridor after even darker water-ice lava tube. Before long, a light shown far in the distance, as the pair walked upward along a gentle incline. The light became orange which became cinnamon, which reflected increasingly off the shiny ice walls, changing them from blue to rust. As they approached the opening towards the open sky the two hurried their paces, raced for the exit and joyously slid out onto the desert sand.

Grace and Manannán stared into the vastness of Titan's great plains. Their hearts sank as they peered into the dense atmosphere where, far too distant to count the numbers, was the caravan of Boll's walkers and hundreds of thousands of enslaved Ruithians headed toward their new doom. Any joy that the pair shared in the prior moment relented once again to the reality that was the terror of Cassius Boll and his new world order.

Crawl, Walk, Run, and Fly

*M*anannán pushed Grace's head into the sand, keeping it down and away from the air which was rippling due to her relative torching body heat as he did the same, but voluntarily. She reacted instinctively resistant with a huff but relented after understanding herself what he was trying to avoid. They dared not move curled in a ball as they shivered in fear for being discovered. Sounds of walker-steps resonated through the thick atmosphere, which made their pitch seem low and ominous. Above them were the wails of Ruithian humanity being pulled along in shackles, on foot, herded away from their home to the mines of the Triple Cities, far to the east. Thousands of walkers raced around the perimeter of the mass of humanity, reigning in the hundreds of thousands terrified Ruithians whose views of escape were blocked by the barrels of rifles pointed at their heads. The collective wail was like that of an innocent child feeling a burn for the first time in its life.

"God! My people! There is no light in the world anymore," Grace pleaded in sadness.

"At least yours are alive, Grace. Mine are all dead. Which is worse?" Manannán asked from his own grief.

"I'm not sure, at that, Man. I know. A fate worse than death is death, or is it *that*?" Grace asked rhetorically referring to the marching slave caravan in view. "We can't just lie here, crawling around," Grace uttered in a loud whisper, deflecting the overwhelming emotional state between them.

"That, I think," Manannán answered. Then he replied, referring to the second part, "We have to stay as low as we can right now. We need to crawl before we can walk. So just hush," Manannán ordered.

"I can't just... lie down and stay here, Man," Grace pleaded. "Stop pushing so hard," referring to her face being pushed harder into a hill of tholin dust by Manannán's hand.

"Right. Sorry. Just a bit tense," Manannán offered.

"Yeah, I know. Me too," Grace agreed. "How long should we risk staying here out in the opening of this massive cave entrance everyone can see for kilometers?"

"Funny," Manannán poked. "As long as it takes for the caravan to move away out of sight or until we need to."

"So, hours then. Great plan." Grace's frustration was illustrated by her hand gripping the sands tighter and tighter so that the grains were forced between her fingers.

"Relax. We're raising our body temperature, making things worse. We need to settle our emotions. We're becoming irrational." Manannán's tone was increasingly calm, in reciprocal to Grace's increasing irrational emotional state which was trumping her ability to reason and all logical thought.

"Shut up," Grace flatly replied as she allowed the tension in her hands to relax and her breathing to slow.

Minutes passed as the marching stomps of Boll's walkers dimmed in the air. Manannán dared to look up and said, "They're nearly gone. Maybe another hour and they'll crest over that hill. Then we can move." He looked at Grace and pointed to a distant hill with his eyes. Grace followed and agreed when she saw it in her gaze as well.

Grace then offered, "If we keep to the craggy ridge here along the opening, maybe we can blend into the topography of the ice-rock formations as we move, now that we have several kilometers between us and them. We'd just be a blip of heat on their infrared sensors, which from there could be anything, and nothing to be worried about.

"Fair analysis," Manannán affirmed. "I still would feel better to wait a bit longer. Minimize the risk to as near to zero as we can make it. Or just make it zero by simply waiting for them to move past our line of sight."

"In what? Another two, three hours?" Grace debated. We can get so far in that time. We're going south. They're going east. By moving we get farther away from them. Faster."

"True, true," Manannán relented. "Just give me a few more minutes before we move. Fifteen. That will be better. Concur?"

Grace paused and agreed, "Concur."

"Good. Just be calm. Just be still."

"Okay."

Fifteen minutes passed and the mass of humanity that was so large hours before was a small swath of grey in the distant orange horizon. Barely a sound could be heard for all the steps being taken on rock-hard frozen ice.

Manannán said, "Okay. They keep going east. We'll go west along this ridge and turn south in a few hundred meters, guaranteeing a blind of rock between us and the caravan."

"Yes. My thought exactly," Grace agreed. "It cannot fail."

"Right. No way for them to see us through the ridge, unless they're looking for us with active infrared pulses pointed at us looking for movement. But even then, the ice-rock is meters thick.

"Right," Grace again agreed. "Let's go."

They quickly crawled left, in a westward direction and kept crawling against the ice-rock wall that curved around away from the caravan, the cavern-opening, and the danger both represented for being discovered.

They rose to their feet after a time, coming around the arching ice-rock face. Walking briskly but carefully, the pair walked right up to the back of an outward-facing walker, and Bollan Rider occupying it. Shocked, they stopped dead and their tracks and instantly held their breath.

Grace froze in fear, while Manannán's thoughts rushed in silence. He quickly assessed the distance, strength and needed force in order to relieve the guard of his walker in a way that would not draw any further attention than was necessary. Was there another? He saw none, but why would only one be out this far away from the rest of the marching herds? He couldn't know until he engaged. Fear and panic left him and in their place were only force and momentum calculations, vector analysis, and predictive analytics, that made him feel at peace and calm once again, all occurring in the moment he took to formulate his attack.

Manannán's weapon of choice was a retractable titanium pike, that when closed fit in a small pocket. But when released, exploded into a two-meter long pointed spike that would skewer any enemy from a distance before they knew what hit them. One firm thrust through the center of the back of the head would do it, and all would be quiet. Not a sound would be heard or carried in the wind. Manannán took a long breath.

In one swift move he leapt to his left onto the ice-rock wall, jumping up its side in one strong pace, and using his momentum, leapt forward towards his target, while in the air, released the spike that punctured cloth, skin, flesh, bone, and brain. Manannán flipped in the air and landed feet-first in-front of the walker, retracted his spike and held out his arms, catching his victim before he was able to hit the ground. He carried the body in the next seconds behind the ice-rock wall and left the guard's body in a small crevasse at its base, burying it in tholin grains, masking his dying heat signature from the world.

Grace was stunned in silence, having witnessed never-before-experienced stealth, grace and military perfection she never considered, or conceived. She was in awe, her heart racing in both inspiration and fear.

"How... how in the world did you do... do *that*?" Grace asked, dumbfounded.

Manannán looked at her and flatly stated, "Emotion is the mind-killer. Leave it behind Grace. You see the result."

"I've never seen anyone do that before, not even in all my training, or in my visits to Ergon. How did you...?"

"It's a personal training I have developed and practiced most of my life," he answered, cagily.

"U-huh, right. But who taught you all that? You can't just come up with it on your own, out of nowhere, Man. I'm not stupid, you know."

Manannán sighed. "Fine. It's not something I share with anyone, for fear of public reprisal. But seeing how there's no *public* anymore, save you my dear, I suppose it doesn't matter anymore, right?"

"Yes, if you've been paying attention, clearly," Grace responded sardonically.

Manannán paused and stated flatly, "I learned it from Justin Forsythe."

Grace retreated in stunned disgust, and denial. "No you didn't. Not *him*. He's the worst human being to have... he's *not* human... he's a..." she trailed off towards Manannán's interruption.

"He is *not* those things, Grace. I know what the public history has led you to believe, but *he* was the one who discovered, well, everything! He was the one who sacrificed himself to save humanity! And there were others too... His wife, Jessica, and a woman named Sherrie Donovan. They all died to save us! There are things that happened on Yurpa no one talks about. Aliens, tens-of-thousands of years of prior history, Miracles! We only know about the voluminous realms and all of it because of them!"

"He destroyed our civilization! Obviously!" Grace was weeping. "You say you know. I don't know any of it. It's all crap, Man.

"Did he really destroy it? Did *they*? I don't think so. I think they were used," Manannán was finally letting down barriers that came so difficult to release. "I know history that was never shared or known before. I pieced it together on my own, over years. The fragments, the memories of so many people and what they used to call, 'AIs' all needed to be patched together. It was daunting. But I did it."

"AIs?" Grace blurted. "What the hell is an AI?"

"Artificial Intelligence. It's what Yurpans referred to as people who were printed, instead of genetically produced. They were considered slaves back then."

"Slaves... Like my people now." Grace began to nauseate.

"Yes, unfortunately."

"Boll will die for it, you know."

"Someday, he will. While I'm breathing, he will," Manannán resolved.

Grace paused and blurted, "We're off topic. Ugh. Justin Forsythe. Ugh. I hate saying his name. He destroyed us. Jessica's even worse. The arrogance! Yurpa was our last hope. Now it's gone and here we are being hunted by a madman. We'll all be dead in a hundred years. He should be forgotten. It's that simple."

"I don't agree. But I think you know that already."

Grace rolled her eyes.

Manannán continued, "History wasn't lost, Grace. It wasn't. I found it. In the ether. In the voluminous realms. It's all there, in time's second dimension."

"What the hell are you talking about, Man?" Grace was fuming once more. "The ether? Time's second dimension? You know we can't access that unless we have those old mind drives, and no one's had one working since the Ripping. The system was torched along with Yurpa, and Gabriellium. We are alone, and stuck on a one-way trip into oblivion! So what are you going on about?!"

"I can access it," Manannán calmly stated.

"It? What?!" Grace raged.

"The ether. Time's second dimension. All the information that was stored there. I hear it, see it... experience it!"

"Bullocks! You don't. You're a liar! You are one because you want to know why? Because you're a liar, first, and I hate you second, third, you are a liar *and* I hate you and forth, you don't have a damned mind drive you idiot!"

"You're right Grace. I don't have a mind drive," Manannán's flatness returned.

"What?! Now you're agreeing with me. You've lost it Man. You have jumped off the precipice into the deep dark hole of mental incongruity."

Manannán laughed slightly at the sudden, surprising metaphor from Grace. He stoically replied, "Yet I access the ether."

"And how the hell do I know that? Your word? Did you hear the first part of what you are? 'You're a liar and I hate you?'"

"I thought that was number three."

"Shut up! One, three. All the numbers say you're a liar. So you're a liar and I still hate you."

Manannán paused and grinned at her childish kinesics and said, "I can show you, if I must."

"Show me? Really? Grace was no longer playing. "But how?"

"I'll just intend it to you."

"Intend it? What's that mean?"

"Not to worry... I'll just *will* it. It's like telepathy, they used to call it."

"What the hell is 'tell – eh – peh – thee?'"

"Using my mind to connect to yours without talking. Mind drives. You know. Think thoughts and everyone hears. You remember at least that part of history don't you?"

"Yes, obviously. I'm not stupid."

"That's one word."

"Shut up. I still hate you."

"I know. It's alright. I hate you too darling."

"No. I hate you. That's all that matters. You can't re-hate me to make it even."

"Are you literally a child right now?"

"Shut up."

"As you say." Manannán began to love the banter, knowing how benign it truly was. He thought how beautiful Grace became when she showed her strength that was raw from emotive dishevelment; that it was somehow powerful, albeit insane for him to think so. And he loved disarming her ferocity with facts and reason as much as he loved rattling her cage with weaknesses in her character he exploited readily. "Yes is your answer," he concluded.

There was a moment of silence as the Titan air breezed by them with a soft caress calming their spirits. Grace then blurted, "Wait. We're all printed, right?"

"What?" Manannán asked.

Grace repeated, "We're all printed. Now. That's how we procreate. We print copies and change the genetic sequence a bit to make us unique. Is that right?"

"Yes Grace. That's how it works."

"Ok. But you said before that in Yurpa that those AI things were printed, and that they were artificial, like they weren't real people."

"AIs. Right. They were printed. People thought AIs were printed and people, while sterilized from radiation from the Purge, were reproducing genetically in laboratories in Gabriellium."

"Okay, but if we're all printed now, doesn't that make all of us 'artificial?'"

Manannán paused at the concept and replied, "It was Justin and Jessica Forsythe who discovered the truth on Yurpa. They met someone who told them that everyone on Yurpa and everywhere since the Purge were actually being printed, and the story of genetics laboratories was a front to ease the psychological burden of wondering if they were all 'real,' similar to what you're asking now. I assure you Grace, you're real. As am I. If you just let me show you, all these questions will be answered in moments for you, and it won't be so cumbersome for you to comprehend."

"I said I wasn't stupid."

"Ugh! Stop! You're not stupid. You're just missing color and details and facts that I cannot possibly begin to describe with this meat in my mouth and this mundane language! Come here. Please."

"Meat in your mouth... what are you going on about?" Grace was splintered and getting lost in the jargon and allegories.

"Grace, please come here. I'll hold you. You'll be fine."

Manannán felt her body melt into his, signaling the banter was over, and she relented to the deep-rooted trust she had in the man she loved more than life itself. In the next moment, all that Manannán knew of civilization's history, Grace knew. Images and scenes of Justin and Jessica Forsythe in Gabriellium, in Level Zero, on the Bridgewater Crossing, and within the Gardens rushed into her experience in a menagerie of endless informational wealth, like a fountain of truth left only to those who could still see it to drink from.

Grace saw the corruption of the State destroy humanity's last hope of natural reproduction be killed on the order of a morally conflicted soul who led them. She then saw the Purush, the sentient halophiles of the deep ocean in league (and at odds) with Argus, the twenty-thousand-year-old grudge match between them, and...

"...the Midge!" Grace yelled out. We're going to where *he* is?! Are you completely out of your mind?! He's sure to deliver us right to Argus! He's his father for pity sake!"

"No! Grace no! Well yes, he is his father but not like what you think. Look again. He was printed after. *After* Argus. He was printed fertile! He was... is an experiment. Just like everyone else in Gabriellium. Just like everyone else after the Purge was! It was Argus who used him, his own father for his own selfish desires to bring the Yurpans, the real Yurpans to their proverbial knees. If we can trust any of them it will be Midge."

"Them? Who else is here now?"

"Well you see what I see. Argus, certainly, somewhere. Maybe even Sherrie Donovan. She's God's messenger! She is bound to be here."

"Messenger? That poor woman lost a baby, lost her mind, and lost her life, the latter three distinct times, and for what? Just to be reprinted back here in some unknown printer room with a resonance sphere with a location lost to time itself? I would not call her a messenger. I'd call her a lackey!"

"Is there a difference between messenger and minion?" Manannán asked reflectively.

"Yes of course there is... well, wait. Now that I think about it maybe not so much then."

"You can see it now can't you?" Manannán asked genuinely. "You can see everything, now."

"I can. I, I do." Grace was stunned. "I see *everything*! What did you do to me? Do I have a mind drive?"

"I don't know," came the honest answer. "Near as I can understand, the technology known as mind drives were destroyed in the Ripping. But, after centuries of use, implanting and printing directly into the atomic structure of the human genome, I have come to the conclusion that they, or more precisely, whatever it is they do (quantum entangled particles, spins and suchlike) occurs naturally in me. And now I see it does in you. But yours lay dormant until I, well, turned in on."

"You mean activated it. Like opening an eye you didn't know you had, right?" Grace asked wisely.

"Precisely."

"I didn't believe you, Man. I, I couldn't. You know that right?"

"Of course. I knew all along. We had to follow the path in the dark before the path could be illuminated before us. See the way before us, now!" Manannán pointed skyward.

"The Way was never dead, only hidden. 'Yaldabaoth has hidden the truth....'" Grace muttered.

"Exactly!" Manannán stood and exclaimed, "We have a Walker. We have the guard's gun. We have a chance. We have to go. Now."

"I see the truth of it," Grace beamed, climbed with Manannán onto the Walker's back, took the hands and began running south as fast as they could.

Not a minute passed before light aircraft and walkers from Boll's caravan were on them. Blue fire rained around them as Grace and Manannán's walker did everything it could to avoid the onslaught.

"Where'd they come from?! They're everywhere!" Grace cried.

"They were on to us apparently. Hid in a ditch, while the main group marched on. We haven't much time! There's no cover!"

"Go faster!" Grace again cried to anyone who could hear.

"I am Grace! I don't think it can go any faster. I keep leaping about but you may fall off!" Manannán's rapid breaths overtook his vowels such that all he had was panicked response as an exhale of exertion.

"I'll hold! Don't worry about me! Just keep dodging!" Grace assured. "The planes are coming around again, strafing!"

"Got it!" Manannán called out and jumped his walker high in the air and flipped head over feet to his right so that the aircraft missed their target completely.

Grace held on for dear life to Manannán's narrow waist, and let out a grunt as the walker landed on the ground with a thud, Titan's lower gravity permitting ground-to-aerial stunts that could not be fathomed on the old, good Earth from before the Purge.

She said, "We can't keep that up for very long. It's only a matter of time now. What's the plan?"

"Keep going! That's all we've got. Find cover."

"There's no cover out here!" Grace yelled. "They're on us!" She let out a scream just as another strafing run from the planes was about to overcome their position. But it suddenly stopped and blue fire against cinnamon fuel explosions all around them were frozen in time; her scream, lonely in the new-found silence.

Grace and Manannán's heavy breaths were eerily absorbed into what seemed to be a great nothing, a quiet and a respite that excluded all sounds of moving craft, munitions, and air around them. Light itself appeared to have stopped in mid-journey from the chemical explosions that created it to the intended targets' own eyes. The environment around them both darkened as a result of the suspended photons, and all noise utterly disappeared from their perception. They looked up, around and behind them to see teams of walkers, meters away in mid stride, seemingly defying gravity itself.

Grace asked, "What the hell?"

Manannán held Grace's hand and said, "Wait. I've seen this before... in the Gardens. Look for a silver disk."

"What, like the one we both saw in orbit before in that vision, or whatever it was?"

"Yes. That too. Exactly."

The sky suddenly darkened as a silver disk several meters across descended above their heads. One from below the ground rose them up where they stood to meet it and stopped so that the two disks sandwiched the riders like a super-voluminous meal prepared with great care.

From above them a figure appeared, silhouetted by the faded sunlight, walked forward, followed the surface of the upper disk so that its feet were above and head was below. His eyes met there's from this inverted position when the figure said, "Hello. You are Manannán mac Lir of Ergon, Vinculum Mare, and you are Grace Blieh Amadán Dubh of Mug Ruith, and you need my help... *desperately.*"

Manannán bravely replied, "And what of it. Who the hell are you?"

The figure snickered and said, "I am not Argus; rest assured that I am not he. Rather I am 'the father,' he would say I am."

"The *father*?" Manannán asked. "Ah... So you are *the Midge*! Yes?"

"*The* Midge?" The figure laughed at the title. "I've never been called *the* Midge before. But I suppose there's a first time for everything, Justin might say."

"You mean Justin Forsythe," Grace asked pointedly, "don't you?"

"I do indeed, Mum," Midge replied. "You have questions, I see them. They will be answered. As you can see, time is irrelevant at the moment, which in itself is a funny little phrase, don't you think?"

Grace and Manannán didn't reply and stared blankly at the inverted face.

"Ah quite right... a lot to take in. Where are we going... yes, all of that... Not to worry, I won't harm you. You are safe with me. We have much to share... since our time in space before... Ah yes that was real... no you're not losing your minds... patience. We'll be far from this place in an instant where Boll's forces cannot find us. Shall we go then?"

"Do we have another choice?" Grace poked.

Midge laughed blatantly, "You always have a choice, my dear Grace. You can choose to stay here and die in the very next moment after I return you to linear time's first dimension, or you can come with me and follow what I light before you. It's always your choice."

"Umm, yeah. Alright. I see... I see your point. Shut up Grace. Don't be an ingrate. The world hates ingrates. So, shut your hole. Got it," Grace relented, covering her insecurity in the situation with rough-hewn humor.

Midge laughed again, heartily and said, "You have a singular wit Grace, which I like very much. You remind me of Jessica, a lot, and Tanya as well, when she was well, still Tanya."

"I can imagine," Grace offered weakly.

Manannán remained silent while the two bantered in order to find comfort in the circumstance.

Midge then said to both, "You've crawled, walked and run to fight for your lives, for the right of humanity to be *human*. But that's not gotten you very far. And it would've ended in tragedy but for the Way before us.

There is always a way, and it became my time to show it to you. So I know you have much to discuss. But for right now, in this moment, it is time for you to fly."

In the next moment, Boll's walker teams, within meters of their prey, suddenly saw nothing but dusty, frigid air before them, as well as walker tracks that ended in both the Xanadu desert sands and the sands of time.

Ontario

idge was as tall as he was calm, a force of stolid resolute to behold that held no sway of anything that would emotionally disturb the strongest of others in to a psychotic episode. To Grace and Manannán, he towered above them, standing on the same disk as they, by nearly two meters. The pair was startled, cautious and alarmed, to say the least. Yet, relief filled the still air as the winds of Titan's vast deserts whizzed by as the transport disk traveled through the cinnamon space, but not external time. As a result, startling images of dust devils, in perfect isolation and suspense could be seen, that somehow made the whole scene look phony, like a bad movie set in a low-budget production, as still scenes caught their eyes.

After long minutes of dead silence filled the space on the disk, Manannán broke in and asked, "Are you aware of the stories my people tell to the new ones about you?"

Midge, who was looking outward, silently absorbing the rushing landscape in a seemingly meditative state turned toward them and said, "Yes, I am aware... more than aware actually. It was actually me who gave it to your people."

"So then there is a Wonderland! Do you actually keep track of everyone's words, deeds, activities and judge them accordingly?" Grace broke in.

Midge laughed slightly that sounded like a forced exhalation through his sinuses and said, "No child, I do not do that precisely. While I have the capacity to, I can think of nothing less fruitful. And that would be a bit demagogic of me, wouldn't you say? Actions of a maniac. We already have too many of those on Titan, I think."

"You can say that again," Grace conceded and trailed off. Then, having another sudden thought blurted, "So wait a minute. If you were on Yurpa a half a millennium ago how are you still alive? How'd you get here after the Ripping? I just don't understand how anyone can live for five-hundred or more years."

"You mean, Europa, of course, Grace. Yes?" Midge corrected.

"Yerr-Oh-Puh?" Grace genuinely asked trying to reproduce his cadence. "I don't know it as that, it's Yurpa to me."

Manannán interrupted, "Grace, five hundred years is a long time. Language changes. New dialects form. It's actually quite surprising that we even understand the common language at all from the Ripping. In our history, whole new languages immerged after falls in far less time."

"That is very true, Manannán," Midge answered. "I commend your peoples' efforts to piece together history from the stored knowledge you recovered from the Ripping. There's a lot going on here happening spontaneously we did not expect. Your ability to access the ether without a mind drive, for example, is fascinating to me. But as for language, after the fall of an empire called 'Rome' which existed long ago, deep in Earth's history, several knew languages immerged in only a few hundred years that were later called the 'Romance Languages.' Our common language came from those and was influence by several other, unrelated ones. After millennia, any similarities to the original Latin spoken in Rome were so far removed, few could make the connection today. Yet the root of how we speak is there, buried beneath perhaps seven thousand years of linguistic evolution."

"English," Manannán offered. "The common language is called 'English.' It's right there, in the ether. It came to me. I needn't search for it."

"English?" Grace judged. "What kind of funny word is that?!"

Manannán continued in response, "England was another empire that colonized much of Earth a couple of millennia after the fall of Rome. As a result, many of Earth's inhabitants spoke it. It later became the global common tongue used for trading, negotiations and diplomatic endeavors, before the Purge of course. After the Purge, well, there weren't that many people left to carry on now dead languages. English became the only one. We then almost lost the spoken language altogether with mind drive technology. But the Ripping took care of that. Then in the centuries since the Ripping, many differences in our lexicon have crept in, and here is where we are, with 'Yurpa,' instead of 'Europa.'"

"Precisely," Midge affirmed. "Nicely done."

Grace rolled her eyes at the pedantic dialogue she was compelled to listen to. She expressed her discontent by sighing audibly and asking, "So when are we going to be there... I mean wherever it is we're going? Not that I'm ungrateful, mind you, for saving our lives and all in that mess back there, but I'd like to know we're not in for something worse. Exile has really not agreed with me thus far, so I'm hoping for a long, hot bath and a molt-scrape, if you please."

Midge laughed aloud, an act he caught himself realizing he was not accustomed to and said, "My dear Grace! You are truly the Mum of Titan! I would expect no less. Yet, I have. All your needs will be met, I assure you. Where we are going has everything a person would want. Merely think it, and it will appear. It is quite a 'Wonderland' as Manannán called it earlier."

"I think it and whatever it is I think of, simply appears. Right. Got it. And there are purple shkins flying in the air above our heads too. Sure." Grace's sarcasm had no filter any longer.

Midge laughed again and said, "You sound just like Jessica sometimes... Wait, Mum. You'll see. I assure you. I am incapable of lying or omission of any kind. So you will be shown that I mean what I say. A little patience, however. We will arrive within the hour."

"Ugh... Jessica Forsythe again. Shut up about it... Arrive? Where?" Grace asked.

"Ontario. Ontario Lacus to be precise, in the south polar regions."

"You were right, Man. There is something in Ontario. The story *was* true," Grace affirmed, whispering to her unlikely partner.

"Well every story or legend has a foundation of some truth," Manannán replied.

Turning back to Midge she pressed, "So you never answered my question. You know, about your age and how you got here."

"Yes Grace," Midge answered. "Now that you are beginning to access the information stored in the ether, you may begin to understand the answer better than just my spoken words can convey. But for your benefit, the history goes like this: Several of us reprinted ourselves within one of the resonance spheres located on this moon. We did the same after the Purge, making our way to Europa. However, I am not the same Midge as I was on Europa. I am an atomic copy, printed based on the molecular map of who I was on Europa precisely at the moment of my departure, seconds before it exploded. When I arrived here, I was that person, for the most part, age-regressed. But at the same time, the copying and reprinting process has a degradative effect... something about the state of entangled particles disentangling, causing an accumulation of error over millennia, if I recall. Some of us also used transport disks like this one to travel here through space, without moving through time. So relative to anyone on the outside, we all simply disappeared right before their eyes, just as you have right before the eyes of Boll's walkers."

"So we're moving right now, but time is flowing around us, and not through us?" Manannán asked intently. "And that was what we experienced in orbit in that vision earlier?"

"Exactly," Midge agreed. "However, I did not bring you up there to witness the extraction. That was someone else's doing."

"Someone else?" Grace asked. "Who?"

Midge looked visibly disgusted and blurted, "My son, Argus."

Grace and Manannán simultaneously sensed the spike in emotional energy coming from Midge and glanced at each other.

"Apparently you're estranged or something?" Grace poked.

"Putting it minimally, yes," Midge mumbled in response, collecting himself. "*Beyond* that. For certain, dear. He's changed a great deal more than I have over the ages. He's gone insane I think."

"I feel like I should be sorry," Grace replied. "Should I be sorry?"

"There's no time for feelings of sorrow or regret, Grace. We are trying to survive, just like you are, in a way far deeper than I think you realize."

Grace was worrying. "What do you mean? You *are* us. So we're 'all in the same boat,' as they used to say."

Midge smiled at her, like a wise old man appeases a child with an agreeing grin and said, "I think you might be right about that. At least I hope so." Deflecting, he continued, "Isn't the horizon so beautiful this time of orbit? The sun is facing us now, and casts long shadows. It's quite beautiful, wouldn't you say?"

"What?" Grace asked confused by the topic change. "Oh yes. Quite beautiful. The sky's nearly white out here. Must be a thin spot."

"M-hmm," Midge grunted, "Or it might rain soon."

With that, the winding conversation gave way to a few moments' reprieve in silence as the terrain continued to move on by the travelers, safe in their silver disk. Grace allowed exhaustion to set in, having been pursued for days by Boll's walkers. She sat motionless staring at the orange haze. Manannán also stood motionless, seemingly blank-stared at a random spot on the surface of the disk on which he stood, while Midge stood erect staring in the direction the disk was traveling at the horizon ahead. It was a forced peace for all after so much chaos inundated their lives. Grace felt safe for the first time since the assassination, which seemed like forever ago to her.

Midge broke the silence after several minutes with, "When we get to Ontario, there is someone I'd like you to meet."

Manannán joined in as Grace looked up towards him by asking, "Oh really? Who?"

"A survivor," Midge replied.

"Really? From where? Ergon? Although I can't imagine how anyone from Ergon was able to get here before us unless you rescued them with this device before us, I suppose," Manannán analyzed.

"Sort of," Midge affirmed mildly.

Grace then added, "Hold on. Why is this playing in my head now?" She was referring to the vision she had in orbit above Titan's atmosphere, the broken ship, the saucer, and the extraction of the cryo-pod, asking, "Why is this playing my head? I'm not thinking of it. Man, are you showing me something again?"

"No, Mum," Manannán replied. "I'm seeing it too." He turned to Midge and got the answer.

Midge stated, "I'm intending these events first, to assure you that they in fact did happen, and second, to reinforce your memories so they are refreshed to what unfolded in detail. I became aware of a badly battered and broken vessel entering Titan orbit a number of days ago when a new presence entered the ether."

"What, in the mind drive network?" Manannán asked genuinely.

"There is no mind drive network anymore, Manannán," Midge replied. "Not since the Ripping. But this presence—her name is Elizabeth Hawthorne—her mind drive was unaffected somehow. She still had access and I could feel her. Her mind, although still in cryogenic suspension was a morass of tortured thoughts, loss, destruction and sadness. The S.S.V. Deadlight was a lost cause, having been sent on a one-way elliptical orbit to Titan space from Jupiter, just slow enough for someone to see and investigate it before spiraling and burning up into

Titan's atmosphere. I retrieved her before that could come to pass and I took her to Ontario, where we're headed now."

"Obviously," Grace blurted. "So who is she? Where's she from?"

"She's from Europa, or what they used to call, The Belt. She was a miner, with her husband, Daniel. She fostered several children as well. Her memories are mottled, but from what I've seen in her mind, her ship was nearly destroyed when the moon exploded and cast it into a nearly unrecoverable orbit, save for a final, desperate rocket burn that launched it into an elliptical one that placed it here five hundred years after the disaster. She's a relic."

"I'd say," Grace added needlessly. "So we are to do *what* with her? Is she in exile too? What is she going to do about what we have to deal with now? She may regret having come here, or surviving at all, with Cassius Boll killing or enslaving everyone in sight. She'd be better off dead, I'd say."

"You don't mean that Grace," Manannán interrupted. "Right? I mean, can you imagine a Yurpan surviving that disaster having witnessed it from Jupiter's orbit? The horror! But she may have a lot of insight. She may have a lot to share with us once she's conscious. She may be one of the most important people on Titan right now."

"Well it does seem a bit circumstantial that she arrives right when the world's gone to hell," Grace commented.

Midge added, "It's providential. I know this because there's more to her story. I'm certain of it. There has to be."

Manannán then asked, "You don't *know*?"

"I don't, actually. Very perceptive. Yes there are parts of her psyche that are closed off, even from me. I'm not sure how that's happening, but it is the case, regardless. But that fact makes her all the more important in my mind. There's something else going on, clearly that we're not meant to see right now."

Grace added, "Well I don't like it. We have enough of our own problems in the here and now. I don't think an ancient traveler sent here on autopilot is going to matter much when all of my people are working the mines of the Triple Cities. I see what you see now Midge, so I don't see anything that you see that's a golden lit path towards a bright future."

"You assume much, young one," Midge retorted pointedly. "You are wise, as you should be to be made Mum, but you're young and naive in many ways. Your distempered racing thoughts you insist on saying aloud show a lack of maturity... experience. Remember. You still need my help.... *desperately*. Check your opinions... Not all of them are valid. Check your premises... not all of them are valid, either. Think through them before speaking, if you please."

Manannán defended Grace rapidly, "Hang on. She's right Midge. One person in this mess won't amount to a granule of dubgrin against the backdrop of this unceasing nightmare we are living. It's too big for one person. It's like a drop of water in an infinite sea. It's worthless."

"Yet all the drops are needed for the infinite sea to exist, wouldn't you say?" Midge asked rhetorically.

"I would, but that's academic," Manannán replied sharply. "She's a bug pushing a planet. End of story."

"As you say, Manannán. But so aren't we all then? I believe time will show us otherwise," Midge offered. "It doesn't matter right now. We've arrived."

"Nearly," Grace blurted. "Not quite yet. I have a question."

"Yes?" Midge asked.

"Why'd you save us? Why us? What does it matter? We were dead anyway. Titan wouldn't have noticed otherwise. Our people are gone, our cities destroyed. We are leaders of extinct races."

"Extinct?" Midge asked in response. "There are hundreds of thousands of Ruithians headed to the Triple Cities right now, and as far as Ergon is concerned, yes most were killed. But there were a few, perhaps twenty or thirty thousand, that were spared and taken as well. Surely you can both sense them if you focus your energies."

Manannán walked closer, surprised and suddenly very interested in the discussion. "I see them. They're in Áed Rúad, Díthorba, and Cimbáeth, but not alone... not as people. It's like they're all joined somehow. I'm not sure how to interpret what I'm seeing. It's not like *joined*, like a mind drive technology. This is more physical... permanent."

Midge said, "Yes, that's what I sense as well. A mystery. That's two now. Elizabeth Hawthorne, spared Ergonites. What's the third? The third must be, and is usually the most important one."

"The Nautilus!" Grace called. "It has to be. That's probably the biggest mystery on Titan. Let me show you." Without thinking about it, Grace naturally and automatically intended her memories of seeing the life sustaining Nautilus in the ice-lava tube from which they emerged. She said as she was sharing, "It was beneath this old space probe called Huygens... how it got there, I haven't the foggiest, perhaps buried by eruptions from Selk... But the point is we thought... we *surmised* that microbes from Earth survived the journey and found a way to survive, and even thrive in the ice."

Manannán then added, "Yes we analyzed the microscopic organisms closely. They metabolize the ethane and methane in the air by breathing it in and eating the water to create oxygen in some sort of natural electrolysis. They eat their air and breathe their food. They emit these beautiful colors in the process for meters up and down inside the Nautilus. It appears that Amadán was the one who first found it and returned there often right after the Ripping destroyed civilization."

Grace continued, "Right. But no microorganism could adapt and evolve so quickly. Evolution doesn't happen in years or even centuries. Timescales on the order of millions of years are required. I at least know *that* much. Evolution doesn't happen in an instant. So I say... I say it's divine. It's *creation*... literally before our very eyes!"

Midge then offered, "Yes... Is it evolution or the divine creative force? That is probably the biggest mystery of all and would certainly qualify! I am glad you've found your faith once again Mum. We are all going to need it in the days to come."

"I should say so," Grace agreed.

"Looks like we're landing," Midge said. "Watch outside. It's dramatic when the time flow resumes. It'll be a bit noisy though. The winds here are quite strong."

The silver disk came to a stop and the environment around the three travelers swirled into motion with a hissing whine that carried the force of dense cinnamon air behind it. The bright sun which was low on the horizon aligned with a rare clear opening in the haze only moments before gave way to darkening clouds, rain and thunder.

Large methane rain drops smacked the ground around them hard as the trio made their way to a small structure several meters ahead, which appeared too small to house them in the ethane fog that accompanied the pummeling methane projectiles. Their layered fabrics muddied in the thick tholin soil that covered the ice bedrock beneath their feet that sloshed in the sinking liquefaction. Quickly, puddles and moving streams formed around them in mere moments as large volumes of falling liquid filled every low point around them. Gravity transferred it to even larger, deeper depressions farther away. Off in the distance, a swath of liquid methane drew out Titan's horizon like a blade. Black as pitch, Ontario Lacus was only partially softened by dense ethane mists in the storm. Lightning strokes blanketed the darkened rust-brick sky with blue-white surges of power which shocked the travelers' highly sensitive eyes.

Hurried, Midge, Grace and Manannán made it to the door that open as they approached and closed behind them as they raced inside. Heavy breathing and dripping garments, quickly evaporating in the warmer, enclosed space, were the only sounds reverberating off the metal walls of the tight enclosure they were forced to find spots to stand in.

Midge said in a reassuring tone, "Don't worry. This is just the entrance. Now we go below. This is just a lift."

Manannán replied, "Ah. I figured it was something like that."

"Well it stinks in here, certainly," Grace coarsely stated.

Midge smiled and said, "Well that's probably because you've not bathed in a week Grace, and you're beginning to offend even the sands with your smell. Even your garments are offended."

"What, is that some sort of joke, Midge?" Grace targeted. "If it is, I am *not* laughing." Manannán let out a snicker of his own, which prompted a disgusted grunt from Grace, followed by a prompt, "I still hate you," directed toward Manannán's direction.

Manannán simply diffused her bear-poking by responding, "Of course, Mum." The lift began to hum and everyone felt light on their feet.

Before long the door to the lift opened and revealed a sight that neither Grace nor Manannán could have imagined in their wildest dreams. But before shock and awe overcame Manannán, his deep access to the memories stored in voluminous time spoke to him and he blurted, "It's a Garden! Like on Yurpa—I mean Eur-O-pah."

Midge smiled as the golden light of some distant power source shown bright like the sun, an hour before setting on the old, good Earth. In a vast cavern no one could see the end of, forests, fields of wildflowers along rivers and lakes, made of water (and *not* methane) glistened in the light. The smell of humidity and moist soil, made of organic material instead of frozen tholins, greeted their sinuses. Insects flew into them all with a subtle hum and buzz that startled Grace remarkably.

"Ah! What are those?!" she yelled, terrified and cringing behind Manannán. "Get them away from me! Do they bite or sting or anything?"

Midge calmly replied, "Yes. Some of them do. But your molt is too thick for them to get very far. You won't even feel them if they decide you're a tasty treat. Is that all you have to say about the sight before you?"

"Sight? I don't even know what I'm looking at," Grace stated frustratingly. "What's all that green stuff out there? What are those colored things? And why is it so hot in here? How'd all this get here? Is this the 'Wonderland' Man told me about?" Grace asked in a run-on list of 'no-ideas' that revealed her complete ignorance of organic life forms, and their significance within the frozen world as the home of all she ever knew. "God, I'm so hot!"

"It's over three-hundred degrees Kelvin in here," Midge offered. "You will indeed be hot. I suggest stripping those layers so your bodies can breathe," he said to both in a concerned, genuine way. "I don't want to treat you for heat stroke."

"Heat stroke?" Grace asked. "What's that?" she asked dropping cloth layers to the ground

"Hopefully you won't need to find out," Midge answered. Speaking to both Grace and Manannán he said, "Your bodies, everyone on Titan, have grown accustomed to ambient air temperatures barely over a ninety Kelvin. Going from that to this, will, well, be a shock to your system. You may even begin to sweat."

"Sweat?" Grace asked frustratingly once more. "What's that now? I have no idea what anything your saying means." Manannán tried to comfort her by hugging her gently at which point she pushed him away in a physical flurry and a thunderous, "Get off! You're cooking me!"

Manannán backed away and rolled his eyes at Midge looking for an ally in his bewildered frustration in dealing with Grace, the child, instead of Grace, the smart and maturing leader. All Midge could do in response was to grin and lightly shake his head, knowing full well the challenges Manannán faced in being Grace's primary guide through a difficult transition from thinking like a child and into the strength of adulthood. His patience was solid, but now having another man to share his challenge with, gave him a reprieve that he never thought he'd get.

Manannán thought to Midge through the ether, "She's a spoiled rotten little brat you know. But I love her fire. And I love *her*."

Midge thought, "Yes, I can see why you'd be drawn to it. It's very stimulating. She needs to find an inner calm though. Her wail is powerful. Her om is weak."

"Like all children, I would say. That perspective is the source of my patience. But I understand she was handed power under duress before her time. She is coping the best she can, given well... being hunted."

"Indeed," Midge agreed. "In my youth, a very long time ago, I was as volatile as she. It took years and great pains through direct experience to transform me. But I did change, as all people do through growth. She'll find the Way within her."

"At what cost? At what damage? She's already barely holding on. The child within needs something stable... a Mum. She's lost hers. I can only be so much for her. I love her, certainly, despite the... *noise*, but she needs her Mum. I can't be both."

"You're doing well," Midge offered. "This point in the journey must be passed in order to reach the next. But I believe I may have a solution to your dilemma... Elizabeth Hawthorne."

"The relic? Surely not," Manannán defied.

Grace then blurted in the thought exchange, "You idiots know I can hear you, right?"

From the ether in both their minds came a new voice, a female voice, relatively deep and booming. It was that of Elizabeth Hawthorne who interrupted, "Who are you calling a relic?! I'm only thirty-seven."

Thought-laughter overwhelmed the exchange as everyone glanced at each other while a two-meter tall relative giant approached them from the greenery, but who was still nearly a meter shorter than Midge. Elizabeth Hawthorne's imposing stature beside her one-meter tall counterparts gave Grace and Manannán pause as she reached out a gracious hand and said, "Hello there, Manannán, Grace. I'm Liz. Nice to meet you." Liz's hand completely enveloped Manannán's dwarf-sized one with only four fingers to return the grip of Liz's five. Grace reluctantly also took hers in a trepidatious gesture of goodwill.

Grace looked down at her torso and noticed it bulging and asked coarsely, "What's that? What's wrong with you?"

Liz looked down at her belly with tears in her eyes and said, "I'm pregnant, I guess. Midge says so. Although I am still not quite sure what all that means. You have no idea what I've been through, have you."

Midge interjected, lowering the quickly rising emotional tension in Liz and said, "Yes, apparently she somehow going to have a baby... naturally. No printing."

"Not possible," Manannán blurted. "Not been possible for millennia, save Sherrie Donovan's case."

"Don't be so dismissive, Manannán. After all I was the father of that baby," Midge defended. "I was printed fertile five hundred years ago. I presume that trait has been copied over in the reprinting events I've had since then.

"Oh right... I'd forgotten that detail. But that has nothing to do with her," Manannán gestured upward towards Liz.

Midge gestured reassuringly and said, "Forget it. It's just not part of your mode... your 'normal' as it were."

Then turning to Liz he said, "Maybe you can enlighten them on your experience... I know it must be difficult for you. It must feel like it was only a few days ago when it all went to hell. So I understand your trepidation if you wish to wait."

Liz said, "No. That's fine. Getting it out in the open now will help me grieve I think. This is actually the first time I've not felt totally alone here. So I think it will be good." She paused, tapped her left temple and intended the memories of her last days with her family on the Deadlight to her new acquaintances. Rushing forth in the following moment was Europa's destruction, her husband Daniel's frantic attempts to escape with their lives, the loss of her children, and finally, the greatest sacrifice a partner could make in the realization that only one of them would make it: Dan's sacrifice for her one-in-a-million chance at survival. She played what she saw from a spiritual realm, as she was being frozen. Her beloved husband's life snuffing out as hard vacuum took him so that her cryo-bed could be powered was her last image of him. With it, she remembered how the Deadlight's orbit was adjusted to reach Titan—in what was to be for her at the time, five hundred years hence.

Grace began to weep uncontrollably.

Manannán was silent, in shock and introspective.

Both felt what Liz felt, as they never before experienced the full effects of the mind drive, which included all the physiological repercussions that went along with visual scenes that their natural perceptions were incapable of until that moment. Like the opening of yet another unused eye, Grace and Manannán's natural access to the records in the ether suddenly were accompanied by the emotions and endocrine excretions each observer recording them left behind during the

Ripping. And like a quantum leap in perception, Grace and Manannán suddenly shared the full effects of mind drive augmentation without having need of one.

Grace thought, "We're on equal footing, you and me," she stated pointedly to Midge in his mind.

"Don't be foolish," Midge retorted. "Do you think I would actually allow you to have that privilege? As much as I admire you young Grace, I have been doing this a lot longer than you have... by about twenty-five thousand years. You of course know that by now, hmm?"

Liz interrupted through recovering tears, "Please. Both of you. There's been enough conflict for me, loss. Can you think of anyone besides yourself for a moment?! Take a step back. Please. I'm so tired, and there's so much I need to share, that goes beyond experience I can just intend to you."

"How's that exactly?" Manannán asked.

Liz glanced silently, then answered, "My babies. They speak to me. Only to me."

"*Babies*?" Midge blurted, shocked. "I sense only the one. We've confirmed this in the laboratory tests we conducted when we got you out of cryo-stasis. You got pregnant right before you were set asunder, and in five hundred years, your fetus has matured nearly nine equivalent months. You are ready to give birth soon. There's not two coming."

Liz came around to Midge and looked him square in the eye and said aloud, "There are two. And I know their names."

"Excuse me?" Manannán asked. "They tell you *their* names? Please enlighten me."

"You won't like it. But it will be the truth. They say they are Justin and Jessica."

Stunned silence gripped them all.

Grace blurted, "As in Justin and Jessica... *Forsythe?!* Not possible. They've been dead for centuries. You're lying."

Liz wilted. "Please Grace. Please believe me. I have no reason to lie to you. It's not that simple. They're saying, 'We are union, one great being.' Right now. That's what they're saying. 'The Justin and the Jessica are union.' They say, 'We are the union of unions, as one.' They say too, 'See the way before you.'"

With that utterance, Liz doubled over and grunted in the pains of labor no human being had experience since Sherrie Donovan's disastrous birth in level 3909 five hundred years before. Midge called for assistance from many of the other inhabitants of the Ontario Garden, as it came to be known, and moved Liz to the laboratory where her delivery would proceed in safety.

The grandest event in human history, unfolding before their eyes, left Grace and Manannán in struck silence as they witnessed the first natural childbirth in over five hundred years take place over nearly a dozen hours of labor pains and tortured screams from Elizabeth. But before too long, Midge delivered a healthy baby. Liz passed out from exhaustion and pain as the group stared slack jawed at what came forth when Midge called them in.

"It has no gender," Grace blurted. "No parts! It's not right. Right? That's not right. Why isn't it crying? Isn't it supposed to be crying?" Grace asked as floods of new information about newborns came rushing in from the ether against her will.

Everyone just looked blankly, stunned, exhausted, and depleted. Then, from the voluminous realms, as well as in the audible physical world, the newborn baby said in a child's whisper, "I am Geradamas, and I am the Way before you! In the ether, they asked for a child out of themselves, as one self, from their union, in order that he may become father of the coming immovable, incorruptible race, so the dead aeon may finally dissolve. And thus there came forth from above the power of the great light, planted His seed within this seed to bring forth the Coming. I am that seed. I am Geradamas."

The baby Geradamas closed its eyes and appeared to sleep suddenly, startling Midge, which was a feat in-and-of-itself for him. Hurriedly he took the baby with Liz to another section of the laboratory for testing.

Midge ordered openly, "Take the baby. I want a full genetic and atomic analysis of its structure. I want to know what we have here. I have no insight to the child. It's as if it doesn't exist in this universe! So hurry before it awakens again. Keep it sedated if you must. But get it done. Take care of Liz as well. I want her genetic structure and atomic pattern loaded and fully analyzed as well."

Not an hour went by before the results were being communicated via the ether to the waiting group.

"They have how many?" Grace asked aloud.

Manannán analyzed, "Ninety-two. Ninety-two chromosomes, forty-six karyotypes. Precisely double the twenty-three karyotypes humans have. This child is literally two people in a union, *physically*. And their gender chromosomes are paired accordingly as well; one set X-Y, the other, X-X, which explains the lack of parts. There are no parts right now. But maybe it will have both, eventually. But now it is itself a genderless, androgynous being. Its name is fitting, for as I'm sure you can find on your own, Geradamas was the one from whom the first humans were created from by God in the ancient biblical teachings. What did it say? It will 'become father of the coming immovable, incorruptible race, so the dead aeon may finally dissolve?' Does that mean this aeon? This race will be replaced by a new one? The proverbial New Man in Gabriel maybe?"

"No. We are that," Grace replied. "I know I'm young but I do know my scripture and my faith is based firmly in the believe that we, *we* are the New Man. That's why we abandoned all the rest of it in favor of Gabriel's teachings. It overarched the ways of the Old Man in favor of the New. They, *it*, mentioned a Coming. What's that? This new race?"

Midge said, "Speculate all you want. I'm more interested in the atomic structure. There are particles bonded within atomic nuclei that have negative mass, like this resonance sphere we're inside of right now, and the little one on Europa, the Bridgewater Crossing. There's dozens of these scattered about the system, not even my people know who built them."

Manannán then added, "Wait we're inside a resonance sphere now? This whole place? That's remarkable to say the least. But yes, I see it. That would explain our lack of parity with it. It doesn't exist in this physical universe by much at all. Therefore, time for it exists in super-voluminous plane that stores its information in dimensions we cannot access. Time's fourth dimension, as it were, paired with space's fourth, given the negative mass. Much of it will flow backward in time relative to us as its forward, like the spheres do, opening up many other possibilities in voluminous time that transcends our understanding of it. Every one direction we perceive in the ether could have four in its universe. Sixteen times the complexity of what we experience in the physical, at least."

Grace then asked sharply weary of the technical discussion, "What if it's here to get rid of Boll? It could be why it's here now. Boll is evil. That is clear to everyone."

"Except the millions of people in the Triple Cities," Manannán retorted in mid-sentence.

"That's clear to everyone who's been victimized or certainly killed by Boll's army," Grace concluded. "Why wouldn't God send a warrior to destroy evil? That's His job, isn't it?"

"The Mum of Mug Ruith has to ask a question like that?" Midge chimed.

"I think so. God allowed evil to run rampant for millennia before we almost went extinct before showing up again. Now here we are, nearly extinct, again! And here this Geradamas is, with a message about the Way before us. What else would God send us to save us but a warrior?"

"A messenger," Midge answered flatly.

"We don't need another messenger!" Grace blasted. "We need a Savior! And what do we get? This relic and this Geradamas thing, whatever it is. What do we call it? 'He,' 'she,' 'Sh-he?' 'It?' '*Them*?' It's infuriating. I hate it."

Midge approached Grace and tapped his left temple. "Peace," he said aloud and in everyone's mind.

Grace relented and collapsed in the space where she stood and went silent. Manannán, startled, went to her and held her up to prevent her from falling over.

"What'd you do to her?" Manannán asked Midge.

"Be not alarmed. I just gave her the peace she needed in the moment. It's just a bit of emotional will to strengthen her foundational stability. Her wail is awfully strong, more so than I would expect from any Mum of Mug Ruith. It's... *concerning*."

"Well she is still growing," Manannán offered.

"Yes, but even at this stage, Mums before her have been established, quite established. Hers is a unique departure."

"Yes I forget you've been here for all of them, haven't you?"

"In some form or other, yes."

"She'll come around, Midge. Give her time. Her situation is certainly unique.

Liz suddenly approached the debating group, who were surprised enough still at her stature, but then now pale and fatigued. Midge clamored to catch her as she listed in her stance.

Midge asked with a grunt as Liz's full body weight landed on his, "Wait, Elizabeth. How did you get out here? Why are you out of bed? Let's get you back there."

Liz in her physical disarray and weakness grew whiter in his arms, in her terror she pleaded, "No. No. Dear God, help me," in a waning vocalization that landed in a whispered grunt, as she let out a long exhale that ended her unforeseen consciousness in a sudden, mysterious event that dumbfounded everyone. Manannán and Grace, newly alerted, rushed over to Midge as Elizabeth's falling body went limp, attempting to help carry the weight of her massive frame.

"Liz! Liz!" Manannán called out as Midge gently slapped her face in an attempt to rouse her.

Grace, equally disturbed by the event, cried, "Elizabeth! Come on, wake up! I know you're in there. You didn't come all this way just to die now. I'm sorry for what I said... You're not better off dead here. We need you... We all need you to help us with your child. We haven't a clue what to do with it! We can't do it alone! You have to be the Way before us! So you can't go! So, wake up! Wake up!"

With the combined stimulus from all three, including the desperate, yet surprising, incoherent cries from Grace in the moment, Liz stirred, reassuring everyone that life was within her.

Midge ordered, "Let's get her back to her bed. Hurry." The three carried Liz back to the room where she gave birth to the first live human baby in five hundred years. Upon placing her down, she stirred and wrangled against racing thoughts that projected into the ether, before she passed out once again.

Then in the next moment, another caretaker approached in a panic from where Geradamas was being observed and said frantically, "Midge, you'd better come with me. There's something wrong with the baby. It's growing pale and its heart rate is falling rapidly. Pressure and oxygen levels are also falling."

"What?!" Midge asked, frantically. "The baby was fine. Strong. We verified..."

Manannán interjected, "Connected to the mother I see, still, despite the physical separation."

Grace then asked, "What? They're joined? Like psychically?"

"Yes, clearly," Midge's calming voice returned after settling his own nerves. "They were joined that way, as Liz told us. So that makes sense that they still would be, which means that it, the baby, has a naturally-occurring mind drive. It's probably similar to the spontaneous natural adaptation that you have Grace. Manannán, I know yours was printed there, in Ergon. You being an AI grants you that opportunity, having the right mix of exotic metals in your molecular structure."

Grace blurted, "What do you mean he's an AI?!"

"Relax Grace," Midge answered. "It just means he has some augments you don't have. He comes from the line of AIs while you come from the line of natural humans from before the Ripping. Since then, no one's really that different since we're all printed. We all are all AIs in a sense. It makes little difference."

Grace relaxed and replied, "Oh. Yes. I understand now. Thanks Midge. So he's real, right? Man's real?"

Midge stared him dead in the eye and stated, "Yes, Grace. Manannán is real. Now stop obsessing and focus. You *get* me?"

Grace nodded weakly in response.

The caretaker broke in, "The atomic structure of Elizabeth Hawthorne is highly unusual."

"Is that so? Let me see the test results," Manannán demanded. The technician handed him a computer pad and there Manannán saw the atomic structure of Liz's body. To his utter amazement he saw the markers of negative–mass neutrons actively replacing the baryonic ones he was expecting, each winking out of existence and back in again with the exotic replacements. "This... this is impossible."

"Yet, there it sits," Midge countered.

"Quoting Justin Forsythe again are we?" Grace chided.

"Of course," Midge poked back. "His lessons on the fallacy of Occam's Razor are required learning here in Ontario."

"Are they?" Grace asked pointedly. "So, how many people live in this 'Ontario Garden,' anyway? Where'd they all come from?"

"About five thousand souls, Mum," Midge replied flatly. "Some are from Ergon, some from Mug Ruith. But most are from the Triple Cities. They consider themselves escapees, of sorts. They managed to sneak out of the ranks of the walkers, or among the raving masses of lunatics in one of the parties in the Main Square to get away from the dogma."

"Really?" Grace asked sarcastically. "So how many of you people are reprinted then?"

"Just me, actually, and my son, Argus, as far as I know. Some others may be scattered about Titan in other printers. But as far as this one, just the pair of us, as peevish that makes me feel sometimes."

"Why so?" Manannán asked genuinely.

"Because my son is a madman, and for all my worry for him, he will never change. He gets worse with each iteration. On Europa he was the President of the AI Population on Europa. Elected. Revered. Here, well, here he's become something of an antagonist."

"In what way?" Grace asked anxiously.

"In the way, my dear, that he has taken Cassius Boll under his wing and has been counseling him for years."

"He what?!" Grace and Manannán asked in unison in a fury.

"It's true. Despite my best efforts to rein him in, I have failed to let his diseased mind influence Cassius Boll. He may be the reason why your people are gone. Argus is probably leading him along the path you've been chased down all these long days. That's why I needed to save you. It's bad enough to know that whole civilizations have been murdered and I could do nothing to stop it. But it's another to abandon all hope for the future. I could not let that hope die with you both."

"I... I don't know what to say," Grace said right before she was interrupted by medical alarms.

"Sir," the caretaker called to Midge, "they are both losing energy. It's as if their very life forces are draining before us."

Midge rose and asked, "What do you mean? Show me!"

The caretaker handed Midge another computer pad which showed the energy levels of both mother and child diminishing at the same rate. And in the same schematic, a vector analysis of energy rushing into them from a single source, represented only by a point on a chart.

The caretaker asked, "Do you see this, sir? This is a point within super-voluminous time, and space's fourth dimension that is feeding both of these people. Liz's neutron replacement is taking up as much energy as the baby's fantastic growth rate."

"Growth rate?" Midge asked hurriedly.

"Yes," the caretaker replied, "the baby has grown nearly a week's worth since we've been standing here analyzing. It weighs nearly seven kilograms already."

"That's incredible!" Manannán blurted.

"Like a super-voluminous umbilical cord..." Midge trailed off staring at the schematic.

Manannán then offered, looking at the same screen, "It's as if there's only enough 'food' for one of them."

Midge looked at him and said, "My God! That's right! The energy source is only enough for one of them, like it's designed that way, on purpose."

"What makes you say that?" Grace asked.

"Because of the tenuousness energy flows to Elizabeth, it appears her essence has tapped into it from her own body. See here and here? Those joins are far less stable than those the baby is connected to. They're not supposed to be there."

"So you're saying she's supposed to have died?" Grace asked in a panic.

"It appears so," Midge stated.

"Well that's just not right! "You don't survive the biggest disaster in all human history just to be the first woman to give birth to anything in a half-a-millennium only to die in the end just as you're being rescued! That's! Not! Right!" Grace screamed at the top of her lungs in a tantrum of denial that was emblematical of everything she felt was wrong in her world all rolled into one emotive explosion. She cried and went to Liz who was stirred by her screams.

"Liz! Liz! Don't die! Don't die! We need you here! I need you here! I can't do this by myself! I'm not old enough for this. I have no idea what to do... help me Liz. Stay and help me." Grace was melting down and grasping at any handhold she could find at the edge of a storming, choppy ocean for fear of drowning.

Liz opened her eyes and saw Grace's decompression before her and said calmly, "Oh, poor child. It is not for me you must fear, but for you. My husband and my children sacrificed themselves so that I may live. All of Europa was sacrificed so that you may see the Way before you. My children, Justin and Jessica sacrificed themselves to save you all from oblivion, through their undying love for one another, and all humanity. They did not destroy our world. They saved it. And they will do it again, just in another form. Geradamas is that form and he has come to save your world as well. For, he is the Lion of God!"

"Liz! No! Not that. He can't. It can't, whatever it is. You can! You can if you stay. You're grown. You can. You're connected to the other... ether, *somehow*. You know. You know you can." Grace panicked.

"Perhaps, child," Liz replied. "But I am just a conduit for what must come. I am not the shore, but a stepping stone towards it. As my family sacrificed themselves for me, and your people have sacrificed themselves for you, so must I sacrifice myself for my child. Otherwise we both will perish. We all will perish. That cannot be the Way."

The caretaker called out, "The energy tether is faltering."

"What?" Grace asked frantically. "No, no, no, no. Liz, please stay! I need a Mum! I need a Mum! I'm alone! You can be that for me! Please... stay!"

"I'm sorry Grace. It's time for me to go. I am being called to my heavenly home once again. I am honored to have been able to use this form to help you. Now Liz Hawthorne will have a place in humanity's history, vindicated at last for all the sacrifices she made in life, while she was a part of this world."

"What are you saying, Liz?" Grace was confused.

Liz said finally, "See the Way before you! Cassius Boll will destroy the world. You must not let that happen, Grace. Geradamas is the Way before you! Sherrie Donovan says so!" With her last dying whisper, Elizabeth Hawthorne took her last breath, revealing her true spirit, that of Sherrie Donovan.

Grace's tears flooded her heart. Her one chance to re-establish a sisterhood with another woman who understood precisely what Grace needed was gone. As was usual in Grace however, she quickly used her emotional volatility to transform her grief into rage—every calorie focused on Cassius Boll.

Manannán mac Lir held her tightly as Grace turned and hugged him. "We will raise this baby, Grace, if you'll have me."

Grace, taken aback briefly said in response, "What you want to marry me now, Man? I'm a pain in the ass you know, that's for sure. Do you think you can handle me?"

"I've done pretty well so far. It can only get easier from here. I love you like crazy, Grace. Let me keep loving you." Grace smiled as she kissed her betrothed deeply and thankfully. He said as their lips parted, "You'll never be alone so long as I'm breathing."

"We will raise it... I mean *him*, Geradamas. And we will destroy Cassius Boll. Maybe not today, but in due course he will pay for the hell he's rout on my world. I swear on my life and my love for it, and on all the power and energy I possess, that I will kill Cassius Boll and this Argus, if it's the last thing I do."

"Not if I kill them first, Grace," Manannán replied with a whispered smile.

The caretaker announced that the second energy tether that led to Elizabeth Hawthorne had finally terminated and that the strengthened one, from beyond voluminous time and space was at full strength, coursing into young Geradamas. He said, "The baby is regaining strength. Vitals are returning to normal."

Midge then added, "Grace. Manannán. This is now your home, to raise the miracle before us this day, in safety. You're exile is ended."

The ether was alight with thoughts of love and hope for the future. Nearly five thousand residents of Ontario Garden rejoiced in knowing that now, after centuries of darkness, light may return to Titan and its downtrodden people. It may not happen today, or even in the next year, but soon. *Soon*, Titan could be free.

~

"You see Boll? I told you I would find them," Argus confidently announced. "I told you that I would make you emperor... *quickly*. After this, there'll be no one left to stop you. You will be the master of the world. You get me?"

Cassius Boll sat on high in The Chair and smirked. He said, "Then it is nearly done. The final nail in the Ruithian coffin is laying there at ease in Ontario. We will dispatch her and that AI garbage with her. That child and that AI have been the bane of my days lately Argus! Now I know where to look after they disappeared—*magically*. Do you still deny knowing how any of that happened, Argus?"

"I swear I know nothing of it at all." Argus lied baldly, flatly, as to not give away his manipulation to his rapidly developing student.

"Uh-huh. You know I am not certain if I believe you still, giant. You would be wise to not test me. You have done well to help me and provide guidance, but never forget who rules Titan. I can snuff you out just as easily as all the rest of the bugs on this world and sleep soundly!"

As those words entered the cinnamon skies of Titan's icy air, the caravan of three hundred thousand slaves taken from Mug Ruith entered the Main Square in a parade of victory for all Xanadu's citizen to regale in. Boll rose from The Chair, and walked out upon his private balcony that overlooked the Square. A feeling of the greatest satisfaction overcame him as he gazed upon his millions of subjects all looking towards him as he appeared. And at once, as if prompted by some great force, from the entire crowd in a low, growling rumble cried, "Boll! Boll! Boll! Boll...!"

End of Part I

Intermission

Cassius Boll exploded when everything he was seeing went dark, as if his own memory failed him in the moment it was made, when those he hunted disappeared from the ether altogether. Argus nervously rung his hands in the hope the emotional display would subside before losing his head, literally, became a real option for him as Boll raced around the hall. Boll fumed. Argus shook. For one, it was a position for which he was familiar. For the other, it was unknown territory where fear ruled the kingdom of his mind.

"How could they just... *disappear* Argus?!" Argus stood silent and motionless as another ten guards entered the Hall for which even Argus's giant-sized stature would be ill-equipped to fend off if they all opened fire at once. Thus, Argus stood silent in fear, and bowed his head before Cassius Boll who returned to The Chair and was at equal height in his seated position as Argus was in his stance. "You will answer me, Argus, or there will be consequences. You get... *me*, Argus?"

Argus's thoughts swirled, mixing lies and manipulations he used to drive his student in the past with the honest truth he needed desperately in the moment to come up with an answer. The honest truth scared him far more than managing the deceptions he had planted over the years to manipulate Boll into what he had become: a dictator demagogue rapidly transforming into the soon-to-be-emperor of Titan. Argus wondered in an instant of doubt why it was Boll he chose and why he hadn't simply forced the Titans into making himself emperor. It would have been, certainly for him, far easier than to train an indigenous from scratch. He thought in that moment that perhaps madness was indeed creeping into his soul, if he even had one any more. And then in the last moment he thought that Boll was going to be his legacy, because in a moment of clarity, Argus knew that death was coming for him, one way or another.

Argus simply told the truth in his moment of fear that he hadn't felt in several tens of millennia, "I have no idea, and that's the truth, Cassius."

Boll stood on the seat of The High Chair so that he was effectively a meter taller than Argus and said, I can read no deception—I'm getting skilled at using this mind drive thing you know?—so I suddenly find myself believing you. Pity. Killing you would have been... well how would you say it Argus? *Delightful?*"

Argus snickered nervously and said, "More like, *delicious.*"

Cassius broke out in hearty laughter as he sat back down in The Chair and slumped in a smug posture. "Yes that's immaculate!" More laughter from the pair echoed in the room. "But enough of that. Where are my prey Argus? Are they or are they not in Ontario?"

"They were. Just for a minute. I was with them in the ether. I showed you. I followed them into a door, and after the door shut, the world went dark for me and I was brought back here. By what, I have no idea. I need answers... *desperately.*"

"By *you*, you mean *we*, right Argus?"

"Of course... *we.*"

"Desperately," chided Boll.

"Desperately," agreed Argus, peevishly. "You saw for yourself. The walkers we sent there found nothing, not even the door we saw. It was as if *there* wasn't there anymore. The ether is veiled." Argus paused reflectively and said, "You know Midge would probably say that the Way is dark right now if he were in my position."

"You mention the Way in this Hall one more time Argus and it will be your head mounted on my wall! There is no god before me, for I am Cassius Boll! There will be no other!"

"Be careful, Boll," Argus warned. If you over reach too soon, everything we have been building will collapse under its own weight. Your people love you, and you sold them slavery, but there is trepidation in the air. They're waiting to see how it all lands. They want to be sure that the slaves you made won't be *them* one day. And for that, you need to continue to earn their trust before the final schism."

"So you keep telling me...." Boll paused in introspection and continued, "Alright Argus. You still have my trust. Besides, your idea about sacking Ergon before Mug Ruith was pure genius. We have their resonance sphere and printer. I have my mind drive now because of it. And now I can see anyone in the System, at any time, right? Now we can print whatever we want, get back to the Ring around Jupiter and bring back your children, as was our bargain. I have you to thank for everything, Argus. But you know as well as I do that, you and me? We're on equal footing now. You may be three meters tall, but remember, I'm *god* here."

"Careful Boll... You assume too much," Argus stated confidently. "You only can see what some may choose to show you. There's no mind drive network any more, remember? So your use of it is well, *limited*.

"No matter. So be it. I have it. That's all that matters. We will send scouting parties for the prey. They're here. *Somewhere*. It's just a matter of time before we find them."

"Time is all we have, my friend," Argus agreed.

~

Grace looked into Manannán's eyes, doe-eyed, and recited a promise she never thought in a million years she would have the opportunity to with the man she had a crush on since she could remember. Midge stood before them both as he followed Ruithian wedding tradition to the letter and recited the invocation to they and several witnesses overlooking the golden-lit green Garden spread out in the vast open plain behind them.

"Friends, neighbors, family," Midge began. "We gather here in this sacred place to ask God for the power of his Holy Spirit to come over these two people: Manannán mac Lir from the city of Ergon, Vinculum Mare, of the great Region of Kraken Mare, and elected leader of the People of the Seas... and Grace Blieh Amadán Dubh, from the city of Mug Ruith, of the great Region of Shangri-La, and divined leader of the People of the Sands. For, in this holiest of times, do they come together now, in the Spirit of Gabriel and all His teachings as two equals, finding within each a complimentary half of a one whole great being that they have found completes one another. In this joyous time, do I, Medjugorje Divy Shaanti, Holy leader of the once great Gibborian civilization, now exiled for time immemorial, bring all these people together to bear witness to Grace and Manannán's declaration of love and commitment to one another.

"For Gabriel teaches that 'through exploration do two complimentary, but equal parts, find in love, the power to come forth together to unify again in the body, and open the Way for the Word of the Lord to come and create the new life vessel within the woman. This cannot happen without the man...In complimentary love and respect do the two become one. Blessed is the One Great Being created by two who follow the Way!' Manannán and Grace have found the Way between them, and now see the Way before them, together! For, their future is bright!

"So then I ask, Manannán mac Lir, before God and His holy Son, and Gabriel and all his messengers, and all these witnesses around, do you bring forth from all that you are, in full openness of your spirit, the unfettered welcome of the pure unification of your mind, heart, body, and soul with that of Grace Blieh Amadán Dubh, to be bonded for all time, in all the voluminous realms here and thereafter, as one great being, forevermore?"

"With all my heart, I do," Manannán replied as he held Grace's hands tightly while saying the words. Inside he was still stunned. His unlikely love to one so completely removed from everything he ever came to expect in a potential partner made the ceremony seem surreal for him, as time slowed down. The world felt more like a dream than anything objectively real, like it did running and fighting for his life in the cold sands of Shangri-La. The world within a world he found himself in left him spinning in altered states of consciousness and perception. He blinked rapidly for a moment as he attempted to process the new feelings coursing through his mind.

Midge turned to Grace and said, "So then I ask, Grace Blieh Amadán Dubh, before God and His holy Son, and Gabriel and all his messengers, and all these witnesses around, do you bring forth from all that you are, in full openness of your spirit, the unfettered welcome of the pure unification of your mind, heart, body, and soul with that of Manannán mac Lir, to be bonded for all time, in all the voluminous realms here and thereafter, as one great being, forevermore?"

Tears flowed down her face with excitement, fear, disbelief and awe. She bounced on her heals as she struggled to form words from her quivering lips on the verge of joyous crying. On the knife's edge of rationality she managed to say in response, "My dear, my love, Manannán mac Lir, I promise for now and ever to take you as my compliment, and promise to make you the happiest man alive with all the skills and faith I have. I love you, Man. I've always loved you."

Midge smiled and added, calling to the audience, "I think that qualifies as a 'yes' if ever I've heard one!" A small interruption of laughter spread further joy to the Garden. "With your promises of devotion and commitment to each other, by the power of the people in audience, by the power of this rite of passage, and by the power of the Divine Creative force of God Himself, I..." Midge was cut off by a new voice.

It was the baby, Geradamas who said, "See the Way before you! Grace and Manannán! God chooses you to bring your people to the aeon from *your* union, in order that I may become father of the coming immovable, incorruptible race, so this dead aeon may finally dissolve. And with the Divine Creative force of God and His great light, has He now planted His seed within this seed to bring forth the Coming. The New Man shall emerge and the Way will be bright forever more!" Geradamas's words ended with a sight none had beheld before: the ice "sky" above them within the Garden brightened sharply, the orange and white cavernous volume gave way to a stunning blue and brightening sun, as it was on the old, good Earth before the Purge. People, looking up in shock and gasps raised their hands and arms to guard their hyper-sensitive eyes against the pain the sun's glare caused.

Suddenly, a warm wind blew through the garden, filled with humidity and the smells of life all around. Everyone within the Garden began to sweat and their white, molting skin peeled from their bodies, revealing pink subtle skin below that grew rosy in the sunlight. Mists of water began forming along the ice-walls as frigid rock-hard ice was met with newly heated air. Columns of clouds rose from the disturbances and rapidly formed darkening thunderheads for kilometers around.

Lightning, followed by the requisite thunder joined the shocked sighs and calls from the Garden's inhabitants. Then, for the first time on Titan, it began to rain—*water.*

Geradamas called out in the torrent, "See the Way before you! The Infinite Darkness is *now* to end the old, dead aeon. But the Infinite Light of the Way awaits you! You are *most* blessed! God has blessed you all! May He keep you and hold you, forevermore."

As the baby said those words, the deluge ceased in an instant as the "sky" above opened up to a clear blue earthlike view that revealed something new in the Garden: the sounds of singing birds all around and in the distance, flying overhead in the brilliance of a cobalt sky none alive had ever seen before. And in the next moment, the image was gone; it having given way to the objective reality of the ice ceiling that was the gaping arch of the Garden's protective resonance sphere. The blinding white light returned to the far dimmer, golden hue. What became so violent a weather event, returned to the calm and barely-noticeable breeze of thermal eddies within its volume.

The molt returned on all as quickly as it melted.

Midge, stunned visibly, and most uncharacteristically, struggled to find words to finish the wedding and simply stated, "I, Medjugorje Divy Shaanti—and clearly God Himself!—now pronounce you husband and wife! You may both seal your union with a kiss!"

The pair locked lips to the cheers and exaltation of everyone within Ontario Garden, filtered by trepidation by their experience. What everyone failed to perceive, however, was that to anyone outside the kilometers-wide resonance sphere housing the Garden, and all the miraculous events everyone witnessed within it, happened in an infinitesimal moment of time, and was completely overlooked. For the hunted escaped their pursuers' grasp by finding not just a place to hide in, but a time.

Part 2

OblivioN: Ad Infinitum Tenebrae

In

eradamas thought into the ether that he was hungry and wanted a shkin sandwich with an accompanying bourbon. For him, the meal was the epitome of all things he loved to eat and drink, as Justin Forsythe—a holdover from his incarnation on Europa five-hundred years earlier. The resonance sphere that was the protective lattice housing Ontario Garden instantly accommodated his wish. In that instant, a semi-liquid metallic protuberance rose from the grass beside his bare feet, formed a platform and upon it, slowly grew out of the liquid shape, a white ceramic dinner place, a shkin sandwich and an algae-bourbon, neat, nestled in a cut crystal glass. He thought of a table and chair, and it rose beneath him and he sat thoughtlessly of the technological miracle providing it all to him in mere moments. He grabbed the meal from the organically-shaped structure and placed it on the table, sat and took a bite.

Grace came up to him, soiled from working a planting of corn she was assisting a group with and asked, "So, are you feeling better then, dear? Your appetite's returned. So has your taste for that brown stuff you like to drink. *Bower-bin*, right?" Grace struggled with the cadence.

"Bourbon, mum. Burr-binn. It's the most beautiful creation of humanity to date, in my opinion." He laughed slightly repeating it for the nineteenth time in a month.

"Yes, I know. You've told me often, Gerry."

In only five standard years they experienced within the sphere, Geradamas, or *Gerry*, as he was called commonly so that the 'G' sounded like a soft 'J,' aged as rapidly as he did when he was born. He was a full-grown person of roughly twenty-five standard years in stature, intellect and genderless form. People adopted the 'he' pronoun for simplicity's sake in referring to Gerry in conversation and thought. The parts of him that was Justin Forsythe were strong, fierce, stoic and powerful. The parts of *her* as the 'she' part that was *Jessica* Forsythe were loving, brilliant, inquisitive, and insightful. Both parts of the whole androgynous union of Geradamas were unrelentingly sarcastic and gleefully playful. Never before was there anyone inside the Garden who projected so much joy, confidence and love.

The nearly three thousand Garden residents adored him, as did his adoptive parents, Grace and Manannán Blieh Amadán Dubh mac Lir, the surnames they both proudly acquired after their wedding five inter-Garden years earlier.

Gerry stood over three meters tall, had never developed a molt, and sported a smooth pink, freckled, nearly hairless body, topped with deep auburn, thick long hair. His eyes were amazingly wide and shown the deepest cobalt blue irises any Titan had ever seen. He was angelic to everyone, in that being in his mere presence projected calm towards everyone inside that formed the foundation of peace in their hearts, minds and souls.

He was the epitome of the 'gentle giant' from long dead tales and legends.

"So papa's feeling the same, I see. He was pretty bad last night?" Gerry stated with continuing concern, genuinely.

"Man is not out of the woods, hon. We still haven't been able to figure out what bacteria or virus is attacking him. It's been days and the disfigurement progresses. It's as if there is something eating away at his very DNA. But that makes no sense to me. I'm not the smart one. He should have what they used to call 'cancer' if his DNA is degraded. But it's not that."

"So you've said, mum," Gerry referred to his mother as mum in the literal sense and not as Mum of the Mug Ruithian culture. "I search and pray constantly for a memory or a record anywhere in the voluminous realms for this eventuality. I find none."

"That troubles me more than Man's illness, darling," Grace remarked.

"Be not troubled, for the Way is bright," Gerry reassured as he took a last sip of his bourbon and swallowed his last bite of shkin sandwich. "The Way will present itself in due time. You are so impatient mum. I told you to work on that in your meditations."

"You even sound like him, you know?"

"Like papa? Yes I know. He's certainly rubbed off on me, like poison ivy." Gerry laughed at his reference to a weed that no one on Titan anywhere had ever heard of until he brought it forth from the ether, and all were enlightened. Grace laughed, albeit delayed, with him at the itchy rash's reference.

"Let's go check up on him and see if he's any better," Grace suggested.

"He's not, mum. I can see from here," Gerry informed. "But how he's feeling, as himself, escapes me."

"I know, I know," Grace impatiently replied, "but we need to see him in person for that. You should hold his hand. He may not have a lot of time."

Gerry snickered at the thought and agreed by saying, "Anything for you, mum. You know I talk with him nearly every waking moment, right? Through the ether? He knows I'm right beside him. But he hides it from me, somehow. Little pain in the—."

"Shut-up Gerry! Smartass. Just do this for me," Grace sternly ordered, frustrated. "He needs our touch just as much as he needs us in other ways. He's alone in that lab."

"No he's not."

"Yes he is. Just him and those robot things you made for him."

"We can't let the others in here get infected. Quarantine was necessary."

"Damn the quarantine! He's your father!"

"Okay, okay, mum. No need to argue and get emotional. Be calm, mum, for me? I of course will come. You need to really check your emotions. They'll get the better of you one day."

"Oh shut it already Gerry. You're such a sh—."

Gerry cut her off before she could finish, "No I'm not, you yummy-mummy-mummy-mum-mum," Gerry said endearingly rising from his table, and tickling and hugging his mother to end the joking spar they loved to engage in.

Laughing, and in a strange embrace that had Gerry towering over her and enveloping her one-third-sized frame, Gerry said, "Come on. Let's go see papa, in person, just for you, because your special and I love you."

"Oh Ger—you make me feel so loved. You're the best son I could have ever have hoped for."

"And daughter too..." Gerry smiled as he trailed off in his gentle reminder of what he was seeped into her mind.

Grace laughed and said, "Yes darling, daughter too. I get the best of both all in one package. What's not to love?"

"Well for one thing, you need a ladder to give me a kiss on the cheek," Gerry played and laughed.

Grace laughed and said, "Well it's not my fault you're a giant pink broccoli. That wasn't my doing."

Gerry in his laughter picked up his mother and placed her on his broad shoulders two meters above her head. She rode like a child playing a game and joy filled her heart, if not for a brief moment.

Manannán mac Lir was unconscious in one of the laboratory beds surrounded by several mechanical robots that monitored and provided continual testing and treatments. Grace and Gerry approached his silent form and took his hands within theirs. Midge and several lab technicians monitored test results and schematics coming from atomic sequencing readouts and genetic marker imaging systems.

Greeting his friends, Midge looked up and stood saying, "Come here, both of you. Take a look at this."

"What is it Midge?" Grace asked immediately. "Has something changed? What's wrong?" Grace grew immediately panicked.

Gerry held Grace by the shoulders, stabilizing her in a soothing way that calmed her frayed nerves and said to Midge, "Well I know that he is in the same coma-like state that he's been in for days now. His molt has certainly cleared up even more. Have you done additional scrapings?"

"No," Midge replied. "It's clearing up on its own due to the destruction of his immune system. It's similar to what the ancients used to call—"

"Plaque psoriasis," Gerry broke in reading the thought and instantly accessing every record and bit of information ever posed on the subject over centuries long past from the ether. "The molt is not that though, is it Midge?"

"You would know better than me, Gerry," Midge said. "You have a connection to a place in the ether that I don't, as we've explored in our sessions. But no, the molt is not plaque psoriasis as far as we all know here. For hundreds of years, human beings have adapted to the cold by building up callused skin all over their bodies where ever there is direct contact with the atmosphere—the face, the hands, etc. It peels off in sheets as it builds up from the epidermis... Gerry, you know all this. I don't need to say it aloud. The point is that Manannán's molt is not related to the cold, at least not entirely. It's this psoriasis condition... a genetic defect."

"Defect?" Grace broke in. "He's a printed man, perfect, from the line of perfect AIs, right down to his titanium-infused bone structure and Teflon muscles and silver nerves. There can't be any *defects*. I resent, even the notion."

Midge smiled smugly and gestured for her to look at the computer pad he was showing earlier. He said, "Here. Look here, and here. There. You see that? Those skin cells are mutated. Not molt. Not just callus. Mutated. The cell walls are damaged. The mitochondria are dying. The endoplasmic reticulum is shredding. These are skin cells in the process of dying because they're being attacked by these antibodies, which see the cell as a foreign invader." The image on the screen flew across to one side and displayed the antibodies midge referred to.

"Foreign invader?" Grace asked with antipathy. "My husband is the strongest man on this whole bloody world. Nothing can touch him. Certainly not a tiny little cell!" Grace's rage began to simmer.

"Yet, there it is happening, in objective reality despite your misgivings, Grace," Midge stated conceitedly. "You can pout all you want, but *this* is what's happening to your husband."

"Bullocks on that Midge!" Grace exploded. "You can tell me all the *'whats'* you want but I want to know *why*! You haven't told me *why* this is happening. Midge, for the love of God you have to get to why!"

Gerry, still holding her shoulders as she burst into tears releasing her abject fear and peevish acceptance of objective reality despite every fiber in her being telling her to fight, squeezed gently and made a "shhh" sound with his mouth. "Easy, mum. I know you're upset. Midge is doing his best. We all love him like you do. He is your *'everything.'* God I understand that better than most, don't you think? We are all figuring this out. I know your fears and it's completely ok. We will fix him. I will stay up here with Midge if my physical presence makes you feel better. It doesn't matter mentally. But I'll stay in close proximity. Have faith, mum. Be not afraid."

Gerry's words as both daughter and son at just the right moment calmed Grace who exhibited its affect by slowing her breathing and calming her mind. Gerry's beautiful mind projecting peace into hers gave her the emotional strength she could not have achieved on her own. Grace's rage was her power. It was also her abject detriment. Gerry was like a spiritual smith forging the perfect blade within her, to be both the sharpest and strongest of temper, while being so flexible she could never break.

Midge replied, "I think it's a lifeform of some kind. But I haven't the evidence yet to support it. Like a parasite. It's a hunch, through the ether, it's only a hunch. I have no objective evidence of one. But yet, the evidence for something feasting is undeniable."

"The antibodies?" Grace asked.

"No," Midge answered. "They're just an effect, so far down the line of other biological impacts at the end of the run that the source is hidden thoroughly. No, the cause, the *why* you want, is deeper, maybe even atomic. I'm just not there yet."

"I've been following paths in the volumes with Midge, even in the super-voluminous realms that I can see. If it is atomic, a pattern will immerge eventually. We just need time," Gerry stated.

"Well he doesn't have all the time in the world. If that's happening to his skin, God knows what's happening to his other organs. You don't even know, do you?" Grace asked Midge harshly.

"Not yet, Grace. Not yet," Midge yielded. "As Gerry said, we just need time."

Grace then blurted, "If he dies, I think I'm literally going to explode and the world will go with it."

Gerry snickered and said, "Well mum, what a *mess* that would be," then took his papa's hand.

~

In the time five years elapsed within Ontario Garden, a mere week had gone by in the Triple Cities. In that time, the slavery of the Ruithian prisoners went into full effect as Cassius Boll opened the Main Square and created an instantaneous market for his citizens to buy over three-hundred-thousand Ruithian slaves as their personal property. Several tens-of-thousands of the strongest were immediately conscripted to the mines. The rest were up for grabs at the highest price for all the citizens of Xanadu to consume. People from all walks of life partook in the societal transformation with glee, from the low-born to the Regents. Cassius Boll's reign was at its zenith.

This included the Regent of Cimbáeth, Xavier Rademacher. He found himself draped before long by the freshly polished skin of two female Ruithian slaves servicing his every desire on a floor full of tufted pillows, luxuriant fabrics, and soft linens all rubbed and stained with essential oils. The room he called his 'sleep space' echoed with the breathing of three hot bodies in the throes of passion that to some, may have appeared contrived. To others, it was the pinnacle of performance by grateful slaves who owed their lives to their master.

A forth, the Regent of Díthorba, Reyna Meade sat in a corner, nude, pleasuring herself at the spectacle before her that satisfied her in ways that no one partner ever could. Reyna, edging relentlessly, timed her release with Xavier's and the room echoed no other sounds but their shared cries as he released his fountain into one of the unnamed women above him. The other released herself on his face, smothering him slightly, thus increasing the dopamine rush that came with oxygen deprivation in Xavier's brain.

Heavy breathing marked the end of a multi-hour session that called Reyna to the threesome. She climbed into the mass of three other tangled, oiled bodies, atop fabrics and pillows and exchanged deep kisses with all, as if genuinely loving each for their roles in her pleasure. She kissed Xavier most of all. Then the truth of objective reality smacked the room like the breaking of a plate on a solid floor.

Reyna said, "Now get out! Both of you. Go back to your hole. I'll feed you later. Dress yourselves. Now!" The two slaves rushed to grab their torn and tattered rags for clothing, dripping fluids down their legs, and wrapping them nervously and rushed to a small closet sized room where only a couple of pillows and some cloth separated them from the cold, icy ground. A door closed behind them where no sound could be heard.

Xavier said to Reyna, "I really love having them. They clean my house, they scrape my molt, and they kiss anything I tell them to, whenever I tell them to. They make me happy. They make you happier I think. And when they get mouthy I get to shut them up however I like and no one can say boo about it. Boll was a genius when he instituted slavery in our society, wouldn't you agree? All that wasted productivity now being put to good use. Our standard of living increased overnight. The people adore him. I adore him! I would do anything for him!"

Reyna smiled, stroked his face and said, "Yes, we all love him, for there is no god here but him. He's proven that by his grand conquest of the entire Three Regions, all of Titan is his. What of you Xavier? Your way to The Chair seems a bit blocked at the moment. You are the next in line. Surely that fact is not lost on you."

Xavier, in a surprise move, flipped Reyna over on her back, pinned her down and spread her legs with his. In a breath he said closely, "You watch yourself, upstart. I do like you, but know your place. I am next in line. The whole damn world knows that! And it's for you to remember now. My time is nearer than you think."

"Oh? And how's that exactly? He's indestructible and what you suggest could be considered treason!"

"And who's going to tell him? You, upstart? The slaves? They'll die before this night is over if they even hear any of it. Their door is shut and you my dear are the only other person in this room. And I'm guessing you have no wish to die just yet."

"You're right my darling," Reyna replied devotedly. "As much as I love our lord Boll, you are the one I feel safe with. Let me be that safe place for you, as you are for me. We are stronger together. Indivisible and indestructible. We control two of the Triple Cities. When the time is right, I am sure we could stir up trouble for him. I won't say his name aloud. But you know who. Not right now. He's too strong. But later, later he won't be as all things with power eventually wane. Later he will make a mistake and become vulnerable. Then, then we can stir the pot and take The Chair as is our right."

"My Chair! Not *ours!* Mine. I am next in line..."

"So you keep saying my darling. This, I know. Truly. There's no need to defend yourself against my ambitions. I don't even want the damn thing. You'll be a target... *forever*. I don't want to be a target. I just want the spoils without all the paranoia. Power is a funny thing, Xavier. Sometimes the ones most visibly displaying it have the least amount of it."

"What the hell does that mean?" Xavier asked pinning her down harder.

"It means that the strings being pulled behind The Chair by those in the shadows are the true wielders of power. It's not all about the show. It's about the stage."

"I will sit in The Chair. I will hold the power. If I wish it I can command people behind 'the stage,' as you so aptly put it, to kill each other, then themselves, right in front of me, just because I'd like it. That is real power. The power over life and death."

"I won't argue the point Xavier. But you can sometimes be too one-dimensional. There's power wielded in the Triple Cities that not even our lord is aware of. You'd be smart to see the grey between the alleyways and gutters."

"Careful Reyna. You're wise, but I'll take only so much insolence."

"Oh shut it Xavier. Save it for one of the underlings. I know you better than that." Reyna flipped him back over in an equally surprising fluidic move onto his back, her pinning him down as forcefully as he did her. "Your power, or what you think you have of it, won't last long unless you pull the strings beneath the stage—my strings. You keep me happy and I keep you happy. Are we clear?"

Xavier angered and flipped Reyna forcefully and clumsily back onto her backside. He growled at her, drool dripping from his lips and said, "I, am, next, in, line! If I choose to kill you, you will be gone, and I still have your strings, upstart. Make no mistake, Reyna. Cross me, and you'll pay dearly."

She laughed loudly directly in his face. "This I know darling. This I know. But the strings you think you gain from my death will evaporate like the very air coming out of your little face. You will find the web you take has been woven all around you, and the spider ready for her meal."

Xavier, having his bluff called, exhaled and laughed slightly and said, "Bah! Never going to happen, love. You and I have too much to do to be fighting over where we each sit. I'll guild yours if you'd like that. I will do it, real gold too! Whatever it is you desire. I love you that much, here and now."

In the exhale of the word 'now' he kissed her violently and penetrated everything womanly she ever was. The shock in her eyes, if only for a brief moment, gave way to euphoria and the words, "My god Xavier, how I love you!"

Across the sleep space, Xavier's two slaves wept in each other's arms in an absolute black and silent room waiting for spoiled scraps and grey water to be pushed through a magnetically sealed slot beneath the door.

~

Cassius Boll, accompanied by Argus, entered a darkened room populated by hundreds of technicians, its vast volume masked by mists of exhalation and dimly lit computer panels. Lining the walls of the cathedral-like structure were the remaining captured Ergonites. They were linked together, physically by all manner of biological and mental monitoring devices, and were stacked seven high and stretched on each side of the hall as far as the eye could see. The connectors intersected at a single point in the center of the ceiling, where blue-white light powering a massive machine resting down the center of the room along a parallel path as the walls, drove the workers to attend to many tasks.

Argus regaled in explaining to Boll what his eyes beheld. His excitement, and nervous banter, so unlike himself in the years and centuries before, betrayed his own mental instability due to his own copy-decay that was finally taking its toll. Boll looked in amazement at the sheer scale of the space, and the numbers of the captured AIs—his joy no longer hidden by his stolid introspection.

"Just look, Argus! We've done it! We've captured Ergon's printer! We've culled the heard of useless barbarians and put them to work. And now we have the power...finally, to know our destiny!"

Argus gleefully replied, "Oh yes, Cassius. Let me explain it all to you! I have worked tirelessly these days to prepare it. Permit me the joys of sharing mine with you."

"Of course! Of course, Argus! If it weren't for you, I'd still be sweeping floors in my first guardian's molt and clothing store in the Main Square."

"That's right Cassius. You are in my debt. You will always be in my debt. You get me?"

"Yes, yes. I get you Argus. Now on with the tour, if you please," Boll toyed.

Argus began, "As ordered, we have rounded up thirty-thousand Ergonites from the war, and connected them here, in series. We have fifteen or so thousand still in servitude as replacements if we need spares. We of course killed the rest as part of your cleansing of Titan."

"Tell me something I don't know, giant."

"Yes, Cassius," Argus replied obediently. "Using the printer we created a mind drive detector. We can now scan anyone within a few meters to determine if any of these pedantic AIs have mind drives printed directly into their brains. I have gone ahead and ordered the detectors as military standard issue just yesterday, since we were able to finally print enough for general circulation. They're hand-held and small enough to carry in a pocket. On testing the Ergonites, sure enough, we found that some did, as you predicted, have naturally occurring mind drives, linked to the ether in voluminous realms. Most, however did not. So we began printing artificial ones based on the one we made for you first."

"Yes? But why can't I sense this... well all this? I should, shouldn't I?"

"You should, under normal quantum mechanical rules, certainly. But these are special. We found after several tests with the original schematics we used for you that there was no super-voluminal linking capable with it. Mine doesn't even have that upgrade, Cassius. It took us days to dissect one out of the few who had one naturally to determine what was different about it."

"And what did you find, Argus?"

"Something rather stunning, actually. The naturally-occurring organ in the Ergonite's brain is made mostly of negative mass matter. Matter with negative mass! Can you imagine?"

"What... you mean like the resonance spheres you keep telling me about? Aren't they scattered all over the System on various planets and moons we haven't seen in half a millennium?"

"Precisely. I'm glad you listen to me Cassius. It gives me hope!"

"I'll take away your hope if you don't keep going."

"Of course, lord," Argus checked his place. "Atomic printing is based on the availability of raw material, breaking it down into its elemental components, down to each individual atom after breaking apart molecule after molecule, and rearranging those atoms to form anything we want. Through all that we never form anything but normal, baryonic matter, which has mass. Positive mass."

"Right," Boll replied leadingly.

"So the conundrum was how do you print an atom with negative mass without having particles of negative mass to begin with?"

"No idea. That's your job, Argus."

"Exactly. It's my *job*. So I did *my* job and figured it out."

"And how, exactly did you do that?" Boll wearied at the details

"Do you really want the science, Cassius? I know your propensity for rebellion when bored."

"Well don't bore me with too many details, but by all means. I want to know in case something... happens to you." Boll smiled and laughed menacingly at the call-out.

Argus smirked and offered, "I understand. I'll be brief, I assure you. So, it's really based on ancient technology I found in the ether. You can see it momentarily as I explain. Using a laser and semiconductor, an atom wide, like molybdenum diselenide for example as its target, excitons in the semiconductor combine with laser's photons generating polaritons."

"Polaritons? What are polaritons?"

"Polaritons are subatomic particles which have the negative mass. That's the basket of fruit we needed to harvest."

"Harvest? For what?"

"For the printer, Boll. The printer needs raw material to function, remember? Technically, by adding energy with the laser, it causes excitons to yield some of its energy to the photons, which creates polaritons. In bonding with normal matter, the polaritons bond more strongly than paired photons. Thus, it's a simple matter for the printer to use the polaritons to build neutrons and the rest of the atom by replacing photons with the polaritons, and 'voila!' as they used to say: negative mass atoms and associated molecules to form an Ergonite's brain."

"I actually understand Argus! Is that all then?" Cassius rejoiced in asking.

"Well, and the resonance spheres that are part of the printer we just acquired in Ergon. But other than that, that's all, Cassius. I promise," Argus replied, somewhat relieved. "Whoever made the spheres knew how to manipulate polaritons masterfully. They certainly weren't from your or even my epoch of human civilization."

"Oh yes, your antediluvian period you told me about. What was that? Twenty-thousand years ago?"

"More like twenty-five, actually. But no matter. It's long over. My empire has been long forgotten by humanity, except for you and me my friend."

"Only because you told me your stories, Argus. You are the one with the real memories, if after all your copying you can still call them that."

"I do," Argus replied, mournfully.

"Enough of that, Argus. No feeling sorry for yourself! We have much to do! So tell me about these Ergonites' brains and mind drives we've given them."

"Now that's the real trick, Boll," Argus's enthusiasm rose with the deflection towards himself and his accomplishment.

"How's that?"

"As I was saying, we ended up printing their mind drives with polariton-based atoms, which gave us mind drives built with matter having negative mass. Mass that you and I are familiar with is a resistor to time. It slows time's rate the closer one gets to a gravitational field. Gravitational fields are generated by massive objects; the greater the mass, the greater the gravitational field, and the greater the resistance to time. We see its effects all the time in small scales going from planet to planet—," Argus cut himself off, and clarified, "well, when we used to travel across the system regularly. Clocks were always being adjusted to account for it. Fractions of seconds mostly, but with great distances, those kinds of errors accumulate rapidly and wreak havoc with navigation if not accounted for."

"You're beginning to blather, Argus," Boll said disdainfully. "Get to the point... the Ergonites?"

"Patience, Cassius. You are still so impatient. That is no mode for an emperor. Time will teach you... and... *experience*."

"Mind your tone, giant!"

"Mind yours, little man. You know why."

Boll relented, still minding his manners around his benefactor, knowing full well that there was a long journey ahead to justify his arrogance that he built up in his own mind that had yet to be earned by the people around him. He may have sacked all Titan, enslaved the losers, but there was a great deal to be done before he could be assured of keeping his prizes. He knew it, deep down. If nothing else, he felt he needed Argus for a quite a time longer before cutting him loose.

"Sigh. Just continue, Argus," Boll said peevishly.

"As you say," Argus replied. "Normal matter with positive mass resists time. Black holes stop it entirely. Absence of massive bodies speed it up, all relative to where a person is in the universe."

"All time is local, and relative. Spare me the elementary curriculum." Boll grunted.

"Right," Argus continued. "Now think about those things but with matter with negative mass. What do you think would happen if say a whole star were made of matter of negative mass?"

"Time would... I'm not sure, Argus."

"Well if normal mass is time's resistor, then polaritonic mass then must be time's *amplifier*. You get me?"

"Amplifier? Like make it louder? Like my voice in the Main Square?"

"Not quite like that. It would speed it up. The rate of time would increase and not decrease in its presence. It would suck time into it instead of pushing it a way. It's a time hole instead of a time mountain. Time falls down it faster and faster, pushing matter away as opposed to sucking it in. If a black hole is a time mountain, a hole made out of this would be a time hole and a matter mountain. It's the very definition of *antigravity*. It also means, and this is the important part about the Ergonites, that their mind drives operate on the opposite end of the quantum curve, sucking in more and more time relative, meaning *information*, to where we are in our local reference!"

"Argus! Stop! Speak plainly! Damn you!" Boll's head was melting in the most painful figurative way conceivable.

"Sucking in more time, Cassius, relative to us, means, more *information*, from ahead of where we are. They see into the future as easily as we remember the past!"

"That's it!" Cassius blasted with joy and a sudden surge of internal strength. "That's the answer I wanted to hear! So all these strung up Ergonites are collecting future events in their negative drives, or whatever you call them, right?

"Very good, Cassius. That's quite precise... *actually*. That's the point of the... *wiring*. They will accumulate future events through the super-voluminous ether that we haven't been able to access with our regular drives."

"Ensuring my legacy... Outstandi-i-i-i-i-ing!" Cassius Boll, at the height of power and egotistical glorification let out a roar at the end of his last word that echoed within the massive hall.

Then both he and Argus had them.

"And now we know, my friend," Argus stated calmly, "where and when our prey have gone."

"I can see them! They're all still there in Ontario, crawling around like ants in dirt, hiding in plain sight within time's second dimension. I see them. Bugs. But wait...."

"Yes Cassius?" Argus asked stunned, seeing what he saw.

"Who... *what* is that?!"

"It's looking right at us. Another giant. It sees us," Argus blurted with alarm. "They're inside a resonance sphere! A huge one, the size of a city! That's why we lost them! They're not even in this universe!"

"They are now," Boll corrected. "Now, we attack."

Argus smiled, and saw the inevitability of what had to come next, and within an instant of super-voluminous time, a hundred thousand walkers were marching toward Ontario Garden.

In the Dark

bsolute black. Only breathing and panicked sobs could be heard in the two-by-four-meter windowless room the slaves sat naked and afraid in after being ordered there by the master of the house, Xavier Rademacher. Warmish air blanketed the slaves from above, originating from a blind vent, from a blind duct, coming from a blind reservoir of oxygen that made them both shiver and their molt peel. The pair clung to one another for support and warmth in stammered panic.

A light suddenly appeared where the door met the floor. Two plates of food scraps and a deep metal tray of gray water from Reyna and Xavier's bathing cycles were slid through, presumably to drink.

The call, "Food," came from a male voice through the slot. "Ten minutes. Then clean. Begin now." The slot closed and the absolute black returned.

The pair broke their physical seal from each other and scrambled to grab the dishes placed on the floor they frantically tried to remember fully in space before the darkness took their orientation completely away.

Clumsily finding them and the tray of tainted water, which immediately spilled, the pair sucked down whatever food was on the plates hastily without chewing. They both wanted to prevent actually tasting anything to avoid vomiting instantaneously at any kind of thought of what it was they were actually eating.

The pair did what was necessary to survive. They wondered why they still wanted to, however. Finishing, they resumed their hug-hold on each other, in an effort to stop the shivering that tortured them both.

"Slaveaye," Slavebee said to the other, "I think we have five minutes." The Slaves' Ruithian names were unceremoniously stripped from them all. Their masters gave them replacements; designations, arbitrary and meaningless ones used to fill a linguistic space to call each one, *something*. "What's your name?" Slavebee asked.

"Slaveaye, you know. Oh. I can't," Slaveaye blurted in terror.

"Mine's Leigh," Slavebee offered. "I want to remember it. I have too."

"We can't!" Slaveaye said in panic. "It's forbidden. They'll beat us or worse if they find out."

"At least we'll feel *something*," Slavebee replied confidently. "It's better than being dead inside."

"You're mad," Slaveaye said hurriedly. "Never mind my name. They'll kill you, you know it Slavebee. Just pray with me. We must pray. That's the way to the light."

"The Way is dark, and don't call me that. Call me Leigh. Please I beg you."

"We'll burn, freeze, or worse. I can't."

"What's yours? At least give me that much," Leigh pleaded. "Oh! I see it. It's Dorenda. Dorenda. What an unusual name. What's your family name? Coucoules?! Really? You're one of *them*? Wow. From the rebellion.

Maltru Riegnis's siblings... Helen Coucoules. The Devil's Wife, they called her. I hope you're nothing like her, Dorenda."

"Wait! You read me?" Dorenda blurted without moving her lips. "Quiet about that." Dorenda hung her head in Leigh's chest, ashamed. "I'm not like that. None of us are... or were. We're faithful Ruithians just like Aibell was. But if they find out any of this, I'm probably dead already." They were speaking within the ether suddenly, silently, and spontaneously. And they each scantly noticed.

"Why do you say that?"

"Lineage. Lineage is memory. There is no god but Boll here. I would remind everyone that's not true."

Leigh paused and said, "I see your point."

In the next instant, the door opened, and the light blinded the captives inside.

"On your feet!" Reyna ordered from above, her silhouette towering over their crushed forms. They rose with trepidation and walked out into the open. "Here. Some cloth to wear. They're a bit worn but it's better than freezing. We paid good money for you and I don't want you dying of hypothermia." Reyna pointed to a pile of soiled rags and tapestries on the floor beside her. "And no more recycling trash for you to eat. I need you strong and healthy, so there'll be regular meals for you. Healthcare is expensive and I'm not wasting my money on you getting some kind of infection."

"Yes, mistress," the slaves both said in unison.

"Thank you mistress," Slaveaye said first, quickly echoed by Slavebee.

Xavier broke in and said, "Just remember who's in charge and we'll all get along. Do a good job and you'll get extra food, or some nicer cloths. Cloth is warmth. You'll want to keep them. Be insubordinate and you'll be back in the closet, fast. Clear?"

"Yes, clear, master," Slavebee blurted.

"Good," Reyna continued. "You both can sleep in that corner," Reyna pointed to her left and behind her. "Clean the cooking area and dishes. Then serve us rye."

"Yes mistress," the slaves both agreed in unison aloud with a smile of relief as they walked over to the pile, and selected cloths before retreating to the cooking area to perform their assigned tasks.

Xavier said to Reyna as his property walked gleefully away, "This soft-hand approach better work, upstart. I much prefer my way to motivate them. It pleases me more."

"Oh darling, you are more and more like Boll every day," Reyna replied blithely with a wave of her hand, dismissing the statement as a long-foregone conclusion.

Xavier grinned and said, "Why, thank you dear. You say the sweetest things."

"That's why I love you darling," Reyna was basking.

Leigh and Dorenda communed with one another as they each did their respective tasks in silence, sharing family stories, lineage, events in their lives, and their path through the Way as their life's focus.

"We must keep our faith strong Dory," 'Dorenda' had quickly become 'Dory' in their rapid mental exchanges, "and we will live through this," Leigh supported.

"God will show us the Way. I know," Dory affirmed more for herself than in reply to Leigh. "We are Ruithians and always will be. We are the keepers of the Way in this age of seemingly unending despair. Our city, our Region may be gone forever, but who we are lives on in our hearts."

"Don't say that out loud," Leigh thought to Dory, "Someone might hear."

"Deeply true," Dory replied.

From beyond the ether, in the super-voluminous realm, thousands of other minds blasted the slaves' conversation to tatters, by yelling, "There is no god before *me* and the way you believe lies ahead for you is dead!" It was the words of Cassius Boll, who, through the thousands of interconnected Ergonites with their negative drives had discovered Leigh and Dory's conversation in the ether. The enemy was suddenly aware of their spontaneous activation of natural mind drives, and heard their exchanges. It was treason.

The slaves stopped dead in space in abject terror as they knew what and who was coming for them. The room was eerily quiet as Reyna and Xavier drank their rye in utter ignorance to all that was occurring in the voluminous realms around them.

Within moments a dozen military personnel barged in on Xavier's sleep space with mind drive scanners reading each skull as they ran them down. Reyna was pushed by two of the officers to the back of a near wall, while Xavier was ordered to sit on a pile of cushions seemingly forever away from his lover. The guards stopped on Leigh and Dorenda almost immediately.

"There, Commander," one of the soldiers said. "This one. And this one." The soldier scanned Xavier and Reyna quickly, glancing at Reyna with a reassuring nod, to her affirming they were both in the clear. She sighed and the soldier returned to the slaves.

"Are you certain?" the commander asked. "We have our orders from Argus himself. These two were heard conspiring to commit treason. They have mind drives. Look at the reading. Boll wants to interrogate them, personally."

Xavier angered and imposed himself in the middle of the fray, "What the hell is going on? You can't just barge into my house and take my slaves without so much as a why?! I paid a month's wages for these two! On what grounds does Boll demand their custody?"

"Steady, Regent," the commander ordered. "Argus and the Array heard these two thinking in the ether. Then Boll himself heard them. They were talking about their old lives and original names in Mug Ruith. They were plotting to carry on the superstitions they believe inside them. They conspired to commit these treasonous acts. Their treason runs deep. Here. Four kilos of gold should suffice as compensation for the trouble."

"What?! The Array? Ether? Treason? What are you talking—*Four*?" Xavier asked genuinely shocked. "That's nearly six times their worth, at *least*, what I paid."

"Really? Then you'll take less. Give me these. Here's one." In a rapid movement the commander grabbed back the bullion and gave Xavier only a fraction of his original offering, which Xavier accepted shocked and blubberingly.

The commander offered, "You should really learn how to shut up Xavier. It might serve you well in the future. You're not nearly as smart and clever as you think you are. Remember what we can see. You are always in check, Regent."

"My life is no longer my own then? Is that what it's come to? Yes, Commander. It may at that," Xavier replied obstinately. Reyna walked forward and stood beside Xavier.

Reyna said, "Yes, we both have a lot to learn in the new world. No accounting for this one's scruples, though.

What was it? '*A bird caught in the hand is worth more than two flying around?*' ...or something?" She shook her head slightly a bit confused at her words as she heard them come out of her own mouth.

The commander snickered to himself and said, "I haven't the foggiest. We'll leave you now. Here. You can have these back. Argus himself said to give you four, so it's four you shall have, despite my personal misgivings. There will be another market next week for slaves. You can get a couple of new ones then."

"Oh, we will," Xavier said haughtily. "Maybe more."

"Shut it Xavier," Reyna demanded. "Is there anything else Boll wants of us? Or will you be leaving us now Commander?"

"No. We've cleared your residence for what we came for. The two of them are all we need for the moment. I'll bid you farewell, for now, until the next rally in the Main Square."

"I see," Xavier replied. "Yes. The next rally should be quite a spectacle I would imagine."

"Indeed it will, Regent. The Rally in the Rain. I look forward to it. This is my first spring."

"Ah. Well it *is* a spectacle. You'll see. Goodbye then, Commander."

"Stay warm," the commander said as the last of the troops left the premises. He followed quickly and the door closed behind him with a metallic ringing thud.

"Reyna, what the hell was that all about?"

"I have no idea, darling. I have no idea."

"What did he mean when he said 'thinking in the ether?' What the hell does that even mean? And what's 'the Array?' They haven't been here a week and already the police our raiding our homes because of these slaves.

These Ruithians may be more trouble than they're worth. Maybe Boll has made a big mistake."

"Doubtless," Reyna replied. "But they do scrape my molt in ways I could never have imagined," she said passionately.

"Oh, that's enough. You're like a machine that never stops... a fermenter." Xavier laughed at his own bad joke too loudly, giving away his weakness in the moment to Reyna. "I like having them around though. They enrich our lives in a way I didn't consider before. I want them back. Those ones."

"Relax darling. You will have new slaves soon enough. Those are gone, and you'll like the new ones soon enough as well. But I get how there's never anything like your first time! Am I right?" Reyna laughed at her inference. "I guess you'll just have to wash your own toilet for one more week. Poor darling."

Xavier grunted peevishly. "Yeah about that. It's yours too and, uh, you destroy it. So, you get to clean it. Clear, upstart?"

Reyna grunted in a throttled growl to clearly communicate her discontent but agreement to Xavier's accusation, and acquiescence. "Every other time. That's fair."

"Every third. I'll do every third. Eat less spicy food and we can talk. Every third is all I'll give you. It's vile."

"Fine," Reyna sighed and rolled her eyes at the immaturity of the negotiation, agreeing to its terms just to end the drudgery of it. "We have more important matters to worry about anyway."

"Boll, certainly. But the Array, whatever that is. That's got me going right now," Xavier started.

"Exactly," Reyna agreed. "What's Boll doing over there in The Chair right under our noses? There is a process of approval from each city, despite his position. He has to run major movements, projects and funding through the three Regents for city-wide approvals. We are two, and we know nothing about this 'Array.' I say it's time to pay our emperor a visit."

"Yep, that's a definite yes," Xavier affirmed. "Let me layer up." With that, the pair slammed the metal door shut behind them which rung even more loudly than at the commander's exit minutes before.

~

Boll and Argus stared at the slaves brought to them from the Regent's house from across the Main Square.

"Naturally-occurring mind drives," Argus stated, "are an eventuality we did not anticipate in anyone other than the Ergonites. This may become a problem that will spread."

Seated, Boll was picking his gums in agitation with a silver pick, making them bleed in some sadomasochistic ritual that showed his power over pain within his own body. His face showed the pleasure response through his eyes as he dug especially deep in one diseased section in the back of his mouth. Drool ran down the side of his lips which made him appear more like an animal than a human being to everyone else. Through his contorted mouth he replied, "We should take one out, while it's alive and see what happens," gesturing to Dory with his pick. "I need to know if this keeps coming up in them that we can still keep these slaves and they'd be useful. Otherwise all these abominations will likely need to be exterminated."

"That would be expensive and... *disappointing*... and there's the treason," Argus added. "We can't have some subculture in the Triple Cities holding a candle to some ill-gotten religion in an underground somewhere. We need to root it out. Now, while we can."

"Yes, yes. That will be addressed also. I have a plan for that," Boll said in the ether.

Argus, seeing his thoughts in his own mind drive linked to Boll's, smiled at the prospect of what his future emperor had in mind. It would be an event the world would remember. Argus said, "Yes, that will do. That will do nicely. The spring rains are here. The lake is already filling in the center of the Main Square."

Boll said aloud, changing the subject, "Get a surgical team up here. We'll extract that one's organ. It's in the brain, so we won't need anesthetic. It won't feel anything. If it dies, we'll know what we need to do with the others."

"Yes Cassius," Argus obeyed.

Within a half-an-hour a surgical team arrived in Boll's hall. The two slaves were tied, hands behind their backs, kneeling, and tied to their ankles from around their necks with polyethylene twine that was heat sealed so that there were no knots to untie.

In the ether, the two terrified newly-bonded sisters in bondage prayed together, a fact not lost on both Argus and Boll. Boll walked up to them both and said in the ether, "There's no god here but me. So I suggest you start praying to me instead of that false god you seem bent on worshiping. Ha! It won't matter though. Death comes for us all." Then he whispered aloud close to Leigh's face, *"Carpe diem, et cras enim moriemur."*

Standing and directing his gaze toward the surgical team, Boll gestured toward Leigh and said, "This one," referring to Dory, "Pick out the organ from its brain. Try not to kill it."

"Yes, lord," the surgeon replied. "We shall endeavor to achieve the most favorable outcome."

"I know you will. Bear in mind I understand that there's no guarantees. If it dies, I won't hold it against you. We want to find out if it will kill it, to take it out."

"We will. Thank you, lord. Shall I begin?"

"By all means. Argus and I will observe from here."

The surgeon walked over to Dory, to Leigh's right and scanned her skull. Finding what she was looking for, she began shaving a spot on Dory's scalp over her left temple. She pulled out a machine that resembled an electric drill with a hole-saw at the end. The whirring sound blanketed the room.

The surgeon said, "Try not to move and you may live."

Tears rolled down Dory's face in terror, while Leigh tried to remain calm, struggling with the emotions her friend beside her was thrusting into the ether, which she was a part of.

The drill landed and Dory screamed in pain. So did Leigh. Blood splattered from the metal as it penetrated the skin due to its centrifugal force. But within a few moments, the drill reached the end of its work and a slug of skull bone revealing a hole giving a view of Dory's brain was removed. Blood from the scalp dripped down to the floor and once the drilling was completed, assistants cauterized the blood vessels. Smoke rose from Dory's wound creating the stench of burning flesh in the air.

Cassius Boll continued picking his teeth in pleasure as he watched the barbarism unfolding before him.

The surgeon asked for a laser probe, and she penetrated the gray meat that was Dory's brain. She said, "I'm going to attempt to extract the organ, whole, and pull it out. I want to perform a biopsy, maybe several. I will find out what this thing is. And we will find a way to kill it."

Argus, watching intently replied, "I would expect nothing less."

The surgeon continued, asking for assistance, "I need some retraction here. A few more centimeters."

Dory's expression was drooling, dripping terror, heavy breathing and utter submission. She waited for what she felt was the inevitable.

Leigh was looking at the floor, but reassuring her friend in the ether, "You'll be okay. You'll be okay. Just a few more minutes and it will be over, one way or another. Be strong. The Way will guide you."

Dory's emotions didn't allow a coherent reply.

The surgeon announced, "I've isolated the meat that I need. I'm resecting now. Clamp."

Dory began to shake, as did Leigh. The rhythm of their shaking was in perfect unison, such that it was like viewing the same image, but doubled.

The surgeon pulled a three-centimeter wide lump of bloodied flesh from Dory's brain and placed it in a sample jar. She said, "Take this to my laboratory and await my arrival. Be sure it's sufficiently chilled to avoid any decay." The assistant she spoke to shed his bloodied gloves and protective sheet onto the floor of the Hall, and promptly left with the prize.

In moments, Dory's shaking became a quaking convulsion. A seizure raked her body and she flailed violently over the floor, unconsciously dislocating her shoulders, elbows and wrists due to the bindings keeping her firmly entrapped. White foam flowed from her mouth. Her terror-filled convulsion racked her bleeding skull upon the rock-hard floor of the hall until its bone collapsed under the force. She was dead in seconds.

Blood pooled from her broken head slowly under the dim methane flames lighting the space.

Beside her, Leigh shook in fear. Her own shaking continued on even when the surgeon removed Dory's organ. Leigh collapsed onto the floor, limp from the physical exhaustion transferred to her from Dory up until the moment of extraction. She stared catatonically at her friend of only few hours, as her corpse stiffened before her eyes, in horror.

Boll placed his silver glinting pick beside his Chair and approached the surgical team, Argus, Leigh, and Dory's deceased body. He said, "Now we know what happens when we yank them out. *This.*" Boll pointed to Dory, standing purposely in her blood pool, as if in some gesture of dominance over her. "Argus, we'll need to find a way to disable them without killing them. That's now your job. Find more of the slaves with this spontaneous mind drive awakening. It happened to these two, it will happen to others again. I don't care where you get the slaves. Just get them. I'll pay two kilos of gold for each one. Get as many as you need to find a way. Make one if you have to. But get it done. I don't want some damn slave rebellion in the ether slitting my throat in my sleep."

Argus replied dutifully, "Yes, Cassius. I will make it so. What of this one, then?"

"Oh *this* one. Yes, she's mine for the Main Square rally. Treason shall not go unpunished. You'll need to find others."

"Of course, lord. I shall assemble teams. Oh, and one last question."

"Yes Argus?"

"The mines. Shall I search the slaves in the mines as well?"

"Do what you must. This needs to get done or we'll have more problems than obstinate slaves to worry about."

"As you say," Argus bowed slightly and left to assemble teams to scour the Triple Cities for anyone with spontaneous naturally occurring mind drives. Anyone was a target, and with the help of the Array, finding samples would not take long.

"Slavekay! Slavem!" Boll ordered. "Take this one to a cell. It will be on display for the Rally in the Rain tomorrow. Guard! Accompany them. Make sure they don't get any rebellious ideas. Escort these back to me. I need my molt scraped and some other... *matters*... that need attending to." Three men approached the master of all Titan and obeyed his exact words in silence.

Boll had his own team of twenty-seven slaves, men and women making up a near even distribution, of which three answered his call, as well as two of his many guards that protected the High Chair and the Hall from unwanted visitors. The remaining slaves came to their lord's side and began undressing him in preparation for whatever needs he wished fulfilled.

A standard day later, the Main Square was flooded with the masses of citizenry that occupied the Triple Cities, and methane rain from ongoing spring storms that were a spectacle in and of themselves, replete with thunderous light shows and howling winds. The citizenry stood bravely under cloth canopies and metal roofs in anticipation for the 'Rally in the Rain' Cassius Boll planned for days following the arrival of the Ruithian slaves. It was his way of taking the pulse of his people, and reinforcing the schism in society that he brought forth on Titan. There would also be a show that none had seen before.

Slaves were put on parade and marched around the central lake, as everyone stood in awe at the magnificence of lightning, thunder and falling drops of methane smacking the ground and flowing towards it. The slaves' necks were tied to the bound wrists behind the back of the ones in front of them such that any resistance choked the one behind them. Other ropes shortened their strides to almost no distance, so the whole train shuffled along like wandering otherworldly beings. It was a crude but effective restraint for large numbers, in this case tens of thousands, found the night before by Argus, as ordered. They were placed on display like trophies of a glorious war and were emblematical of Cassius Boll's solidification of power over all Titan.

Boll's face on stage was repeatedly seen by all on the large view screens placed every few hundred feet so that none in the Triple Cities would miss this show of shows. Their lord's likeness prompted everyone in the Main Square to chant, "Boll! Boll! Boll!" in that loud, low, slow tone heard for years resonating through the thick cinnamon air and echoed off the surrounding buildings in the Triple Cities between thunder claps.

Boll began, "*Carpe diem, et cras enim moriemur!*" to cheers and wild applause. In a moment, letting the rabble quiet some he went on, "*We* are the masters of Titan! The Three Regions are no more and we, the people of Xanadu and the Triple Cities have demonstrated our supremacy over the human animal. For we are all human animals, all struggling to eke out some kind of survival in this wasted world that freezes our skin and bones. But we persist! We persist in spite of it! We persist because we are strong and we persist because I have led you, my wonderful people to the pinnacle of our civilization! None now stand in our way or leech out our resources by floundering around as unproductive parasites to society! I have put them all to work... *finally!*"

Cheers of millions reinforced Boll's theme and he stopped his speech to soak in the sweetness.

Boll continued, "We have conquered Ergon, Vinculum Mare, and with it we have finally a resonance sphere that allows us to print anything we want. No more are we slaves to the Ergonites for resources, and reproduction. And no more will we be in the infinite darkness of having no access to the voluminous realms, for I... I, Cassius Boll, have my very own mind drive!"

Cheers and roars overwhelmed the loudspeakers.

Boll, unabated, kept going, "And now I can see... *everything*! I see the history of humanity, the poisoning of the Earth, the destruction of Yurpa, Luna, Mars... the Purge *and* the Ripping! The corruption of laziness, weakness, greed, and sloth all splayed out before me to share with you! I share it not to scare you. No. I share it to serve as a lesson of what we cannot let repeat! I have access to the memories of our ancestors. Everything they lived for, achieved, fought for, died for is all right here, now, finally, in my mind.

"It is a gift, a great wondrous gift that human ingenuity created centuries ago and stands as a testament to the power of the human mind. It's also a gift of hindsight, of knowing what not to do, how not to govern, and how *not* to proceed. And in all that history there is one common thought, one common theme that all the fallen, long-dead civilizations throughout time share. That thought, that theme is this: Free people become parasites! They loaf, they linger, grow bored, and complain. They become corrupted and corrupt all those around them, like a cancer for the world. They become obsessed with feeling good without regard for the good of others. They contribute nothing, or as little as they can get away with. Production becomes evil, while consumption becomes a right! That, my beautiful people, is the poison of the past that has nearly made us extinct!"

Jeers and hollers flooded the Main Square in agreement with Boll's projected anger and resentment.

He kept on, "But the one thing that solves all that destruction before it can start is this: Enslave the parasites! Force them to contribute or cut them out like the tumors that they are!

"A people that does not move in unison, fights against itself. Three regions have been fighting against themselves for five hundred years and that had to end. I have put the Ergonites to good use. For, what is left of them are now in my science academy. They occupy the Array which exists so I can see what may come for us. I can see everything! Everything! *Everything!* All that was, all that is, and... all that is to come! I can see the *future!*"

Shocked cries and cheers thundered the Main Square, taking minutes to die down.

"And there are the Ruithians. The loathsome, slothful wastes of life that spent their time looking up at Selk and praying to a non-existent god who could not care less about any of you! Millions of them contributing nothing to the growth and development of what's left of us, leeching our resources away and dumping them into a bottomless pit of so-called needs for some so-called benevolence that they used to blind us all from the truth. What truth you may ask? That truth is: *We are on our own!* We are on our own and we have always been on our own, alone in the infinite darkness. But hear this: we are on our own and we like it that way! That is the way we see the world, as it is! And that is the way that I choose to lead you all! For there is no god but *me* here! For I am Cassius Boll, your father, your brother, your confidant, your provider, and I do dare say to you now, your *emperor!*"

Thunder roared from all around the Central Lake at the center of the Main Square, with applause and approval. The court of public opinion finally elevated Cassius Boll to what he desired most of all: *Emperor of Titan*. All around him from the high place where he was speaking knelt before him, accepting in gesture the rank of Emperor he just bestowed upon himself. Among the faithful gestures included those by Reyna Meade and Xavier Rademacher.

Minutes passed before the roars of the crowd quieted sufficiently to allow Titan's newly self-anointed emperor to address what needed to be addressed. He savored what he planned next with great anticipation and an oblate salivary response.

"I gave you slaves. I gave you the schism our great people deserved. And you all are a loving grateful people so thankful for all I provide, and I love all of you for it. For, I am nothing without you, and you are nothing without me!" He laughed. "Well, my brothers and sisters, you are always something better than anything else on this moon, with or without me. But I as your sovereign have taken on the burdens to provide you the best way forward, out of my undying love for you! And for that I feel your love for me, right here, and right now.

"And yet. And yet, there are those among you who have taken my gifts and have forsaken the great provisions I have bestowed upon you. And there are those among you who have chosen to think only of themselves and act only in some shortsighted selfish desires. So even today, in some of my closest circles treason and corruption grows like a hidden cancer, bent to destroy us all. And this both angers and saddens me, for I have done nothing but give.

I have been nothing but good. And I have worked so hard to provide the clearest of paths that would free us from evil! But no. All was for naught, and there are those of you who would conspire against me despite all I give. I am hurt to the core."

Boll gestured to guards stationed around and behind him. In a flash Reyna Meade and Xavier Rademacher were captured, restrained and forced to the ground, the screens focused closely on their faces for the world to see.

Boll angered and said, "Now that I'm connected to the mind drive, I have discovered that others, our Ruithian slaves have spontaneously sprouted biologics in their brains that do the same thing! At first I was horrified at this prospect. But then I learned that having access to more perfect information is more important than killing the very slaves I gave my people to serve. They will be my eyes and ears, my presence in every home, in every building, in every room, and even in your dreams. For I, as your emperor, know all, sees all, and with this new knowledge I will guide you, my brothers and sisters, to the greatest heights ever seen by human kind!"

Applause and cheers drown out the world for more moments in the rain.

Boll marched on, "In the ether, this one, she calls herself Leigh, but to the rest of us she is known as 'Slavebee,' and she is a hero of the people! She shared with me the treachery of Reyna Meade and Xavier Rademacher, Regents of the Triple Cities and their plot to overthrow me. Xavier Rademacher has repeatedly insisted that he was, 'next... in... line,' a hope which Reyna Meade supported because she wanted to avoid becoming a 'target,' out of fear and weakness."

Groans and awes came from the crowd.

"Oh! And it gets worse. Meade kept going and said that she 'just wants all the spoils without all the paranoia.' A classic parasite! Cancerous! Evil! But hers... her treachery runs deep. She also said that my 'power is a funny thing... sometimes the ones most visibly displaying it have the least amount of it... the strings being pulled behind The Chair by those in the shadows are the true wielders of power. It's not all about the show. It's about the stage.'

"It's not all about the show, it's about the stage?! Really! Well none can deny the treason you both have sunk to! And is on display on this stage, *my* stage, where you will find your justice. Since you are so deluded to believe that there are those in my employ who wield more power than I, let me show you what real power is!" Boll was reaching his momentous climax. Let me remind you all that there is no god here, *but me!*"

Meade thought to herself in panic, "How does he know?! How did he know?!"

In the ether between breaths, Cassius Boll thought to her, "Because I can hear *you*, too!"

Meade wrangled in her bindings shocked and utterly defeated in one intellectual blow that was both enlightening and defining. Meade had a biological mind drive and it activated without her knowing when she was with Xavier only one day before. And even in the moment of realization, she could scarcely believe it.

Boll continued verbally, "Now treason cannot go unchecked, unpunished. Would you all agree?" He yelled.

The mob yelled back in complete approval.

"And so you shall have justice. You shall have it for me, your Emperor. But most importantly, you shall have it for you! For treason against me is treason against you, my brothers, sisters, sons, and daughters!" With those words the sky opened up and another spring methane storm rained hard over the Triple Cities.

"Guards! Remove their cloths!" Boll ordered. The tent they were under was pelted by fat drops to which both traitors looked up in terror at. "Fetch the boom!"

On the Emperor's command, a boom, like a crane, swung around from an area of new construction in the city. On its end was an aluminum hook which swung slowly before the stage.

"Tie them tight," Boll said in almost gleeful anticipation. "Now hang them on it."

The crowd cheered with him, reflecting in the same anticipation.

"Swing it!" Boll ordered. The boom swung around so that the end, with the two former Regents hung in midair, directly over the rapidly filling lake of liquid methane. The pair writhed in agony from the direct exposure to Titan's atmosphere, and every methane droplet striking their exposed skin, which molted at a frightening rate as Boll smiled.

Boll said, "Lower them down."

The crane began releasing line into the lake, lowering Boll's victims, in slow, aching centimeters. Before long, feet were in the lake, then knees, then waists, then chests. Then all convulsing, crying, screaming, and hope for Reyna Meade and Xavier Rademacher utterly ceased to the roars of a glorified and grateful nation.

In that moment, the silent and stout remaining Regent, Conrad Holmes, became the sole heir to the Imperial High Chair of all Titan.

Boll said in parting, "Remember, my brothers and sisters how I love you. Your slaves may have access to the ether, but I have access to them. And anything that is treasonous will be rooted out, I assure you! The thousands parading before you have them. I have paid you handsomely for their use by my scientists. But now you may have them back, returned to you whole. The gold you were paid for them is yours! For I shall never renege on an agreement I make with you. But be warned: never mistake my kindness for weakness, for my power has no bounds! *Carpe diem, et cras enim moriemur!*"

The Main Square exploded in revelry and exuberance as the waves of low flowing sound unified and rose to the surface in the form of, "Boll! Boll! Boll! Boll...!"

~

Manannán mac Lir opened his eyes to the view of his son, Geradamas and his beloved wife, Grace, each holding his hands in prayer above him. He asked in stunned amazement, "Grace! Grace, are you alright?" Grace's body had changed wildly from what he expected to see. Her skin had smoothed, she had shortened, and her body mass was a full third less than he remembered. Her legs had shrunken; her hair and fingernails disappeared leaving only a bright pink smooth figure with the largest blue eyes he's ever seen before him.

Grace and Gerry smiled to one another and thought, "Even now he thinks only of others."

Grace said aloud not realizing that what she thought was sensed by both, "God, I love my husband."

Gerry took her hand, looked her in the eye, smiled and thought to her, "I can hear you."

She stepped back, stunned at Gerry's voice in her mind. Her reply was a stammered mix of thoughts and vocalized words that left no coherent message. Gerry came around and held her shoulders, calming her. He said, "Mum, just relax. You are awakening. Now, just listen to my voice and I will stop speaking aloud at some point and just think to you, and you'll hear my voice in your mind. It will be a bit louder but you won't sense too much of a difference." He did what he said as he told her what would happen. She noticed nothing.

"You're thinking to me right now?" She thought.

"And now so are you, mummy. Listen. Focus your thoughts on Papa."

Grace looked at Manannán, concentrated on his face and heard, "My lovely Grace, always so afraid. Be calm and nothing will harm you so long as I live."

Grace's eyes widened and checking herself she thought in response, "I know my darling. I've always loved you... you almost died... it's been weeks... you're not the same... so much has happened... I love you... but we may be ready now."

Midge entered the conversation and said, "Ah I see you've come back to us. That was a bit concerning for a time. But you've pulled through."

"Pulled through what, Midge?" Manannán asked, oblivious to his own situation. "How long have I been out of it? I've been sick?"

Grace looked at him and said, "Man, you've been in a coma for seven days. You collapsed in the corn, remember? Before that you had a fever and fought it for days on end."

Manannán dishearteningly replied after a swallow, "A week? More? Ugh... last thing I remember was falling asleep with you... but I guess that was a while ago..." he trailed off.

Midge then said generally, "We've isolated the culprit. Finally."

"Culprit?" Manannán asked genuinely.

Grace thought, stricken with shock, "You did? Really? Okay, then. What the hell is this... disease?"

"It's a bit difficult to explain, actually," Midge hedged and struggled to explain. Doing his best, he went with the facts and with science, in the hope that it would at least make some sense to his friends.

Midge continued, "We found a bit of a bug. It's an atomically small creature made up of only a few thousand atoms. By comparison a cell in your body has anywhere around a hundred *trillion* atoms. So this thing, this *bug*, is remarkably small for anything we think of as being alive. On the other hand, the human genome has over two-hundred billion atoms, meaning the sum of atoms in your DNA. DNA is made of base pairs, as we all know, consisting of four nucleotides, which are essentially sugars—energy for making us. But sugar itself is predominantly carbon, hydrogen, nitrogen and oxygen chains... thymine, for example, is a ring of only thirty-five atoms consisting of twelve carbon atoms, seventeen hydrogen atoms, four nitrogen atoms, one oxygen atom, and one sulfur atom.

"Ribosomes come into play when they replicate base pairs... I'll spare you the details, but they are made up of amino acids which are mostly hydrogen, oxygen and carbon. Our bug likes to eat hydrogen, and even though it's in all the ice around here, warm flesh and cells are a garden of fruit for them. So what it does is it attacks the DNA sequence itself and the associated ribosomes during cell replication and consumes it, using the sugar to keep going, and replicating itself. I'm still unclear how it's doing that actually... replicating... more tests... but it's during the binding that the correct translation of nucleic acid to amino acid sequences occurs, thus keeping you whole, as it were. Without it, your DNA begins to unravel, literally, without any hydrogen atoms to make nucleic acids or nucleotides. It literally unwinds your DNA and eats it one atom at a time."

Gerry broke in, "It eats our DNA..." He paused and said, "...so the dead aeon may finally dissolve. It's begun. The coming of the immovable, incorruptible race is upon us."

"He's right, of course," Midge affirmed. "This life form spontaneously appeared in an instant, on evolutionary time scales, and adapted within a few hundred years to seek out and find the very thing that makes us who we are and destroy it, utterly. DNA is a record of the millions or even billions of years of evolution it has taken for humanity to become human. Most of it is inactive—old adaptations that have atrophied over the eons. The active bit that makes us who we are is less than ten percent of the code. But the foundation of what we are is in the rest as inert building blocks for the working parts. Take it away, and you change in ways that have deformed you now. Take more away and you may not have eyes, or digestion, or feet. It's as though it was engineered to erase humanity from the world."

Grace asked, alarmed, "What are you talking about Gerry? Engineered? You mean *this* is what you mean? This is how we all die so that some other race can take over? We just go extinct anyway?! It's not enough we've lost all the worlds we ever lived on—Earth, our home, destroyed, and everywhere else but here! We're already fighting extinction without anything else's help!

"And isn't it enough that your real mother, Elizabeth Hawthorne died after infinite odds of survival just to have you? She sacrificed herself for you! Your father sacrificed himself for her! And I see now that even Justin and Jessica Forsythe sacrificed themselves for a chance of saving their world. You are their... what... reincarnation maybe? And you know how many souls have been sacrificed for the good of so many innocents! Now you're saying despite all that we just die anyway?! What god in heaven would be so cruel? The Way... The Way is a *lie!*"

Manannán interrupted from his bed, "Grace, please, that's not what's happening. You know this. We have our chance as we predicted so long ago. Think past all that. Think of the real enemy right here. Cassius Boll. We gave Boll exactly what he wanted. And now the time has come to exact our revenge. We can use this. We are still alive, albeit differently. Be we are who we are regardless of the changes. We beat it."

Gerry added, "That is the Way, mum. God has many plans for you, and papa. I'm but a conduit for His plan. You beat it because He chose you... He chose *us.*"

"Maybe," Grace said, unmoved. "My faith is shaken to the ground. I don't believe any of it. Where'd this bug come from anyway, Midge? Let me guess, sprouted from the ground in some miraculous creation event?"

"Well now that you ask," Midge replied, "Yes, mostly. It appears to have developed spontaneously, in a relative instant of evolutionary time, as I said before. Like it was built, or... *seeded.*"

Manannán lifted up by his bare shoulders and remarked suddenly, "The Nautilus. I picked it up in the Nautilus. Had to be. So did you Grace. I still have the records from when I studied them. The ones I saw were far larger, but their building blocks are the same. Breathe food. Eat air. The bugs there eat hydrogen in place of oxygen and metabolize it with acetylene in the air instead of glucose, and exhale methane instead of carbon dioxide. These have to come from something that did both at once... eat food and air at the same time, anaerobically. That's what these do. And we gave it to Gerry. But Gerry's different so he scarcely noticed... like a cold to him. But we took days to recover... weeks even. How's that possible Midge? You just learned of its existence I assume. How did we beat it?"

Gerry took his parents' hands and said calmly, "Because your God chose you for this task. You are worthy. The ending of this aeon falls to you. You carry God's will within you. Evil has reigned on this world for far too long already. Thus, He has shortened your days of suffering and placed His grace upon you both so that you may carry His message to the world."

"You also have a fair amount of atoms in your body that are built with polaritons," Midge added. "The bugs can't eat them. They're literally repulsed by them. They die in nanoseconds, running out of energy to burn quite quickly. Since all the molecules, including all the water in your bodies—sixty percent of you, are now built with polaritons instead of photons, they work in reverse, having negative mass, traveling backwards in time, curing Grace before she was treated, as it were. Think of it as like a vaccine for a virus before you get the virus. Funny thing, that." Midge snickered at the obvious illogic of what he just said, but accepting the objective truth just the same. "It also enhances your exposure to polaritons, polaritons attract more polaritons. So exposure to them invites an increasing rate. This also means your body has nearly net zero mass; you're barely in our frame of reference at all. You should feel incredibly light."

"I hadn't noticed. But polaritons? Negative mass particles?" Manannán asked, alarmed. "How would you even know to approach a solution like that?"

Midge responded calmly, "Argus is my son, and he's built an Array of..." he trailed off.

"Of what?" Grace asked.

Midge replied reluctantly, "Ergonites. You know why, Manannán. He's strung them up with negative-mass mind drives. He's trying to see the future. I can see him, and *that*, and I had my answer."

Grace turned to Manannán stunned and scared. As she saw what he experienced in his mind, he explained to her, "Polariton saturation is what I see. It's a side effect of using the resonance spheres for so long. Our people were just beginning to understand it. Boll has someone who figured it out... Argus, Midge's son. The Array... an abomination. He's taken mind drives and printed them with polaritons to make up the molecular structure. Now he's placed them into my people. Those mind drives look into the future... *a* future. So the more observers he has the more futures he can see. That's why he's strung them up in series. It's horrifying. We can only view into voluminous time in the moment we see it. It's different. We can view it, but we can't normally travel through it. That's a big difference. The polaritons in the sphere radiate slowly and inculcate everything around them. We're in one now, and I believe Midge has access to more polaritons than any person in human history."

"Besides the people that built them, of course," Midge added. "The polaritons decay off of the resonance sphere and embed into normal matter, lodging into chemical orbits left vacant inside ions. It acts like radiation in some ways. But its properties create a net mass effect that accumulates over... time, our local time. You've both been here for over five standard years by our frame of reference. So there was plenty to use. But the fascinating outcome of our exposure is that while five years has elapsed inside, a week has elapsed outside in the time's first dimension."

"Wait," Manannán interrupted, "Not zero?"

"Not zero. Actually for you, Grace and Gerry, it's a week. For me it's a half a year. For others in here who came at different times, have accumulated different elapses unique to each relative to the duration of their polariton exposure."

Gerry then offered, "You have gained the ability to move in two directions of time at once, readily, more than you believe, due to the infusion. You will be able to see the past, present and future timelines, all at once, just by... 'looking,' for lack of a better term. But be warned. You can also find it very easy to get lost in the voluminous realms and may not be able to get back to where you started. And, as the particles inculcate your minds further, and your mind drive organs, you will become nearly massless. Massless existence means your local rate of time is near infinity per second. You will find that *moving* through time in any direction is as easy as walking *physically* in any direction, easier in some respects. That will be an awakening no human has ever achieved. It will be glorious. But it will also be terrifying."

"I'm already terrified," Manannán blurted. "I cannot begin to explain how we will control this, Grace. We're changed, forever, I would say, which seems a bit longer now than before. But we need to go find and recover all our people. That was always the plan. We can hear them now. Now they can hear us, and now you can hear everyone, even Cassius Boll."

"And he can hear *us*, right?" Grace asked pointedly.

"Maybe," Midge replied, "but not while we're inside the Garden. The sphere protects us, as we travel mostly in time's second dimension. But Gerry has access to super-voluminous time—time's second dimension's multi-dimensions of its own. He perceives the whole universe as a point of infinitesimal nothingness. We don't, despite your new perceptions. Everything we are is like one something inside a whole nothing from his eyes."

Gerry stood tall and looked at Midge, curiously, "You, creature, are more perceptive than the rest. There is hope for you. I should say, 'Midge,' but there is more to you than what you show here." Gerry paused, studying Midge carefully and said, "But he is right. All the force in your frame of reference inexorably evaporates into the relative nothing of the interdimensional super-voluminous realms I perceive. Yet the force you exert in Creation must exist for Creation to persist, because Creation itself is the result of the energy behind the creative force flowing into the world. Do you understand?"

Grace and Manannán shook their heads in bewilderment. Midge, however, did not. Grace then said, "It's the Way... the creative spark. It's what makes reality, *real*. Right? Or am I oversimplifying... Ugh!"

Midge said, "The drop of water in an infinite sea... has no value, yet leaves a ripple. An infinite amount of them must exist for there to be a sea at all... so one is both something and nothing, at once. One in infinity is like one in nothing; one still exists. But in a space of limitless value, it contributes limitlessly little towards it. It is a conundrum in this frame of reference. But for you, Geradamas, you see all too clearly, don't you?"

"You know all too well, 'creature who calls himself Midge.' You and Grace are right."

"I understand!" Grace announced. "It's no different than a nearly infinite supply of something being essentially valueless, like the tholins in the desert. I see it! There's so many granules they each have nearly no value.

But each is needed to make the whole desert. So from the desert's perspective, they're priceless because it couldn't exist without them."

An awkward silence stole the moment, and then Gerry announced, "They're here."

Outside, a hundred-thousand of Boll's Walkers bombarded Ontario Garden, which from within sounded like low hum, due to the time distortion, barely noticeable at all.

Gerry announced, "We'll get to the disk. I will accompany you. You must escape and I know the perfect place."

Midge said, "Not me. Not the rest of us. The end is approaching. I must reprint elsewhere, else-when. You'll find me in the system of the blue world in some future time."

"What?!" Grace screamed. "What do you mean, 'you must?' Coward! What are you running from?!"

"My son. He'll be coming after me. He'll want to kill me in the instant this place is destroyed in his timeline. His Array will see to that. I've done all I can for you... for your... *race*. There will be punishments for those who deserve it. I promise." Midge closed his eyes, thought into the ether, and the resonance sphere delivered his immediate wish with the same steadfast efficiency as it did with Gerry's favorite meal. With Midge's departure, every living thing that was green and warm was gone.

Within seconds, the only residents of Ontario Garden were Grace, Manannán and Gerry who ran as fast as they could to get cloths, breathers and find their way to the silvery liquid metallic traveling disk they arrived in parked on the surface. Finding the elevator, real fear stoked panic in Grace and Manannán, because they knew once leaving the confines of the Garden, time's first dimension would flow normally, and the fury of Boll's Walkers would be upon them.

The sounds of blasts and bombardment went from a low hum to a dull roar to the full impacts of explosions and concussive destruction as time's first dimension flowed freely once more.

Outside Grace shuttered at the view of menacing mechanical death aimed toward them as the elevator door opened, revealing their presence. The silver disk was nowhere in their line of sight.

Gerry stepped forward out of the elevators into the open, right in the path of oncoming fire as Walkers targeted him specifically. Grabbing his mum and papa's hands together with his left, he raised his right and called, "No!" And in that moment the Walkers, the weapons fire, and explosions disappeared from sight. Grace gasped when she saw the traveling disk that was lost before, appeared magically before them merely a few meters away.

Roundabout

erry let out a sigh in the frigid Titan air as Grace and Manannán scrambled for their rebreathers. Placing them on their faces, they both gasped deeply for saturated oxygen which was rapidly depleted after taking their first breath of Titan's naked atmosphere before getting them on. It was always humid at the poles. It was like drowning. They coughed relentlessly at the taste of putrid, saturated nitrogen air with methane droplets. White exhalations vaped in the wind away from their heads and life-supporting oxygen returned to their bodies.

The world was quiet in a way that spread an eerie feeling over Grace. She looked around on the ground searching for Walker tracks, blast craters or anything that evidenced the battle she experienced just moments before. Finding none she asked, "Gerry, what did you do? Where are we? *When* are we?"

Gerry, sans rebreather and not seeming to mind replied, "Find the way within you. You should see the 'when' just as easily as you see the 'where.'"

Grace quickly rebutted, "How? That's not how I can... I can't just... Where's your rebreather?!"

Gerry cut her off and held her shoulders, saying, "Calm, mum. I don't need it yet. Focus. Look at the time around you and see the 'when' you're in. It's only a matter of turning your mind, the same way you would turn your head to see hills on the horizon, or seas by their shores."

"Ugh! If it was easy don't you think I'd just go and do it, Ger?" Grace asked frustratingly. "And put on your rebreather, please!"

Gerry complied. Suddenly and without warning, Manannán rushed up to her and slapped her across the face. Grace yelled out in shock and horror as the man she loved struck her in anger. "What the hell did you do that for, Man!? How could you?!" she asked, horrified, with an angry death stare pointed directly at him.

"Wait, darling. Not in anger. Wait. The adrenalin..."

Grace's heart rate exploded as her fight response kicked in and flooded her system with cortisol and adrenalin, locking her senses into overdrive. In the next moment, she could see all the *when*, out to the horizon.

Grace gasped and blurted, "My holy god... Man... It's like nothing I've ever seen! It's chaotic but strangely beautiful in its way. You were right. Not the way I'd prefer. Remember that. But it worked."

Manannán asked, "The element of surprise does wonders to gain objectives. So, what do you see, Mum? Is it what I see?"

"Well I don't know what you see, Man. It's cloudy. I can see only my perception. But in it, I can tell you I can see layers upon layers of events; scenes playing out in parallel lines all at once, before my senses. It's not just sight. It's *experience*. Sounds, smells, touches, emotions, energy consumption, breathing, the cold, the wind, everything an experience provides... hundreds, thousands even, all at once."

"But are you there, or seeing, eh, *experiencing* everything through someone else's eyes... err, presence?" Manannán asked genuinely, getting confused in a language breaking down when describing things that it never described before.

Grace answered, "I see Walkers... battles... here and in Xanadu. I see Mug Ruith. Ergon. The invasions... oh God, the genocide..." She trailed off. A pause of increased breathing and panic interrupted her. "What is this? The Triple Cities? Yes. The Main Square. My people in ropes, gathered in the Square, Cassius Boll is laughing." She inhaled in terror. "He set them ablaze! Oh no! They're being set on fire with bright blue-white flame!" She stopped, took a breath as if watching a horrible accident. Then she cried, "Now the whole Square in blue flame... Oh God! Millions are burning! It's spreading! The screams! A blue tumult spreading like a... like, like—ugh!"

Suddenly, Grace began shuttering that rapidly broke down into a stammering mess of a person who had taken in more information than her mind could process. She let out a series of incoherent grunts and panicked breaths before pleading to her family, "Help me. Please God, help me!"

Gerry immediately stepped over to Grace, lifted her up, and cradled her relatively tiny physique in his three-meter-long frame, and stroked her head.

"Calm... caaaalm," he said in a slowing softening tone as the 'a' was stretched to alliterate his emoting to her. He closed his eyes, focused on her consciousness and in a moment, Grace was opening her eyes and seeing the love above her.

"Ger," she asked, "what was that? It was like I was living out my own moment of death."

"Sensory overload, mummy. Be calm. It's an effect of being thrust with more information than your brain has ever been exposed to in such short order. Your mind isn't ready for infinite information coming from every time line ahead and behind us all at once. I frankly don't know how papa is managing. He's different. But yours is... unique in ways that a mind can be. It's visceral. Your heightened emotional levels both bless you and curse you with correspondingly heightened reactions to everything you just witnessed."

"I'm not sure," Manannán interjected. "I am seeing what she's seeing, I think. I see only a dead city with lingering straggling people—but not *people*. They're not all there. Something's happened to them. They're not human any more. And not many. Maybe a dozen or twenty. The world is dead around them, yet they persist. And then they get into a machine and leave, into the sky."

"A machine?" Grace asked. "What kind of a machine?"

"Not sure, really. It's large and close in field. I can see only a door, and its silvery-metallic polished surface. I cannot see a shape. Wait... There's a marking. A circle within a square within a triangle. The Way symbol. Must be one of ours. I'm getting in." Then Manannán realized the truth of what he witnessed. "I'm one of them."

"One of them?!" Grace began to panic once more and asked in a desperate plea for something solid for her mind to hold onto, "Was—*is* that real?"

"Yes, mum, in a way," Gerry answered. "All of it is, was and will be real, in a sense. You both saw events of the past, present and *possible* futures."

"In a sense?! In a way?!" Grace chided. "My sense is that I'm horrified! Gerry, stop talking in circles and just give your mum what she needs in the moment for once, without the half-lessons. I just want to understand and know it's going to be alright." Then she looked at her husband and asked, "And you Man, you see none of this, or all of it and what, have no reaction? At all?! Our whole world is going to die and I'm the only one who's worried?! I hate both of you. Both of you really suck and I hate you more now than before." The old Grace returned for a visit.

Manannán smirked and replied sarcastically, "Oh Grace! When did *you* get here?" Approaching her still cradled in Geradamas's arms he carefully stroked her face with the love he had shown so many years ago in his timeframe, before they married. He looked at her aging face and felt sorry for her, for it was quite clear to him that the immature, emotionally-driven girl hadn't really grown up at all, despite evidence to the contrary displayed in the previous five standard, locally relative years. "Shall I explain it to you, or will you get bored if it gets too—well, *boring*?"

Gerry offered, "I will. What you both see are optional futures that have likelihoods to transpire based on a probability curve in the macro-quantum world. They appear so real because they are likely to occur based on your relative position in space and time with the culmination of all forces acting on this world and on you at this moment. Those forces are based on the actions and choices every person on this world has made, with all the momentum in every particle in everything around us has, and how they interact with everything up to this point by pushing and pulling at everything else. These are like chaotic waves of turbulence within fields of intersecting force lines. Just as in the quantum realm of the very small, one cannot know both the speed and momentum of a thing at once. That chaos applies to us as well.

"We cannot know the momentum of macro probability curves to the surety of a constant. We have only a likelihood of an event occurring within a hierarchy of probability. Thus, we cannot know the future, but we can see *a* future in the form of probable outcomes more clearly than others. What you both experience looking through time is unique to you, based on your observation of it, closing the wave function. The two outcomes you experienced both will happen and won't happen until you observe them—until you *experience* them. They happened for mummy the way she experienced them and they happened for you, papa, in a way that is most likely from your experiences, choices and observations. But they've not happened yet as a function of objective *local* reality."

Manannán listened intently and responded, "And that's just one layer, at one point of time in the future that we both happened to experience now. There's infinite future destinations we can observe, making the whole 'predict the future' thing a fools game."

"I'm no fool, Man," Grace replied, insulted and confused, hiding her clear ignorance. "It's literally the creative spark. The universe does not persist for us until we make an observation, have an experience, and close the wave function. It's all right there in the Way, in The Secrets of the Construct."

Manannán reassured by saying, "It is at that. No love, you're not a fool. I was saying it's a fool's game to try and predict the future for us, who exist in a very narrow experience of time. Even with polariton infusion, and our ability to recover memories and information stored in the voluminous realms, it is still folly to know what the future brings for us, because of our still limited perceptions. Any outcome is possible, because *probability is not actuality* until you travel in the vector of linear time that records it as *history* in the infinitesimal moment of its creation, called the present. So, despite everything, we are not God. We still follow His plan, so be not afraid."

You know me so well, Man. I *am* afraid. I'm always afraid. My whole life I have been afraid and no one cared a whiff about it. Until you. You made me feel safe. I don't understand most of what you do, but it assures me that you do. It helps me not be afraid. You made me feel unafraid once. Help me more to be that again now. Please just make me not be afraid anymore."

Manannán took her hand she reached to him and said, "You've always been a slave to your fears, Grace. Despite your faith in the Way, which has wavered time and again for you, you still cling to your fears, even now. Why are you afraid? What is it that scares you?—deep down at the most fundamental level? What is the beast caged inside the darkest spaces in your heart?"

Grace fell silent and said nothing for a few moments. The wind of humid air whirred around them as the sun prepared to sink below the last of the southern horizon that could be in a northern spring. Twilight grew darker as the star's illumining faded behind the hills.

Finally Grace said, "Aibell. I saw her die. I saw it coming. I saw it coming and I could have stopped it, but I didn't. At least I think so. I remember seeing it in a future event somewhere in the mess I just went through. I have a memory of a premonition of an event that I still remember as real that Aibell Amadán Dubh was killed by an assassin's pellet."

Manannán replied, "Yes Grace that happened. I was there. I helped you escape, remember?"

"Of course you did," Grace smiled and laughed uncomfortably. "I remember that, certainly. This is different. I remember the forethought of it going to happen, but *differently*. Ugh! This is not making any sense and I do not have the words I need to describe it."

Gerry then said, "Show us Grace. Don't speak, just intend."

Grace closed her eyes and thought of her memory and associated it through her intention with her beloved Geradamas. She, with Aibell Amadán Dubh, within the Sanctuary Cloister before, was talking. Cassius Boll, animals, no creative spark, the selfish wail and suddenly, "I see what you see" was blurted out by the three of them.

"Wait," Manannán asked, "what do you mean she said, 'I see what you see? What did you see?"

Gerry then said, "Her death. Grace saw Aibell's death before Aibell even did. Aibell surely could see the past in the voluminous realms, but should not have been able to see the future. Grace certainly, should not have been able to see the future. A future. Any future. Do you see it all now, mum?"

"Yeah," Grace nodded. "I knew there was going to be an attack. I somehow knew it. I have no idea how. But I knew and did nothing. It was a feeling. It terrified me, and I didn't say anything because it was not my place to. And now she's gone. My Mum, the one who raised me, is gone. I see horror for us now and I can't lose you both too!" Grace wept and retreated into a fetal position in Gerry's arms. She continued in a sobbing breakdown that rapidly collapsed out of control, "Then the chase. Oh the chase. They wouldn't give up. The Walkers... I knew they'd get us sooner or later. It was only a matter of time. And they had us! Oh God! ...until Midge saved us. How did he know? How did he know to be there right when it mattered most? I thought we were just lucky."

Manannán replied, "Of course it was luck. Just good timing..."

"Unless you have mastered the art of seeing through time," Gerry added. "Grace, if she could see what you see, then she also knew that the end was coming. There are no coincidences for us. Our cosmos has grown very large and very complicated, and in it there is no room for luck. The people connected to us are so in all of voluminous time. The things we do in our moments of action, ripple in the infinite sea and create interference patterns in events that intersect at high points, amplifying force. I can see the pattern. I can see the waves. And I can see where we are in it, right now."

"So Aibell knew she would be killed somehow, and Midge knew to be there, just at the right moment before we perished," Manannán asked, "just like you know everything now too, Gerry?"

"She did. He did," Gerry replied. "Aibell was blessed with a natural ability. Perhaps forethought itself interlaced with her natural mind drive's abilities. Midge is not only The Midge, but he is also something else. I sensed it before. Remember? It's familiar to me, to the *Jessica* of me most of all."

Gerry paused, closed his eyes and took a deep breath. "Purr... ...oosh," he said in a long exhale that went on for seconds with the 'sh' sound at the end of the word."

Grace blurted, "Purroosh? What's that you're saying, Ger?"

Gerry opened his eyes and looked back at his mum in his hands and said, "Midge is not Midge... well he is. But that's not all he is. He is the creature, Purush, from Europa—I mean *Yurpa*. It's—he's one of the indigenous creatures that lived in its deep oceans, and existed both physically and naturally with all the voluminous realms; time's first, second and third dimensions. He collected the life forces of many others and became The Purush. But I hadn't considered he'd be re-printed with anyone like Midge and Argus to escape the destruction. I see a room of black glass and a resonance sphere, and the creature Purush trapped inside. I—*we* ran from it—to something—someone, a miracle, and met our fate in the bottom of the world. And then it ended. That's all I see from it."

"From what, Ger?" Grace asked wholly befuddled.

"From my—our lives before. On Yurpa. I can't get any more specific than that."

"You have memories from your past lives?" Manannán asked.

"I do, yes, papa. And more."

"What more?" Grace asked, intrigued.

"I can only say it plainly, but you may not understand. You see likely outcomes of future events. I see them all."

"Okay, so yes. You have access to super-voluminous information. We knew that when you were born," Manannán said. "But what does that mean, Ger? For us. How does that help us?"

Gerry put his mum down back onto her feet, smiled at both of them from two meters above and said, "Because I have brought us back to a *when* that is before everything fell apart."

Grace and Manannán gasped in surprise and futilely looked around Ontario with their eyes half expecting to see something they missed on the horizon that might confirm Gerry's assertion. Finding none, Grace asked, "Gerry... my sweet Geradamas... tell mummy what you mean so she can understand better."

Gerry looked down on his adoptive mother and smiled, "There's no need to speak to me that way, mum. I'm not an infant. But I get your need to find peace in your mind and heart. We are out here, six years prior from when we left the Garden, a few moments ago.

"Six years for us, and what, a week for everyone out here? You mean before everything happened. Before the war... before the genocide... before even the assassination! But why now? Then? I mean then, before... ugh! You know what I mean," Grace said.

Gerry nodded and said, "Yes mum, I do. We are going to stop Boll before he can start. All of those in the Triple Cities will feel God's wrath."

"God's wrath?" Manannán asked, bewildered. "Hasn't God punished humanity enough lately?"

Gerry laughed, as Justin and Jessica's sarcastic side rose to the occasion at the irony of the statement he just made. "Ha-ha! Yes, I can see where you'd think that. Cassius Boll and Argus are a cancer to your race. Argus is from a wicked time, from before the Great Flood on Earth, and he exists only to find others like him who he can train to be as brutal and power-mad as he. His history is replete with those he led to become the wickedest of men. Cassius Boll is only his latest creation."

Grace asked, "But why? What does he have to gain? What's his motivation? Lately he's been losing a lot. I mean you, Ger, said that he was a part of the past life experience of Justin and Jessica Forsythe. How? Do you know? Can you see it? I mean, he reprinted himself to Titan at some point after that, along with Midge, and this Purush thing. But Midge and Purush, they are the same thing here? Like they combined somehow? Is that the right answer?"

Gerry replied, "It seems so. Midge and this Purush, this indigenous life form from Yurpa are one being now. But in exploring the ether, I remember that The Purush was itself an amalgam of souls as well. Not only was it the alien creature, but it was also other names: Tanya, Taree, Vespa come to mind. The alien had no name. Just a description: The Follower."

"That's a lot of souls," Grace blurted, "and horrifying if that what it's doing."

Manannán then added, "If this Purush thing is all that, then there's a strong likelihood that Argus, after reprinting so many times, has also combined with other souls. Perhaps the original Argus is but a fraction of what he is today. What if he collects souls too..."

"...by adding energy to his own to become stronger in the next iteration?" Grace completed.

Gerry replied, "Precisely. It would mitigate his error accumulation built up over hundreds of iterations. But that's what I am too: one being formed from the perfect love of two people who gave their whole selves to one another willingly. I can see it all clearly. Jessica and Justin Forsythe were two people who complimented each other so perfectly, and at the perfect time. They were soul mates. And now they're one, and I am that which they became in the hereafter."

Manannán then analyzed, "If that's true, then Argus could be *forcing* souls to combine with his, as this Purush with Midge, by force to grow and do the same as well. He is your... *antecedent*. Argus seems clearly evil, and that we can see in Boll. You are clearly good, Gerry. But this Argus and Midge creature, I am unsure where it stands. Yes, Midge has been a good and trusted friend these past few years. But The Midge of my childhood, if he's the same thing, could have done something to prevent all this in the first place if I understand the timeline logic, err, anti-logic, rightly. Why have us be involved at all? Why allow all the trauma?"

Gerry replied, "It's becoming something that has yet to exist. God certainly has a plan for it as well. For now I trust that Midge, who has been our confidant, is good, and our friend in whatever way it can be. Regardless, it decided it needed to escape. So be it. We have other matters. We must go to Mug Ruith and Ergon today if we are to do what we need to."

Grace asked, "And what is that exactly, Ger?"

"We have to go infect everyone now that you're carriers," Gerry replied. "That's how we shall defeat Boll and the People of the Hills. It's time we rid us of their scourge before they become it once more."

"Why do we have to infect everyone?" Grace asked, alarmed. "Why don't we just go to when Boll's printed and kill him then? Isn't that easier and it avoids harming innocent people?"

"There are no innocents in the Triple Cities. Remember Sodom and Gomorra. Its corruption runs deep. And going back to kill Boll when you suggest means that you will lose who you are in this timeframe. That's because that which made you who you are now would not have happened for you to make it."

"Same for this. We're here now, before the assassination," Grace argued.

"That won't change. What we do now is not prevent, but plant," Gerry offered.

Manannán blurted, "Aaah! I see what this game is Gerry. We are going to infect everyone with this atomic bug we carry. Then when the week or two goes by, everyone in the Triple Cities will suddenly fall ill, including Cassius Boll!"

"And Argus, if we're lucky," Grace added. "I see the truth of it! Let's get going! We have so little time!"

The three made their way to the traveling disk and once inside the flow of time in the outside world ceased to be once again.

~

Selk rose high over the horizon first, then the blocks of cubist architecture that was the great city of Mug Ruith rose to meet it. Grace remembered only its ruins as she ran for her life from it years before. But in the instant of time the three traveled to it, safe within the traveling disk, the city remained the vibrant nexus of spirituality and metaphysics on Titan, oblivious to what would meet them in the hours to come this day.

Tears welled up in Grace's eyes as she gazed upon her former home as it stood intact, vital and alive once again for her. Wiping them away she asked generally, "So what's the plan? Are we to just wander around aimlessly touching anyone we can in the two hours before everything happens?" The sarcasm, though dripping overtly was mostly unintended because she had no idea how to infect a million lives with a disease in such a short amount of time.

Gerry replied with a warm smile, "Be comforted, mum. We are in this disk, where time flows around us, and not through us. It doesn't have to move in space in order for that effect to be present. We can stay still and touch thousands. Or we can move slowly and touch millions. Remember, they will be still, in the very instant of creation; in their present."

"Oh, right. I get it." Grace paused, thought for a moment and stated flatly, "I have to see her, in her time flow. I have to warn her. I think that's how she knew. I came to warn her before it happened. And that's what's compelling me now."

"Grace is beginning to see, papa!" Gerry announced gleefully. And then he said to her, "Yes mum, that's precisely what you need to do."

"Good!" Grace called. "I have to see her again, before she... before she dies again. I have to say goodbye."

"Yes love," Manannán agreed. "I know that's a must for you." Manannán hugged his wife, kissed her deeply and said, "You are the only thing in the world I ever loved, and I love you more now as every day passes, as you grow ever more beautiful, both inside and out. You are my... saving grace."

Grace laughed, loud and haughtily. An act she had not allowed herself to do since before the war. She wondered why she chose now to drop her guard. Maybe it was because after running from and searching for an amorphous something that would make things alright, she, now, for the first time, had the real hope she'd been looking for within her grasp. It was a hope based on a real strategy, based on real facts, and based on real communion with the man of her dreams. Maybe it was because she knew if it failed, she could always just start over again and again and again, a prospect that made her spirit giddy with joy at its ease.

The traveling disk made its rounds through the markets, streets and alleyways of Mug Ruith. The process of touching another person from within a bubble of fixed time was not as straightforward as those within it assumed. In reaching past the demarcation of force separating time flows, outstretched hands and forearms progressed in linear time while bodies did not, relative to the outside world. This cause pain and numbness in the hands because of the lack of circulation to them from a relatively still heart and absent blood pressure. Each reach—each touch—then was accompanied by a moment of burning pain and a second of advancing age that fell out of alignment with the bodies and minds initiating contact. After more than ten thousand Ruithians were touched, the pain for all became unbearable and more than fifteen minutes of age in linear time separated the threesome's hands from their bodies.

To the Ruithians, the touches were met with startled turns and glances as skin met skin within blinks of instants where something was caught in the corners of their eyes. In the air, ten thousand snaps of touch and time threshold penetrations all occurred in a wave that lasted fifteen minutes, to the utter confusion and amazement of wholly unaware citizens. The wave of sound was like following the swarm of a thousand bees flying through an atmosphere no bee could survive in. The wave faded and stopped, and the world of Mug Ruith returned to normal as quickly as it had been distracted, chalking it up to a malfunction in the intercom system throughout the city.

Manannán said, "It will have to be enough. We can get lucky. Boll took three hundred thousand. Even if five or ten of them are part of that group, the bugs will jump and spread rapidly. Within a couple of weeks, all the slaves will have been infected."

"And all the slave owners too," Grace added.

"Indeed," Gerry agreed. "It will appear in the Ruithians first, days in advance of the owners, just because of the march across the desert, which took three days."

"Then it's done," Grace said. "Take me to the Sanctuary Cloister. Let me speak with her."

"As you wish, mum," Gerry agreed. "Remember though that once you leave this disk, time will advance for you and will separate you from this local time. We can meet you back here at a predetermined time in the future; say in fifteen minutes from now? That should be enough time. Make it enough time, because everything starts in less than two hours."

"I understand," Grace relented before making an argument. "It shouldn't take that long."

"I'll push the disk forward fifteen minutes," Gerry informed. "After I find some cover to hide it, I'll shut it down, allow time to flow and start back up again. I need to find a good place to hide outside the wall."

"Do what you need, Ger," Grace gushed. "My beautiful boy. Thank you for this... I need this. Thank you."

"Off you go then, Grace," Manannán charged. "See you shortly."

Gerry then blurted, "Miss me!" and smiled a broad, eye-welled grin as if it would be the last time he'd see her again.

"You know I will," Grace replied. "Don't be late."

~

Grace's eyes met those of Aibell Amadán Dubh in a shocked silent moment inside the twilight of methane torches, dusty dim sunshine, and enriched tapestries.

"*De tribus unum*, Mum," Grace said softly as the Ruithian standard greeting came forth as a habit of speech suddenly finding itself on autopilot.

Aibell, not recognizing the figure before her, jumped in her seat as she broke from contemplating the metallic headdress beside her on a preparation table, one of many in her chambers.

Grace noted the sculpted images of man and woman in a circle, alternating twice, crouched and bowed in reverence. She remembered what Aibell had told her of it the day she died, "It's all very Gaudi," she blurted as she thought of it, which took Aibell aback even more, and then piqued her curiosity that stymied her instincts to call for her guards. Before Aibell could say anything Grace added, "It will be dreadfully heavy and will kink your neck intolerably, Mum."

"Who is this woman before me?" Aibell asked as she leaned forward and leered into Grace's freshly transformed, brilliantly *blue* eyes, and smooth, molt-less pink skin.

Grace swallowed and said in a fury, "Mum, it's me. Grace. Grace Blieh Amadán Dubh mac Lir... err, well, Grace Blieh, Mum. Just Blieh. It is so good to see you. I never thought—," she stopped short before finishing with "I'd ever see you alive again," which was squelched before being spoken aloud.

To Grace's amazement Aibell finished by saying just that, "You'd ever see me alive again, eh?" She paused to study Grace's features again and said, "I see what you see."

"And I you, Mum," Grace's eyes welled up when she sensed her Mum's thoughts intending towards her own, connecting in the voluminous realms for the first time. Grace allowed her mind to open completely. The experience she endured over more than five years, in her local time, filled Aibell's consciousness.

"So Boll is what I feared all along," Aibell reflected, "a ruthless megalomaniac bent on his own power. And I see no way to prevent his enslaving us all. This Argus however concerns me even more. He's older. He's almost a mythic. I can only sense his presence, but not his intent. He's behind Boll. I see it."

Grace blurted in frustration of the analysis, "Mum, they're going to kill you!" Grace fell forward and landed again in Aibell's arms, sobbing. "You can't let them do it! You can't die! You can't allow it! Those animals must be brought to heel. I told you before... I mean I will soon... Ugh! They *disgust* me! They are like animals with big ships and big mouths, the latter being more loathsome than the former. I loathe them. I loathe them all! You can't let them take you! You cannot! They're animals who scream at the sky and you should not sink to their wishes, level or desires in any form!"

"Be calm... caaaalm... my dear Grace," Aibell said in the same tone and demeanor as Gerry had done to settle Grace's heart through the years he matured in Ontario Garden. Aibell stroked Grace's face gently with a warmth and loving caress she'd never shown her before. She said, "Listen child—well no longer, I see. But listen anyway. Listen to your Mum and be comforted. There are things that must happen to complete the journey we are all on... Gerry called it the end of the dead aeon. It cannot come to pass without you being who you are, right now. My death, as horrifying as that is for you and for me to think about, made you—will make you—who you are in this very moment. Without it, Grace Blieh Amadán Dubh mac Lir will cease to be." Aibell held her face. "Would you believe that you and Manannán would be together without pushing though all the walls you both had to while running through the desert escaping Boll's Walkers?"

"No," Grace sighed, "of course not. He's a cold arrogant, conceited—."

"And you love him anyway." Aibell snickered softly, cutting Grace off. "And would you have met Midge in Ontario, and raised Gerry after Elizabeth Hawthorne sacrificed all that she was to save him, and her husband to save her? There's soul after beautiful soul committing acts of complete selflessness and good, so that others may live. They're acts of heroism and necessary sacrifices needed for us to continue. It would appear that Gabriel wishes this of me as well."

Grace frustratingly replied, "Yes but now they're all dead. Such pure souls should be here, alive, now, helping us all to be saved from Boll and his empire!"

"But they have my child. They have. Their sacrifices are like torrents in the sea of magnificent volumes we can look into but not yet swim. Most just leave a small ripple. Think about it this way, child: when you push a cart down a hill and you kick it with your feet at the top, doesn't it go off into an entirely new direction by the time it gets to the bottom? The force of your choice of kicking the cart changed its path dramatically as it got further away from you."

"Cart?" Grace asked, "Like a trading cart of goods?"

"Exactly."

"Yes, I see it. If it hits a hole or a rock, unless you control it, it will go down the hill in a whole different direction. If I kick it, it may end up somewhere else entirely."

"Well, child, the sacrifices of Elizabeth and Daniel Hawthorne, Justin and Jessica Forsythe, Sherrie Donovan, and other names like Tanya Arcadian, Vespa, and Taree, all are like kicking the cart, moving it in a direction that has a destination it cannot get to by any other way but for their sacrifices. Their energy transmits through the ether like tidal waves, not just ripples, in the infinite sea. And for all of them, their cart landed in Geradamas; your Gerry."

"Gerry? I do know that he—*it* is the embodiment of the pure love Justin and Jessica Forsythe shared as soulmates in the hereafter. But *all* of them? How can you know that? Who knows where the cart's supposed to go, except the cart?"

Aibell laughed slightly and said, "My dear child. You know your scriptures as much as anyone in Mug Ruith. You know that God is the only one who knows where the cart is supposed to go."

"Gerry says this, here and now, is when the dead aeon ends. There's the disease caused by these, bugs, and..."

"I know child. I see them. They're inside of you still, lying still. Except now they're inside of me. And I see inside of most everyone else in the city. Fifteen minutes is a long time when you are traveling in timeless space, you know."

"Oh, you know about that already—I mean too... already."

"Of course, child. I see what you see. The plan is sound. When you've completed your roundabout, everyone on Titan will be a carrier except for those in the Triple Cities. We will give them what they want most, our lives, and they shall die for it, because they won't be exposed to the stolen resonance sphere long enough to absorb enough polaritons. Whomever is left of us, in whatever form is spared for them will be the ones to move to the new aeon, into the unending light. The New Man, the incorruptible race, will come. But be comforted. All the souls who perish today will be here tomorrow. You'll see. All you need to do is look down the right road."

Grace looked up at Aibell, perplexed and said suspiciously, "I don't understand the last part."

"I know, child. There's no more time. Your disk is back and you will be coming to these chambers to help place this awful headpiece on my head. I promise to be kinder to you this time than before. Always know I have loved you and will always so. Find me in the ether, child. Look down the right road. Now go," Aibell finished and pushed Grace off her body and waved her hand, shooing Grace away, back into the shadows of the Cloister from where she came.

From the darkness Aibell heard, "I love you, Mum," in a fading whisper before the main door to her quarters opened and a younger Grace Blieh happily greeted her.

~

Manannán mac Lir outstretched his arm to pick up Grace as she ran and jumped into the traveling disk, on time as promised. Gerry smiled satisfyingly to see his mum back within his reach and he hugged her small form happily as time froze around all three of them. They left Mug Ruith and headed north, to the city of Ergon, Vinculum Mare, in the Region of Kraken Mare. Manannán looked stressed for the first time in a genuine way since escaping the war, while running for his life from Mug Ruith.

Gerry, sensing Manannán's trepidation asked, "Papa, are you afraid to meet yourself? Because you won't. You're not there to meet yourself. You're going there to infect those who were caged after the invasion, those who were set aside to not be slaughtered; those who end up in Boll's Array. We're not going to Ergon before the genocide. We're going there *during* it."

"During it? That's insane! It's suicide!" Manannán cried, flustered and uncharacteristically emotional.

"Calm, papa," Gerry assured. "Caaaalm. We need only infect the survivors. And we don't want to take any chances with further corruption of the ether. This is for Argus. Argus will be working close with them. He will be touching them. There's a good chance we can infect him, as well as Boll himself."

The calming nudge worked. Manannán took a breath and said, "Boll's a long shot, but I see the logic. If Argus or anyone in Boll's organization gets an idea that something's amiss or wrong with the Ergonites too soon, they may suddenly realize we have this one traveling disk, and Argus will just print one of his own once obtaining my resonance sphere and do what we're doing, seconds or moments before or after us."

"Yes papa. That's it," Gerry agreed.

"But isn't the same risk there for my people?" Grace asked.

"To a degree. But keep in mind Boll wants the slaves. He's not looking for an examination of your people mum. He wants free labor. And he wants to punish your people because of his hatred for anything metaphysical that you represent. He is so blinded by his hatred and need for instant gratification that he will fail to anticipate any of what we are doing. Argus is who we must worry about. Argus is the real threat behind Boll's stage."

"It's the Trojan Horse from the ancient stories in the ether. I'm seeing it now," Grace blurted in a wide-eyed surprise upon unintentionally becoming aware of it for the first time.

Both Manannán and Gerry experienced Grace's awareness and smiled. Gerry said, "Just when we thought that we were being original, you find out you're eight thousand years out of date!" Gerry laughed at the irony as Justin Forsythe's sarcasm came out for a visit.

"Indeed," Manannán agreed in his own, stoic manner.

Silence and solitude draped over the threesome as the disk made its way north to Ergon. Its opalescent white tapered spires rose from the horizon as the mists of Kraken and Vinculum Mare dominated the landscape with a wide view hills and shorelines, marking their start. Streams and rivers of methane flowed from the hills and formed white capped waves in the northern breezes, replete with showers in the springtime schismatic weather. Dense ethane fog blanketed the atmosphere so it looked like a twilight scene from an ancient Scottish loch.

"I'm bringing us to the center," Gerry said. "There's a make-shift detention camp in a guarded public square in the center of Ergon, across from the Capitol Building. There's about a hundred-thousand people being held there."

"Yes," Manannán replied, "the Magistrate, the Ministry of Science, the Section, Centa, Milla, Bimilla leaders, on and on, are in that cage. I, as leader of the Transmillum should be there with them."

"I'm certainly glad you're not, Man," Grace blurted as she elbowed him in the gut. "We have a chance now that we wouldn't have had lest you'd been with me. So this, as much as it is my escape, it's *our* escape, is for a reason—a bigger purpose. Surely after everything, you see it."

"Still, my duty," Manannán started.

"Duty!" Grace blasted, "It's our duty to serve the highest purpose...the *greatest* good, not just the greater! Surely Gerry's existence is proof of that!"

"Still, my people..."

"Are already dead," Grace said flatly. "That's the only way we continue. We need to accept the things we can't control."

"I think we can. But not without consequence," Manannán relented. "Don't worry. It's a rare moment of remorse. It will pass. I know what must be done."

"Then let us get it done," Gerry concluded.

A minute went by. In that time, the traveling disk appeared in the center of the camp housing the Ergon elites. Manannán mac Lir, to the surprise of everyone pleading for a way to escape in the seconds of synchronized time there was, touched one life in the center. With his mind, he intended to the rest to physically connect with everyone else in the cage. In the next minute after that, the one-hundred-thousand doomed Ergonites understood what needed to be done to bring war and justice to Cassius Boll and Argus.

Back inside the traveling disk, the three left Ergon in silence and in secret. None of the invading forces sacking the city became aware of the flying disk buried deep inside the center of the mass of prisoners, so anyone not explicitly looking for it, would know that it had come and gone in the moments it took for Manannán to plant his seeds within the seeds of the chosen.

Grace asked, "Alright Ger. Now what? Where do we go? When?"

Manannán was intrigued by the question and added, "We have a traveling disk. We can apparently go back to any point in time, thanks to you Gerry. We can observe anything we'd like and maybe change a few things."

Gerry laughed to himself, "They see, yet they are blind." He turned to the couple and said, "The traveling disk is a wonder of technology, and its range is remarkable. But it does not go forever. It, like its predecessors from ages past, eventually run out of energy. This one is almost depleted. We've traversed most of the world twice already. It's depleted its resources meant to last years. Without a place in the system to be refitted, it will come to a stop soon. Once depleted, it cannot be reenergized."

"Why's that?" Grace asked.

"Because it runs on bosons. Mass is indirectly proportional to the flow of local time. Meaning, mass resists the flow of time, by definition. Mass-carrying bosons *are* mass; they're what gives everything we know weight and gravity. The traveling disk warps time around it because it strips positive mass bosons from atoms in its core, stirs them at close to light speed adding artificial mass to the surrounding space. They collide and form photons, neutrinos, muons, and anti-bosons. Anti-bosons accelerate away from mass. They're anti-time, instead of resisting time, they amplify and accelerate it. They're anti-gravity as well.

"That stirring mixture creates a chain reaction that neutralizes the time stream in the local area. Energy is produced in the form of magnetism which can be directed, and is used to propel the disk through space. As more bosons are used in the process, atomic structures decay into their principle parts: quarks, leptons, gluons, and so on. All of them escape into the space and time volumes at differing vectors in all directions. After enough local time has passed, no more bosons can be pulled from the core's atoms. The mass runs out. The core disintegrates and the reaction stops. No core means no more traveling disk, mum. And yes, before you ask, that *is* the whole thesis!"

"How did I know you were going to say that, Ger. At least it wasn't *boring!*" She poked him in the stomach as high as she could reach and laughed at him, showing him her mental inferiority to understand such complex matters of technology.

Manannán sighed in an internal struggle to understand the nuances of what Gerry was describing—a science so beyond his own capacity to understand that it was scarcely believable to him to accept it on face. He said, "Ger, you'll need to sit papa down one of these days and go over all of that in detail. I don't see it in the ether. But you clearly can."

"Because it's been hidden from you. This kind of control is for the coming immovable, incorruptible race. It is both *from* it and *for* it, at once."

"It's from the future?" Grace blurted.

"In a manner of speaking. Language is so limiting. The answer is yes, and no. Both and neither," Gerry struggled with the language.

Grace rolled her eyes and exhaled with a growl that signaled her limit of endurance to the conversation. She asserted, "We need to go back to a when and a where, Ger. We need to do that before we get stranded out here again, and I have no interest in reliving those chase days again. Pick one."

Gerry, anticipating his mum's displeasure said, "I already am *en route*. It is the day of the Rally in the Rain, in the Main Square of the Triple Cities. We are to observe the... *festivities*." Gerry closed his eyes and muttered something incoherently and said, "There. Time is back to when we started. We'll just make it to the gates. The disk will disintegrate, and we will be on foot for the rest of the way. We'll need to blend in.

"Ger," Manannán said, "one day you'll need to explain how you're doing that."

"Yes papa," Gerry replied. "All days are just one to me."

"Ha!" Grace burst. "Easy for you to say. Maybe you can tell me why the long days seem longer every day, one day?" Grace snickered at her own joke and the family shared a last happy, peaceful moment before the end of time.

Jordan G. Farrell

The Lake

The Triple Cities were bustling with chaos and activity that left a person overwhelmed, utterly, in trying to keep up with sensory overload. Street vendors and flying advertising signs begging anyone to buy what they were selling at painful volumes by screaming as close to one's face as physically possible was enough to warrant a violent response in anyone. Grace didn't waste time calling attention to herself by smashing a flying sign with a block of ice she picked up off the ground, not caring about its frigidity.

Gerry, Manannán and Grace walked barely noticed in the din of the Main Square however, despite nearly a million people and traders in view and the loss of one of a nearly infinite quantity of roving, screaming billboards. Sparks spewing from its motor flew across the ground and became a momentary distraction for a few curious onlookers who were bored enough to care about the new experience. Still, after a few moments, the flying sparks, like hardened steel being ground away by an angle grinder died off, and so did everyone's waning curiosity.

The three walked on, without a specific destination in mind. Still, without saying a word, Grace and Manannán followed Gerry, who seemingly knew where he was going, despite never having traveled to Xanadu or the Triple Cities before. The spring rains opened up above them in a thunder-filled darkening sky.

Grace, looked up on high at the towering buildings, filled with light, sound, and screens in a wondrous amazement that was as far removed from her home in Mug Ruith as New York City was from a Buddhist temple in Tibet, on the old, good Earth from before the Purge. She walked into several others in her dazzling spinning gates which did more to attract attention than her destroying the floating, screaming billboard.

In a slowly pouring rain a strong male voice pierced her focus, asking aggressively after colliding with Grace, "Hey! What the hell are you doing? What are you lost or something or just freaked out from some drug I bet?! Idiot! You've never seen a skyscraper before? Moron. Watch where you're walking and not at all the pretty lights, slave!"

Before Grace could answer, Gerry stepped between them and said acting as her owner, "Yes of course, sir. It's my fault for bringing it out. It's her—its' first experience. But I need it to fetch my groceries and it can't do that unless it can navigate the Main Square."

"'The Main Square?!' You mean *the* Square don't ya? No one calls it that whole name...," the man broke off in suspiciousness looking at Gerry's towering height, dismissing it with a hard blink and shaking of his head, and asked, "Where are you from anyway?"

Gerry grabbed Grace and blurted a, "never mind, sorry for the mishap," and hurried off into a large crowd, as Manannán followed in silence behind. The man leveled a sneer in disgust, turned away and kept walking to wherever he thought he was going, and then was instantly distracted by a vendor. Gerry said after a moment, "We'll head to the lake, and get a good spot since the Rally doesn't start for a couple of hours. All these people will make their way there soon enough, so it's just as well to sit and wait than to chance another encounter like that."

Manannán added, "It's no wonder the whole Square isn't in an uproar. Your height is hard to miss, Ger."

"Yes, papa," Gerry replied, "I wondered about that too. It's as if they don't care a giant is among them. Like they see it, but they don't register that it's highly unusual and they should lose their minds."

"Isn't Argus a giant?" Grace asked.

"Yes, that he is," Gerry replied.

"Ha!" Grace laughed, "Maybe they think you're Argus!"

"That's not so farfetched," Manannán added. "They've probably never seen him up close, just know he's tall like you, and jump to a conclusion. It's easier to assume than it is to explore the truth and check premises."

"Very true, papa," Gerry agreed. "The lake is just ahead."

Grace in the silent march towards the lake began to reflect on the brief experience which reduced her to the level of Ruithian slave in the eyes of the locals. She wasn't marked, but apparently her demeanor was enough to mark her as a Ruithian to everyone in the Square, like some stranger from a strange land whose customs and mannerisms were completely misaligned with the local culture. They stuck out like a metal spike in a bed of pillows.

"That man," Grace uttered, "he saw me as a *thing*, as less than human. Like some kind of vermin." She began to weep. "I never felt anything like that before. It was as if I wasn't even alive. You called me 'it' Gerry. I really hated that."

"Yes I know, mum," Gerry replied. "I had to in order to not call more attention to ourselves than was already there. I certainly didn't mean it."

"Oh I know," Grace said. "I get it, mentally. But it sure feels awful to be on the receiving end. I can't even begin to imagine what my people are facing—enduring. Ugh... the apathy... the... *marginalization*. It's sickening."

"Slavery is sickening," Manannán interjected. "It's inhuman."

"Beyond," Grace added. "No words exist to adequately describe the feeling. It's like a heavy, permanent sadness—a weight on one's soul that can never be lifted, once placed."

"Indeed, mum," Gerry said. "The language is difficult. But I bet that gets close to what all slaves may be feeling."

"Awful. Simply awful," Grace concluded in a growing silent downheartedness, as a melancholy blanket covered the travelers' spirits on their walk toward the lake.

The Main Square, or *the* Square as the locals referred to it as, was bound by the Triple Cities on all sides in a triangular wall of sky-high buildings. In its center was a dried lake bed, around twelve-hundred and fifty meters across, rapidly filling by the rains being fed by three suddenly raging rivers that flowed in from the hills around the area. Pinky-white propane fog hung just above the methane's surface where water ice rocks and pebbles flowed with the liquids like rolling balls downstream into the lake, forming three ice-gravel deltas at the triangle's points.

The three made their way to the lake's edge and watched the rivers' pouring, filling the lake, forcing them to take periodic steps backward up the shoreline to avoid getting wet, despite the rain. The white noises of rains, thunder and rushing fluids pushed back the din of the Square and created a scene of relative tranquility. Grace walked up the embankment a bit further and sat, her cloths hanging wet like a pile of damp towels on the tholin sands. She sighed and contemplated the view before her in silence.

After a few moments Grace said, "Say what you will about these people. But this place is really remarkable. Just look at this! Not even Ergon has views like this. It just had the sea, which kind of just lays there. This is active, exciting. I'm not bored. It's mesmerizing. I love the sounds."

Manannán sat beside her and nodded with a grunt of agreement. He said, "If we have to wait for two hours, I suppose there could be worse ways of spending the time."

Gerry stood stoically at the lake's edge peering across as if desperately trying to zoom in on Cassius Boll's tower and platform where he would be delivering his speech, a task wholly impossible without the aid of a telescope at the distances before him. He sighed, in a distinctively un-Gerry-like act. He said, "Forever. It's like waiting forever."

"Or not at all!" A voice came from behind them, startling them all, forcing Grace and Manannán to turn around in the rain. Argus was before them, smugly grinning down upon them with his arms grasped firmly behind his back.

Grace and Manannán jumped to their feet in fear and shock.

"I didn't feel him! I didn't feel him!" Grace cried.

"Me neither," Manannán added.

"He just came out of the ether," Grace raced. First he was nowhere, and then he was just here in the instant. Now."

"Enough!" Argus ordered. "I suppose you think I'm here because things that you have been doing matter and that I need to stop it, or undo it or something. But remember, you need me...*desperately!*"

"I'm sorry, but what?!" Grace blasted. "Need you? I think not at all. You are the cancer of this world, Argus! I've seen it—you—in all the realms in the ether. I know what you did on Yurpa—to Gerry, to Justin and Jessica—to the Follower! You started this whole series of events in motion just to do, what? Destroy us? Have Boll destroy us? End humanity? What is it, Argus? What purpose do you serve other than to wreak havoc on humanity? No. I don't agree that we need you in any way. And yes, I hate you—I *loathe* you—more than Boll, more than the animals in these three ghettos, and more than all the pain the world has seen in all history for that matter! You must be destroyed once and for all!"

Manannán physically held his beloved back from the towering Argus before her for fear of some unforeseen force of energy coming from somewhere that would wipe her existence from the universe. Of course, that was an irrational thought out of the pure fear he felt for himself and Grace. It was the most human display of raw emotion Manannán had ever conveyed.

He said, "Argus, I know you probably are aware of everything we've been doing..."

"I am," Argus interrupted.

"...and that you need to or already have undone it."

"I haven't. As I said, it doesn't matter."

"What do you mean, 'it doesn't matter?" Grace blurted.

"Nothing does," Argus provided. "Nothing we do matters at all. The world will die, the dead aeon will disappear, and that abomination over there," Argus pointed to Gerry standing by the shore, "will destroy every living thing on Titan. He serves only one master. And that master serves no others but himself. You would be wise to distance yourself from him...*it*."

"Gerry?" Grace asked. "Gerry is kind and loving. He protects me. I'm his mother for all that is good in the world! He would never hurt me."

"But you're not his mother, Grace," Argus clarified. "Liz Hawthorne was his mother. And she that only because the master forced the union of those two incorrigible people from Europa half-a-millennium ago and reincarnated them in her womb. They are the master's slaves...*It* is the master's slave. Geradamas is the real slave on Titan. None of us are. Not even the Ruithians. We all still can make choices."

Manannán charged, "God. You mean God is the master you're talking about?"

Grace looked frantically at Manannán and then back at Argus and asked, "You mean to tell me that you think that God is the master bent on our destruction—that it's His will we all will die? That's ridiculous! God is the creative force of the universe! It is He for which everything else owes its existence. He creates. He does *not* destroy."

Argus laughed haughtily high into the rain and said, "Of course He does! The universe destroys all the time! Your own Gabriel says so when the Old Man dies and the New Man is born. 'The first Creation dies, becoming fodder for the second Creation.' The old creation is destroyed in favor of the new one. Geradamas over there is here to end the dead aeon and 'become father of the coming immovable, incorruptible race, so the dead aeon may finally dissolve.' Those are the words of your God, according to your own doctrine Grace. There is no denying it. That bug you acquired and infected all the Ruithians in hopes of getting to Boll: do you think that God created it just to destroy Boll? Or me?" Argus laughed again. "No! Of course not. God killed my people with a flood. It will kill yours with a bacterium. And I will stand and watch in full glory of it just for the sheer joy it will give me."

Manannán shuddered. He then interjected and added, "He may be right, Grace. Think about it. New stars, planets and life on other worlds can't be formed without the destruction of old stars, which creates new planetary nebulae—new elements that were never there before. Creation and destruction are very close cousins. From a certain perspective, they are in fact one in the same event. This bug we have. It may be the new creation, here on Titan."

"Precisely," Argus agreed. "It's macro-quantum effects on the nature of reality. Destruction and creation are both the same event, in the instant it occurs. But the master—your god—knows everything that will happen, can happen, and has happened before any of us can perceive it. It's a game, a vicious game. And that game is the biggest rigged farce in the universe."

Grace raged and her blood boiled. "Rigged farce? How?"

Argus continued, "Because if the master created the universe, and knows everything that will happen, it doesn't matter what we think we can do to change anything. Nothing can be changed. It's preordained. It's destiny. The universe is the universe and can play out in only one way, which makes this and all of us utterly irrelevant; your one-over-zero hypothesis. You're nothing—we're nothing because no matter how we act or how much energy we push out, it gets dissipated into an infinite sea of nothing because nothing we do makes any difference in the outcome. Remember?"

"How dare you! Grace exploded. "You dare to know better than God Himself what is the good and what is the evil? I know what is evil. Your words are evil. *You* are evil..."

"They're your words, Grace," Argus interrupted, talking over her.

"Unfettered, Grace continued, "Do you know *why* I know that? Because of your own argument. The argument that nothing is good or bad because of a relativistic sense of perception is what destroyed morality—destroyed the old, good Earth, and created the Purge in the first place! You are just bringing it back to further your own ends, selfish as they are, and whatever they may be! Pretending nothing is evil and nothing is good means that nothing matters! And that's wrong on its face. We all matter! We all matter to God and to each other! We matter because God has a plan for all of us! God is the creative force and He has placed the power of creation in each of us. So you're wrong, Argus. Creation is the first force. Not destruction. One cannot destroy what has not been created. By making nothing matter, you usurp God's plan, and that is heresy!"

Argus smiled and glared at Grace as if she were a toy doll with a repeating verbal message he was growing bored with. "No Grace, we don't. We are all just bugs, like the ones you found in the Nautilus. We create? Ha! We create nothing that the universe already has in its voluminous entirety. There's nothing we manipulate that creates something from nothing. It's already there in one of the voluminous realms. We just perhaps move it around to a different place. You call that creation. Grace, your views are so... *narrow.* Your commitment... *misplaced.* Your argument... *irrational.* That's because of one premise you missed.

"What's that?" Grace asked sharply.

"That the god you believe exists is a figment of your imagination and doesn't exist at all. God is nothing in a universe filled with nothing—a giant game that is a ridiculous equation that nets out to zero in the end. Infinity over one equals one over zero. It's an illusion of our limited perceptions. It is that which it is not: *real.* Nothing is real, Grace. It's all a figment in the meat in your head you call a brain. If you don't perceive it, it doesn't exist because observation closes the wave function in the quantum ether, and 'creates' reality for you, and only you. We are ants in a farm of souls that live out their existences in utter ignorance for no reason whatsoever. That is why I have given the ants something tangible to believe in: the premise that there is no god but Cassius Boll here, and I have made him in *my* image!"

"No!" Grace cried. "We exist. I exist! I think therefore I am. It's an old phrase but it's true. I am self-aware. We are not 'nothing.' The world has to have a purpose. Otherwise why does anything exist at all?"

"The Array has shown me that nothing exists. The future is a dream because there are endless paths that change every time they're observed. That taught me that choice is an illusion. And because choice is a lie, life itself is both a lie and an illusion. I'm an illusion and when we die here, we will experience the utter oblivion of everything we ever were, like we never existed at all. We all exist in a plane of infinite darkness and project imaginary light to make our existence try to mean something. It doesn't. If it did, your god would show you. He'd be here, right now, and guide you—and prove to you that there is a purpose. He would strike me down and show the world that I am wrong. He doesn't and allows all this suffering to continue in silence. Why? Because there's no god protecting you, Grace. There is no divine parent making everyone safe.

"'Safe,' like a god, like 'hope,' is the biggest lie in the universe. The universe itself is a lie! We are temporary animals made out of temporary atoms that store temporary potential energy, in precipitated droplets we call matter in an ever-increasing rate of dispersion. It's a temporary realm that both exists and ceases to exist in a matrix of anti-logic that resides in a singular moment of nothing. There is no order because chaos reigns supreme. I say again: *We do not exist!* Because in the end nothing does. And in the beginning, nothing did. All that 'nothing' is the real truth. Everything in between is the grand game of a big lie sandwiched between the truth of infinite darkness. Relative to infinite darkness, the span of our experience is infinitesimally small, and therefore does not exist. 'Everything' is nothing! The darkness is permanence! The light is the temporary fleeting lie! But, you will see for yourself soon enough."

Cold fear took over Grace's heart, mind and soul which her faith was helpless to overcome in the moment. Then she asked with all her strength and pure hatred, "Who's game, you insane monster?"

"Why, the Europans, of course... Midge, or what you see as Midge. He's mostly that thing, the Purush. He is the enemy you need me to save you from. You see? I told you. You need my help... *desperately*. Argus raised his left arm and spun a pointed finger in the air summoning an unseen presence.

A team of walkers surrounded the group, drew a bead of their weapons on them, with Gerry barely taking notice. Grace and Manannán shirked in fear for their lives while Gerry muttered with eyes closed by the shoreline. His words were lost to the wind, falling rain, thunders and mechanics of the walkers. But in the ether, Grace intended to hear him praying and heard the end of something much longer that said, "...I will give freely to him who is thirsty from the spring of the water of life. He who overcomes, I will give him these things. I will be his God, and he will be my son. Blessed are the noiseless, the silent, the introspect, for they are impervious to the wail. Amen."

Gerry opened his eyes and turned toward the fray and said, "You may take my body, but you will never take my spirit. Do what you will."

Argus smiled and said, "So accommodating. Make no mistake, creature. You are not to play the martyr in Boll's world. Not here. Not now. That game has been played time and again in memorial. No. I have a much more fitting end to you. I won't destroy you in the end. I will destroy you in the beginning, so you will have never existed at all."

Then Argus ordered the Walkers, "Take them to the High Chair. There we will finally be done with them, one way or another."

In the ether, Grace intended to Gerry, "Just change time again. Stop this. We can do it again. Don't let them take us."

Gerry thought, "It is what must be, mum. Argus is right. But trust in me. Don't lose faith. See the Way before you."

Sacrificial Lambs

assius Boll sat in the Chair, slumped in a smug lack of posture that gave away the rush of dopamine to his brain he felt in anticipation of his putting an end to all those who believed in anything but himself as the most powerful force in the universe. In his mind, he believed Grace, Manannán and Geradamas were the last bastions of false light on Titan, the only world that mattered to him. He regaled in the thought of their ultimate destruction, which permeated the ether like a blinding flash of explosive fire in the world. The resulting bound energy manifested by his wrestling his own heuristics to figure out where to place his arms in a nervous array of awkward gestures displaying his own lack of control of his body. He fingered his silver toothpick in his right hand and dangled his left foot relentlessly with his leaking, nervous energy.

Argus entered Boll's chamber. Behind him he dragged a wheeled cart, upon which were the bound bodies of Grace, Manannán and Gerry. There they struggled to breathe due to bindings that raised their legs above their heads. The ropes wrapped and tied them each to the necks of two others in a triangle of seated despair that left their hands bound behind their backs as well. Argus's grin spread from ear to ear as his and Boll's faces met at equal heights at the High Chair.

Argus said, "And now it ends, lord."

Boll said, "And so it does, it seems. Fine work Argus. Very fine work. I control the Ruithians and the Ergonites, and now I control these animals before me, thanks to you and to the Array. I owe you so much. It is a debt I cannot repay."

"Nor should you, lord," Argus said. "I made you in my image... *for me*. I am only a few iterations away from my own demise. I required someone worthy and up to the challenge to continue my work. That I found in you, Cassius, a decision I have no regrets about. But it's all in my own self-interest."

"And I'm grateful, Argus. I'd still be just a scallywag in the Square if it weren't for you. Now I sit on the High Chair and rule the whole world."

"That you do," Argus concluded.

"Now what to do with these things," Boll said gesturing with his bloodied, silver toothpick to the tied prisoners. He jammed the toothpick into his gums and grunted in both pleasure and pain. He then asked through it with his mouth half-opened, "What are your plans for them?"

Argus began, "They are nearly faithless. Grace despairs. Manannán has rooted himself in logic and science, so 'faith' never really existed for him. The destruction of the master is at hand. The creature Geradamas is another matter. It is an abomination of the

Justin and Jessica Forsythe, from the Yurpa, from the Ripping. It must be killed.

"Good! I was hoping to have some fun today, although, I do have those two filthy treasonous Regents to play with later."

"Ah, the spectacle! Yes that *will* be magnificent. I too look forward to that. How surprised everyone will be!"

"Those animals are easy to manipulate, Argus. I have convinced—*we have* I should say—convinced them all they are utterly powerless. They have no power over their own lives. They are poisoned by intellectual relativism. They either believe their destinies are all pre-written, and to act in any way that diverts from the mundane is pointless, or, their lives serve no other purpose other than to feel 'good' in the moment, whatever 'good' means to anyone, and has no other meaning at all. They do nothing but to feel even more 'good' every waking moment. A pointless people can find no hope for a pointed existence. They live for pleasure in the moment. And the moment is what I control. *We* control the moment and *that's* how we rule."

Argus clapped and laughed in a sheer joy Boll had never seen before. "Cassius! Cassius! *You* will rule! I am so... *proud!*—*of you*! You have mastered... *everything*! My task here is nearly complete. I know this Titan place will be left in great hands after I am gone."

"Gone?" Boll asked, with a sudden panic in his voice. "Where are you going? You can't go. I need you here. You're my right hand. My guide."

"You require no further guidance, my lord. I have taught you all I can. You have the mind drive. You have the Array. You have subservient, weak, dull-witted cattle at your disposal. All that's left for you now is to rule fiercely and squeeze them all to grow your empire.

Recolonize the System. Recover my people in the Ring around Jupiter. Take back Earth. Make my empire rise again. You have nothing but time in front of you. Use it to its fullest extent."

"Once we've gotten rid of these parasites, right Argus?" Boll pointed derisively at the three prisoners.

"Yes, lord.   Precisely," Argus stated with a masochistic sneer.

"I guess we should untie them for what comes next. They look very uncomfortable," Boll said sardonically with a grin.

"Indeed," Argus said.   "Slaves! Unbind them. Guards! Watch them. If they move in any way that displeases us, shoot them."

"Yes sir," came the audible responses from both slaves and guards alike.

Manannán mac Lir hated listening to Cassius Boll speaking with every fiber of his being. He wanted nothing more than to rid the world of his squeaky voice coming from a stunted grunt that was the beginning of an exhalation of a life that was unworthy of the air it breathed. The slaves and guards approached him and he settled his mind. He became stoic. He opened his thoughts to sounds and breezes around the room. His heart rate rose. He began to perspire. The opportunity was upon him.

But it was Grace who leapt into the air with a fury of instantaneous raw power that stole the one second of reaction time from Argus so that Cassis Boll was directly in line with the heel of her foot. It landed squarely on his rebreather and broke it into many pieces. Red blood poured from what was left of a nose as Boll fell off the High Chair and onto the cloth and pillowed floor two meters below, unconscious. Grace landed next to him and put a death hold around his neck.

But Argus was faster. By the time Grace looked up to address Argus, he had already taken Manannán and pointed a gun downward through his skull. The stalemate was complete.

Argus said, "Release him, or you leave me no choice."

"He's dead already," Grace said referring to Boll. Killing Man will just anger me further." Grace's rage was let completely out of its box.

Argus said, "Your emotions betray you, child. Boll is not dead. You know as well as I do. He's right there, in the ether. Look with your mind."

Grace leered saying, "I don't care. And my anger makes me unpredictable. Haven't you figured that out by now?"

"Oh yes,' Argus replied. "Your anger and emotions make you a free radical in an otherwise ordered system of my creation..."

Grace cut him off, "Yet you anger me!"

Argus snickered. "Be that as it may, you will submit. Now!" Argus glanced at Boll.

Grace and Manannán were distracted and he missed how Boll began coming around. Argus doubled down on his threat. Boll snatched Grace in her moment of distraction. The tables were rapidly turned.

Boll said breathing heavily, "Now one of you is going to die, right now. But you get to choose. Who's worth dying for? Are you of the mind that your love will save you? It won't. You're just two animals who became familiar and had experiences that benefited you both. That familiarity led to a false sense of purpose. Love is a bigger lie than hope or your false god is." Boll laughed as he whispered in Grace's ear while attempting to hold his breath simultaneously.

But Manannán wasn't finished. Despite Argus's grip on his body, he managed to drop below Argus, retrieve his weapon of choice of the retractable titanium pike from his small pocket, and found its mark in Argus's left leg, just above the knee. Argus cried out in surprising pain and he knelt to the floor. Shots rang out from his weapon and blue-white explosions chased Manannán around Boll's chamber.

Grace managed to drop to her knees while on the High Chair with Boll, inserted her hand beneath his death grip, and twist free in one swift, bold motion. While using her foot like a hammer, she cracked the front of his right knee so that it broke unnaturally backwards. Boll cried out in agony as his patella broke through his skin and leg bones poked upward, while his body mass peeled back the flesh around them as he fell to the floor below. He landed next to Argus also trapped by gravity and injury where Boll's relative lack of stature clarified his true nature to the world.

Gerry, in the moment Grace and Manannán acted, closed his eyes. Then all the guards and slaves, moved no more. Time ceased to be for them and they stood frozen in space as if waxen copies of their deceased selves replaced them. Gerry opened his eyes and stood again motionless before the fray.

Manannán struggled to gain control of Argus's weapon which he continued to fire blindly as Manannán came around behind him and climbed upon his back, ensuring he pressed all his weight upon Argus's injured leg. Manannán raked Argus's eyes with his right hand, earning him the moment of distraction required to reach for the gun. Out of reach, he launched off of us Argus's right shoulder, swung around holding his neck and kicked the weapon across the room, burying itself in the cloth floor. But the move left Manannán vulnerable and Argus's massive frame reached out and grabbed him like a child, ready to rip him apart.

Boll, running out of air ran for another breather hanging on the wall, blood pouring from the fleshed opening of his face that was once his nose, Grace in unceasing pursuit. Boll got there first. He grabbed for the breather, placed it on his face and took one deep breath. Grace pounced. The struggle tackled Boll to the fabric floor as he elbowed Grace in her face, stunning her. He reached around her neck with the air tube to the breather and stopped. He knew he had her. She flailed relentlessly, to no avail.

Boll whispered in her ear, "It's over."

"Not while I'm breathing. I'll raise hell first," Grace insisted.

"You may have to." Boll tightened his garrote around her neck and the flailing slowed.

Manannán said, "Grace, don't. Don't let him manipulate you."

"He already has... all of us!" Gerry stepped up and interjected. "I see his treachery."

"What are you talking about, Ger?" Grace pleaded through her closing throat.

"This is a trap. It's not right. Something is off. It's a trap... for... *me*. 'Yaldabaoth has hidden the truth...' I see."

"Was that from Gabriel, Ger?" Manannán let it go and asked, "You mean Argus?"

"No," Gerry said. "Something far worse is coming. And now, it *must* come."

He thought out to Argus in the ether, "Stop. Wait."

Argus obeyed and gripped Manannán tightly so he could not move or surprise him further.

Boll asked Grace in a whisper, "Do you love him?"

"More than anything," she said.

"Would you die for him?" he pressed.

She began to cry, but without hesitation she said, "Yes. Yes I would die for him. He's my... *everything.*"

"If I let him live will you let it end right here, right now, Grace?"

"A bargain?" she asked incorrigibly. "You have us both. You can do what you will. Why strike a bargain now? Just be done with it already you worthless animal!" She yelled in his ear as best she could through a collapsing throat.

Boll said, "My dear Mum," he snickered at the sickening thought of it, "it's not enough just to be rid of you. I want more. I want more than just your life. I want your spirit. I want to not only kill you. I want to defeat you, utterly. That means I want you to admit one simple thing. One easy truth that none of you vermin have ever been able to do."

"And what's that, pig?"

"A simple admission. Admit that you're... *wrong.*" Boll leered at her as close as he could as he tightened his noose even further. Grace's eyes fluttered. "There is no god before Boll. Just say it, and he lives."

"No. I won't lose faith. I've not lost faith. That's what you want, Boll? My faith?" She laughed through her spit and blood. "You're truly insane. I'd die first. And since you're going to kill me anyway, I prefer not to cooperate."

Boll yanked. "You certain? I can make it slow. I can make you watch. I can make it so he lives in agony for *daaaays...* just to have you watch and then die anyway.

You *love* him? I'd say you are being very selfish. After all, it's just the words I want. The ether will keep the truth of your mind. I don't think you love him at all. I think you love yourself." Argus paused and said, "You know, I think I love the way I bring forth the truth. Grace Blieh, you are still a scared little brat. Maybe I'll make the same offer to him and see what he says."

"No!" She grunted. "I'm not that person. Not anymore. I'll die for him. I'll do it for him. I wouldn't be here if it weren't for him."

Manannán could not hear any of the pair's whispered exchanges as the ether was silent. Argus saw his attempt and actively blocked any mind drive communications. As a result, nothing from the ether was coming through, which frustrated and angered Manannán to no end. He fruitlessly struggled as his rib cage began to collapse under Argus's giant grip. Manannán coughed.

Boll again demanded, "Grace, make this easy. Spare him days of suffering and his life. Just say the words: There is no god but Boll."

"Never."

Through the ether, despite Argus's attempts to block all thought communication, Gerry broke through into Grace's mind and said, "My beautiful mum, let go. You have not lost faith, and for that you are very blessed. I will make sure papa survives. But now you are called back home to the Father. You have done well. Calm mummy... caaaaaalmmmmm."

Grace closed her eyes as warmth and peace enveloped her being. And in her mind, a voice from the ether, sounding like the whisper of a child's secret said, "See the way before you!" And then for Grace, all was a flood of warm light.

A crack stopped all motion in an instant of realization: Cassius Boll snapped Grace's neck in the instant of mortal bravery that sucked the very life force out of the ether Manannán drew on for his own energy.

Manannán, having witnessed his worst nightmare, in a moment of purely human grief and heartfelt agony cried, "Graaaaaaace!" and began sobbing from a place that no AI had ever-before discovered.

Then Boll, as expected, reneged on his promise and yelled, "Argus! Kill that animal! Now!"

Argus grinned and began twisting and pulling at Manannán's deflated and defeated body who offered no resistance to his inevitable demise.

Gerry, opened his eyes suddenly and yelled, "Enough!" He raised his arms and the room's ambient light faded. Torches waned. Darkness enveloped the room that appeared to prevent even the daylight from outside from entering. Time stopped outside, freezing raindrops in mid-air. Dark corners and recesses were everywhere. Gerry ordered Argus, "Release him. Now!"

Argus, suddenly in a trance-like state and unable to control his own motions, thoughts or purpose, helplessly dropped Manannán onto the cloth floor. Manannán arose and scrambled to Gerry who was equally as unfamiliar to him as Argus had become. Manannán then froze when he heard the first growl.

The room flooded with cold, from where, no one but Geradamas knew. It was the coldest of colds, as of despair, and of death itself. Clicks could be heard from behind the black ink of lightless space.

Then another growl came closer this time, and meaner. Then another, and a third, fourth and fifth, as a group, like a pack of wolves stalking their prey.

Geradamas then opened his eyes and said, "Boll, you live by a mantra in Shangri-La: *Carpe diem, et cras enim moriemur*, 'Seize the day, and tomorrow we shall die,' right? Today, you *will* die. Oh yes. You will, for God has no place for you in the kingdom of heaven. But before you do, I give you my shibboleth: *'Flectere si nequeo superos, acheronta movebo!'*

What gibberish does that mean, giant?" Boll asked irreverently.

Gerry replied, "If I cannot bend the will of Heaven, I shall move hell!"

From every dark place in Cassius Boll's chamber came forth demons, spirits and minions from the underworld of hell itself, called forth by Geradamas from one of the voluminous realms where they lived.

Geradamas called, "Yaldabaoth! I command you to come forth and do my bidding in the name of God, your Lord and Master, and by the grace of the Holy Spirit! Yaldabaoth! Come forth and rid the world of the wicked before us!" And then he began repeating, *"Flectere si nequeo superos, acheronta movebo! Flectere si nequeo superos, acheronta movebo...!"*

Demons and beasts like black smoke dark as oil, and cold as the force of death itself, targeted Cassius Boll and Argus, swirling in the air around them like sharks in an ocean of never-ending pain. They screamed in terror and wrangled on the floor to get away, finding nowhere to run. Then a large black mass rose from the floor and into the heights of the cathedral-like ceiling, arching over the lower minions surrounding its targets. A great hand of black tar-like smoke reached out for Argus and Boll. As they struggled, their very souls began pulling away from their bodies.

In the next instant, a bright light flashed in the tumult. To the amazement of everyone, Midge appeared and cried, "No! Not my son! Not my son! He is still my son!"

Then, a force of white light formed a brief shield between him, Argus and the monster, Yaldabaoth before them both. The shield became a bubble of warped space-time which distorted all motion, light, and sound, like a barrier slowly growing stronger separating them from the evil flying around them. The bubble grew brighter, until its radiance blinded Geradamas and Manannán entirely. Finally, with an instant flash, Midge and Argus had disappeared.

But the devil's minions weren't finished. They bit and pulled at Boll, who was abandoned to face pure evil on his own. The demons yanked at his life energy from Boll's physical host. Once separated, it was quickly captured, and in a permanent state of terror was taken to a plane of existence no luminous being would dare tread.

Light slowly returned to the chamber.

The emptied corpse of Cassius Boll fell to the floor, shattering from the resulting draining of all heat energy from his wrangled body, into millions of the smallest of fragments even Manannán mac Lir couldn't count.

Manannán arose from behind Gerry, breathing heavily and still broken by Grace's death. He ran over to her body and held it as reverently as nothing in the universe more sacred to him. While normally stoic and full of reason, Manannán found himself without words, without thoughts, and without answers, for only grief and loss filled his mind. He held her close as he said his final goodbye to his beloved in his arms.

Then Manannán asked Gerry, "It's like I lost *my* Grace. That will take some getting used to." He sighed through tears and snot. "Is that it then? Is it over? The timeline is corrupted fully now?"

"Yes papa. It *is* your Grace. They all will be. But this timeline will never see Cassius Boll again. At least not the original. I will fill in the rest of him as I planned. It's God's divine mercy to His children. Therefore, I will comply.

"Will we have to deal with the devil himself every time? God, I hope not. And where's Argus gone? And Midge?"

"What will be done will be. The devil is our servant as much as we are God's. But as for the Midge, and Argus, the Way is dark. I don't see them. And that is an eventuality I cannot understand."

"That's... disturbing," Manannán sighed with trepidation.

"But no matter, papa. Not now anyway. For now, the People of the Hills here will find reason once again after a period of tumult. People will die and slavery will continue for some time. But eventually, order and freedom will return. Harmony will prevail. Humanity will survive. But such is the nature of things, yes? Chaos from order. Order from chaos. Harmony from all. Like the rhythmic breathing of Creation itself."

"It's all relative."

"Precisely. Yaldabaoth has hidden the truth. Relativity is his horror."

"It's another infinity—another whole dimension. I see how, finally," Manannán concluded. "Will it get any easier?"

Gerry smiled and said, "Nothing worth anything is easy, papa. But for now, we're called home."

"Good. Back to our timeline now then?"

"Yeah. The bugs are already making their presence known in the Triple Cities. We'll stop in Ontario. Then it's time we meet Grace again after her meeting with Aibell and go watch the Rally in the Rain.

Manannán paused and as he began walking out of Boll's chamber he said, "Another Grace..." and trailed off. Then he blurted, "That was a long fifteen minutes."

Time remained still outside as the remaining pair walked amongst the crowds and suspended rains. Making it back to the traveling disk which was still powerless after arriving outside the Triple Cities, the pair boarded it regardless.

"Do we even need the disk anymore? And how will you get it restarted?" Manannán asked genuinely.

"Not really. I'll just keep it for mum's sake. Yes I can move energy from the other voluminous realms and channel it into the core, effectively rebuilding the matter that was depleted in this timeline. It's kind of like using a syphon: higher energy states naturally fall into lower ones with the use of a pathway. I am that pathway.

"But mummy's mind is more fragile than yours. Having a home space in the form of the traveling disk for her keeps her grounded. It's the least I can do for mummy. But you saw it before, papa. You'll need the larger one later on when Titan is finally finished for the trip to Triton. The timelines are consolidated now, corrupted, and the wicked, vanquished. Now all that's left is the physical."

"So the bugs are how you are bringing forth the immovable, incorruptible race, and dissolve this dead aeon? You're changing what human beings are at their foundation?"

"Exactly. You are brilliant papa, and I love you so much for it."

"Oh, Ger. You're my child in every way that matters. I love you too."

It was a rare exchange of pure heartedness that came as a shock to both saying the words.

Gerry warmly continued, "Much of the First Man's, meaning humanity's, corruption was due to the animal evolution that built the body before the Lord made you. Ridding the DNA of that animal code in favor of the evolved sequences that came after will produce a nearly pure human intellect and host for its spirit. It will be free of the emotional insanity that destroyed the old world."

"It sounds a bit horrific, Ger. I'm not going to lie. I rely on reason and logic more than anyone, but now that I've discovered what it really means to be alive, it terrifies me to lose it."

"I understand. But, it's not for us to judge, papa. What will come, will come. What will be, will be. But you will be the first. That is a place of great faith and honor, at His right hand."

"God's? I still struggle. But I know the scriptures. I guess I'll discover for myself soon enough."

"Then it will be up to you to rebuild the world from before. You will be the conduit for His creative force."

"I think not!" Argus exclaimed from across the room to two stunned and shocked supposed victors.

"Argus!" Gerry cried. "You are vanquished!"

"Yet here I stand abomination."

"Then here is where you will die, devil!" Gerry again called upon the darkness to come forth. The light disappeared and the sharks returned. This time Argus's life force was dragged from his body in terror and his body shattered into the splinters of frozen matter the same as Boll before.

Slowly, the light returned once more. Mannanan, stunned and confused asked, "Ger, what the hell is going on. Is this Midge's doing?"

Gerry, also suddenly weakened by confusion failed to respond other than to point to the opening of the chamber marked by massive doors. In another second, a flash of light appeared, and then Argus, another Argus, walked forward.

"You see I cannot be defeated, vermin! There is no god but *me* here! Guards poured into the chamber from the doorway firing blindly anywhere they sensed movement before getting a bead on their targets. Blue fire blanketed the chamber. But before immolation could destroy him and Manannán, Geradamas once again stopped time.

Argus was unabated. He foresaw Gerry's actions and suddenly ten, twenty, fifty, and hundreds of Argus versions began filling the chamber. Manannán and Gerry were surrounded, and scrambled to hold their ground which they both knew was in vain.

"It is over, vermin!" Argus called out. "Your power ends here, in this chamber. Don't worry Geradamas I have no plans to torture you. I'll make this quick. I'm done fooling around with you." The Argus foray disappeared in an instant and a fiery light came from all directions. The chamber glowed like a hot oven ramping up its temperature. Heat began baking everything inside, and cloths of all kinds burst into flame. From the ether Argus called out, "You wanted to raise hell, abomination. Well here it sits! You *will* see your doom."

Gerry and Manannán prepared for the worst, but Manannán would not relent. Something occurred to him in the adrenalin flood his body produced in moments of growing agony. He cried out his epiphany, "We're inside a resonance sphere! We're not inside reality! It's all a fabrication!"

Gerry looked at him in shock and said, "Then I know how to defeat him!"

"How?" Manannán asked.

"Watch!" Gerry said. Geradamas closed his eyes and thought into the ether, for the resonance sphere revealed to be around him to produce *another* resonance sphere within the same space.

Manannán saw his plan in the ether and cried, "No! That will destroy everything! It won't work that way! It's not an infinite power source! It will overload everything! You'll blow us all to hell!"

"Hell is exactly where Argus needs to go!" Gerry cried.

"Yeah but I don't, Ger!"

"Sacrifices must be made. The world depends on it."

"What world? *Whose* world?!"

"Everyone's. Yours. Even mine. You'll see, papa. You'll see. It's not the end."

The Chamber of the High Chair, revealed to the pair inside a resonance sphere, the one stolen from Ergon, Vinculum Mare, began to quake. The heat Argus unleashed subsided as energy was diverted from the voluminous realms via polariton-infused atoms, constructing chain after molecular chain of exotic particles, which bonded together in an energetic confluence of influences from the infinite seas of super-voluminous dispersion. The molecular dance of particles and light spun in a fury of light particles, like sparks from a bonfire rising and spinning on currents of heat. Except the currents those followed were of vectors of tangential dimensional force, originating from the super-voluminous realm.

The ether collapsed.

Space and time lost all meaning.

Manannán found himself alone, suspended in space high in orbit above Saturn. To his right he saw Titan's atmosphere turn from orange to blue in a flash of explosive transformation that was demarked by a blinding pulse of pure white light.

In Manannán's mind's eye, the view simultaneously included Saturn, Titan, Jupiter, Europa, Mars, Earth, Luna, and Triton. In what was left of the ether, Manannán experienced the complete lives of millions of souls over centuries, all in one instantaneous view. Time flurried in a chaos that whirled events backwards and forwards in unfollowable patterns, if anyone but he observed them. He observed past, present and future events on all the worlds of man simultaneously. To his surprise, he was able to understand what he was seeing, as is mind was no longer confined to one vector of time. Manannán, in that moment, suddenly knew what it was to observe the beginning and the end, of everything, in one instantaneous moment from a super-voluminous perspective.

In the next moment, his feet were on Titan's cinnamon soil, next to Gerry and Grace, Grace having many copies of she as far as his eye could see, like a repeating reflection in a funhouse array of mirrors. Copies of him were nearby as well. But each took up no space, yet were present nonetheless. They both existed and occupied space, and didn't, in the same view: a quantum conundrum of being within a probability curve of mathematical uncertainty.

"Grace!" he called out. His voice reverberated and echoed unnaturally like speaking into a fan, but far more pronounced.

The Graces, of differing ages and clothing, turned in sequence. The one most familiar was closest and responded immediately, while the others followed independently, according to each's relative sense of urgency. Some followed not at all. One was missing altogether.

"Where are we?" Grace asked, frightened and shaking. Echoes of her reply dissipated in the collapsed ether.

"We're in 'every-when,'" Gerry replied on Manannán's behalf. "I've collapsed the ether, the voluminous realms, and coordinated their vectors into one direction: yours. The best I can explain it is that by intending a resonance sphere to create another resonance sphere, it was like asking a mirror to create itself, not as a reflection, but as a real object. It can't be done, despite the obviousness of a mirror's ability to cast images into infinity. It was like asking *one* to fit into *nothing*. It drew on the other realms' energy vectors, and pulled in as much as it could, never getting enough, because it was trying to fill a super-voluminous sea of infinite dispersion with a relatively infinitesimal droplet. This collapsed the boundaries between the voluminous realms, the resonances, if you will. Now all the realms are in one view. Our view."

Grace looked and studied her surroundings, struggling to make sense of it all. Then she asked, "Is this what God sees? Is this how He sees us and becomes all-knowing?"

"Only God can answer that, mummy."

"But it's close," Grace persisted. "Right, Ger? Man?"

"Perhaps, mum. Perhaps. We can't know, for we're not God."

Manannán then asked, "That thing—those things, the cold, black mists. Those were real?"

Gerry paused and sighed. Finally he said, "That was Yaldabaoth, and I assure you, despite his efforts to make you believe he doesn't exist, he, the devil, is very real."

"He's in this realm too? In here with us, somewhere? Some-when?" Manannán asked with intense trepidation.

"He—*it* is. He has hidden the truth. It's up to us to discover it. But what we have now he doesn't."

"What's that?" Grace asked, pointedly.

"Light."

"Light?" Grace asked, confused. "What's that got to do with anything?"

"Everything is made of light. Nothing is made of dark," Geradamas spoke flatly. "When God's word created the world, it was pure and timeless. It is light. It was Yaldabaoth who trapped pieces of the Word inside massive particles, hiding the Word of God from the world. Now, not only is the dark realm collapsed here, but the heavens are as well. Angels and demons occupy this place now as much as we do. And now God will see His Word freed once more."

'The Creative Force, the Spark," Grace blurted. "It unravels the pieces of the Word that have been hidden from the world. It's the Secrets of the Construct. It's the creative force within each of us. We are inside the very creative force driving the world forward! My God! I see the truth of it!"

Manannán added, "Well, perhaps," which itself echoed through the resonances.

"It is not for us to know, fully," Gerry concluded. We must go back to a space, now. Our physical bodies are already dissipating in this super-voluminous sea. You know where the last bastion of humanity will be in our timeline, Manannán."

"Triton," he said immediately.

"Triton," Geradamas said simultaneously. "But we can't just go. Not anymore. Everything I planned before must be changed. We are in a different state of being. The rules of the dead aeon are destroyed along with the aeon itself. We exist now in amongst the guff of souls. To travel anyplace, we have to be born into it, just as I reincarnated from the prior construct into this one. And it must be like it was for me: from the union of the perfect love of my progenitors."

"We have perfect love," Grace called out. "We, us three. We have perfect love. We're a family! And we, for all our flaws, come together and are stronger than who we are as individuals."

"You have intention, mummy," Gerry agreed.

"Will I die then? Is this death, then?" Manannán asked, uncharacteristically scared and worried.

"In a way," Gerry said honestly. "But in another, it will be like your becoming immortal. Faith, father, is what you need in me to proceed. Put aside the reasons, and just know that it is, despite the fact that you're unsure, and no physical facts are yet in place for you to support it."

"I... I think I can do that, now, Ger." In that moment, Manannán mac Lir found the faith he never had before.

Grace added, "I'm ready."

"And Cassius Boll and Argus are gone, forever?" Manannán asked.

"Forever has no meaning here, papa. Possibly."

"Neither does 'now' I suppose," Manannán added.

Gerry laughed a little and said, "Well yes, papa, that is mostly true as well. That was from the dead aeon has fallen away. What comes next only the Creator knows."

"But we know Triton is our next purpose. Somehow we know that. How though? *Somehow*?" Manannán pressed.

In the next moment, a radiant light burst forth, from everywhere and every-when. Startled, Grace and Manannán raised their arms to shield their eyes from the blinding white light and moved closer together in a defensive gesture. A moment later, a figure walked toward the threesome.

It was Elizabeth Hawthorne and Aibell Amadán Dubh who both walked forward, singularly, like Gerry was, and glanced at the people before them.

Grace, stunned, and wide-eyed in disbelief called out, "Liz! Aibell! Is that really you? How could it be? I mean, you both died, so long ago."

The figures, looking stunned, as if projections of a memory that was once who they were, stared blankly at the person speaking to them. Their large black eyes blinked a few times as their heads tilted.

Liz said, "I was the Elizabeth Hawthorne. I was she and the Daniel of the same name. I'm for Geradamas, my beautiful child."

Then Aibell said, "I was the Mum, Grace Blieh's Mum, and I am for she, who was my beautiful child."

Grace welled up immediately and ran to Aibell, hunger her hard. Gerry became visibly emotional as well and moved in the ether towards his birth mother, reclaiming a voluminous familiarity with her that existed when the Justin and Jessica Forsythe unified as the one great being, then reincarnated themselves into the Geradamas through Liz.

Gerry said, "I remember."

Liz simply said, "I'm here for you my beloved."

Gerry replied, "I see the Way before me, and it includes my family bathed in the light of perfect love."

"Yes, it does," Grace added, peering into Liz's eyes in disbelief. With Aibell, she approached closer to Liz as she said it, studying her. She then felt her mind with her own and blurted, "God, it's really is you."

"Yes, Grace. See the Way together before you, all of us," Liz said as a whisper in the interdimensional breezes.

Manannán asked, "I sense it's time; time for us to move into the light, and continue our journey."

"As one great being," Gerry added.

"Yes. As one great being, from one family filled with perfect love," Liz continued.

"Thank God," Grace said finally.

With her words a flood of light surrounded them all, growing from the center of where they stood. The construct of the collapsed ether everyone perceived began falling away into pieces of dimensional energy as interdimensional tangential vectors returned to their previous orientation in the super-voluminous sea. Aligned energy flows rapidly misaligned again as energetic resonances returned to their original vector, direction and right-angle orientation to one another, like a lattice of snowflakes made up of ice crystals inside a super-voluminous ball of snow.

Then, the never ending light enveloped everyone and cosmic harmony prevailed once more.

Jordan G. Farrell

Ad Infinitum Tenebrae

(The Infinite Darkness)

aldabaoth's minions pulled what was left of Cassius Boll's life force away from its physical body. The world around him began rapidly whizzing by as if accelerating through a tunnel of starlight. Through whatever perception of time was left for Boll, the bright illumining of his world began to grow dimmer, moving into a grey mist where light waned in every direction away from him. The demons clawed and scraped at his soul. The terror of permanence and hopelessness rapidly inculcated his very being.

The grey mist gave way to twilight streaks of sparks flying by and to his rear which shifted wavelength from white to yellow, then to orange, and finally to red. From there the red began to blacken. The sense of cold grew colder. The finality of permanent death grew stronger, and what was left of his soul wrangled in otiose despair.

The thick, even blacker mists of Yaldabaoth approached Boll's spirit, the only light remaining in the ether. As it did, the being that was once Cassius Boll cried out in agony as every photon, lepton, muon, quark, and still smaller vectors of potential energy making up those were pulled over all eternity, one at a time away from his soul, and into the infinite super-voluminal realm reserved specifically for hell itself. In that realm, where the rate of time was infinite, and experience infinitesimal, Boll felt his soul's unitary energy disperse, one infinitesimal droplet of life at a time, over both the instantaneous moment of creation, and never-ending sea of the infinite darkness.

Then, it was as if Cassius Boll never existed, at all.

THE END.

Epilogue

In this second installment of the OblivioN series, I leveraged the technologies introduced in OblivioN: *Ad Magnificum Volumina* such as the concept of atomic printing and the mind drive. In that first installment, the artificial implant called the "mind drive" was a device that uses the quantum entanglement of particles' spin to discern a binary language which allows the transmission of information instantaneously; no matter how far away the communication occurs. Einstein's "spooky action at a distance" paves the way for a communications device that bypasses the light-speed barrier and is the basis for quantum communication technology being developed today.

At the end of first installment, the catastrophic failure of the mind drive network based in Europa, in the city of Gabriellium, which in this book I call, "The Ripping," throws the human experience back to a relatively rudimentary and cumbersome communication mode: verbal speech. This wreaks havoc on the futuristic society I build on Europa in the first book and devolves mankind to its baser instincts. This book showcases human flaws and frailty in all its colorful, and horrifying, grotesqueries.

In keeping with the premise that creation keeps creating and nature always finds a way, I reveled in the idea that because the human physicality became hopelessly inured with mind drive use, that evolutionary forces found a way, hundreds of years later, to grow natural replacements and additional organs in the brain, which created a supernatural outward affect which connected awakening people to the voluminous realms in the cosmic ether.

As for atomic printing, which occurs today regularly in the laboratory using light tweezers (photons regulated to move atoms individually), as well as the greater concept of the mysterious resonance spheres, I pushed the concept of materials science to its limit. The resonance spheres are an integral part of a network of ancient atomic printers that humanity is rediscovering. They are found all over the solar system in my story and no one knows who built them and why. They are constructed with materials made from negative mass atoms built by generating atomic structures using a specific kind of polariton recently discovered to have negative mass in very recent literature on the subject. I use these properties as the basis for the instant generation of goods inside the Garden at Ontario, as well as the source of motive power in the traveling disk. Both of these manipulate the flow of time as a force as well as the interchangeability of matter and energy, which harnesses the creative potential in all matter.

The biological components of this story are rooted in the premise that as we explore our solar system today, we inevitably will seed our destinations with life. Most recently, it was discovered that an Israeli space probe which crashed on the lunar surface carried tardigrades that may have survived the impact and have been known to be able to survive in very extreme environments on earth. It will be fascinating to see what became of them in the decades to come as we explore earth's natural satellite even more.

Carrying that forward and applying it to the Huygens lander, which the Cassini space probe delivered to the surface of Titan on January 14th, 2005, I surmised that if microbes attached to the lander's surface from earth survived the journey, they could perhaps evolve rapidly to survive in an entirely new enriched environment. I found theoretical metabolic constructs which would plausibly function as a motive source for life on Titan. Organisms would inhale hydrogen in place of oxygen, metabolize it with acetylene instead of glucose, and exhale methane instead of carbon dioxide. Titan's surface is replete with liquid hydrocarbons, including methane, ethane, propane and acetylene. Its rocks are made of water ice, and its air is mostly nitrogen. Thus, a plausible basis for life exists, albeit wholly different than what is found on earth today. These scientific principles form the basis for a biological foundation to what the characters in the story experience, which I thoroughly enjoyed developing in the story arcs each face.

This book has no heroes. In fact, everyone is an imperfect anti-hero, as human as human can be, full of flaws, doubts, inconsistencies, neuroticisms, and fears. Because I introduced a religious foundation for the society on Europa in the first book, paralleling human civilization on earth for the past six thousand years at minimum, I continued that vent, and it is used throughout the story as the undercurrent of the story's goal: how would we as mere mortals understand how God views the universe, and His creation. What would that even look like? Can we get closer to the Creator, no matter the form He takes in various belief systems? Can we transcend our own narrow views of the world and view what we would consider un-viewable or know the unknowable? Those are universal questions that humanity has struggled with in one form or another for centuries. They are the same questions both cosmologists and astrophysicists ask alongside religious scholars and those with the greatest faith on earth. And we still ask them today, as function of our ontology. Thus, I believe it is a foregone conclusion that we will continue to ask these same questions far into our future, within the same peaceful dichotomy.

Within the physical context of Titan itself, I felt the need to ground the story in real places that any reader can look up on the internet and see for themselves they exist. Therefore, I based the story on named places on Titan, given them as a result of the Cassini probe's mission to Saturn.

The people of the sands and the capitol city of Mug Ruith, are based in Shangri-La, a real named region on Titan, near the Huygens Landing site on the eastern peninsula of Adiri Region, west of Antilia Faculae, and south of Dilmun Region, and the cryo-volcano, Selk. I enjoyed using Selk as a backdrop for Mug Ruith and a very hypothetical cryo-volcanic experience I wrote which provided the opportunity to contrast Titan's unrelenting orange with its opposite color, blue. It also made sense from a cultural perspective that a religious center may be located in the shadow of a volcano, because of some buried tribal memory that worshiped volcano gods on earth, before the Purge.

The people of the seas and their capitol city of Ergon, Vinculum Mare (The Connecting Sea), is a fictitious place based on the northern polar region's greatest body of liquid, Kraken Mare. Kraken Mare is also real, being roughly the size of the Black Sea. It provided some beautiful visuals of Ergon's location, saturated with methane waves and propane fog.

The people of the hills and Triple cities lay to the east of Mug Ruith in the actual region of Xanadu. The Triple cities are Titan's urban center, where most of the population lives, and is emblematical of our major cities, populated by folks from all walks of life, including a desperate poor populace yearning for a better life, any way they can get it.

Enter Cassius Boll, who for all intents and purposes is an allegory for Adolf Hitler and Nazi Germany of the 1930's and 40's, representative of humanity's darkest hours. In an infinite darkness, it was necessary to come up with a villain of all villains amongst of group of barely likeable antiheroes who swept the world into a darkness that a few holdouts (Manannán and Grace) would fight for their freedom against. Boll's is the story about the acquisition of power by any means necessary by a person of low character unable to earn it himself and uses that power to bury his own weaknesses. Specifically, Boll's rise would not be possible without the Argus's intervention. Boll is the quintessential one-dimensional power-mad dictator who never gets it, even in the end. I especially enjoyed writing his demise in the last chapter—I won't hold back about that.

Finally, OblivioN: *Ad Infinitum Tenebrae* is truly a human story. It's not nearly as lofty or utopian as OblivioN: *Ad Magnificum Volumina* is, a condition I enjoyed exploring. It is a story about how the love within Grace's family transcended the flaws of each individually. In OblivioN: *Ad Magnificum Volumina*, it was Justin and Jessica Forsythe's perfect love that permitted their reincarnation as the Geradamas, a real Gnostic figure who precipitated Genesis's Adam and Eve. In OblivioN: *Ad Infinitum Tenebrae*, the perfect familial love which transcended the former combines multiple imperfect souls in a reincarnation into the next great being, because of their perfect love as a family unit, which ultimately will become the main character in the final installment of the OblivioN trilogy.

I can't wait to see what happens next...

OblivioN: Ad Infinitum Tenebrae

Post Script

Grace's spirit, the one who was sacrificed, the one version of Grace who gave her life for her greatest love, Manannán mac Lir, saw her body fall beneath her as she rose above in a weightless, warming peace. Gerry's words echoed in her mind as whisper and emotive force:

> "Focus. Look at the time around you and see the 'when' you're in. It's only a matter of turning your mind, the same way you would turn your head to see hills on the horizon, or seas by their shores... But be comforted. All the souls who perish today will be here tomorrow. You'll see. All you need to do is look down the right road."

Grace looked towards home. Mug Ruith raced towards her like the zooming of a lens, giving her no sense of her own motion, but of the motion of the world working around her.

Her city glowed bright of white light, cutting the dinge of cinnamon air and pushing it back. The view shimmered in the relative heat, powered by the ones who remained. Her kin, her subjects, her community, once killed by Cassius Boll, found their souls trapped and lost within the city's attached walls. They glowed like beacons of life in an otherwise dead vector of spinning energy, which was Grace's view. Her life force, attracted by theirs, flew toward the hundreds of thousands wandering aimlessly in desperation searching for the light of all lights to take them to their home in the super-voluminous realm where their souls were born.

To anyone still alive on Titan after the massive explosion which nearly ripped the atmosphere off the moon, Mug Ruith was a haunted, ghost-filled ruin, where no living person would dare visit out of fear because of their failure to understand that being a ghost was simply a soul who's path to the afterlife was diverted into an eddy of voluminal energy in a circular vortex, needing a simple nudge to find the way back to the source of all things.

Grace was that nudge. Her brilliant illumining life force, like a beacon of a pulsar in distant space, attracted all the people left behind. Her faith, newly reborn and as deep as ever guided her soul to that grand end, a bright light that blanketed the world. She cried out to all before her in the voluminous ether of light, "See the way before you!"

Finally, they all gathered and followed Grace as she turned and led all those trapped souls into the arms of an undying, unending sea of perfect spiritual unity.

www.ingramcontent.com/pod-product-compliance
Lightning Source LLC
Chambersburg PA
CBHW020534020726
47494CB00006B/1756